THE AFTERB[...]

OPERATION MOTHERL[...]

I'd managed to fly thousands of miles, refuel twice without incident (if you didn't count that psycho in Cyprus, but he wasn't that much trouble) and make it to my destination unscathed. Then, on arrival, I descend to within shooting distance and wave my wings at anyone who fancies a potshot.

I bloody deserved to be shot down.

I pulled hard on the control column, trying to raise the plane's nose and climb out of range, but it didn't respond.

"Oh shit," I said.

I was at 500 feet and descending, nose first, towards a suburban street littered with abandoned cars and a single burned-out tank. I tried to shimmy the plane left or right, pumped the pedals, heaved and wrenched the control column, anything to get some fraction of control.

Nothing.

Too low to bail out, nothing to do but ride the plane into the ground and hope I was able to walk away.

My arrival in Iraq was going to be bumpy.

An Abaddon Books™ Publication
www.abaddonbooks.com
abaddon@rebellion.co.uk

First published in 2009 by Abaddon Books™, Rebellion Intellectual Property
Limited, Riverside House, Osney Mead, Oxford, OX2 OES, UK.

10 9 8 7 6 5 4 3 2 1

Editor: Jonathan Oliver
Cover: Mark Harrison
Design: Simon Parr & Luke Preece
Marketing and PR: Keith Richardson
Creative Director and CEO: Jason Kingsley
Chief Technical Officer: Chris Kingsley
The Afterblight Chronicles™ created by Andy Boot and Simon Spurrier

ISBN: 978-1-906735-04-3

Printed in Denmark by Norhaven A/S

THE AFTERBLIGHT CHRONICLES

OPERATION MOTHERLAND

SCOTT ANDREWS

Abaddon
Books

WWW.ABADDONBOOKS.COM

Thanks to my trusty readthrough crew: Danny, David, Griff, Chris, Phil, Joe and Justin.

Extra special thanks to: Simon Guerrier for encouragement, advice and the wielding of the red pen of doom; and Paul Kane, for the pleasure of collaboration and letting me play with his toys.

This book was written during a particularly challenging year, and couldn't have been finished without the steadfast support of my wonderful wife, Emma, and the superhuman patience and generosity of my editor, Jonathan Oliver.

This one is for Justin Rowles, whose younger self was slightly less terrifying than his fictional counterpart. Slightly.

PART ONE

Lee

CHAPTER ONE

I celebrated my sixteenth birthday by crashing a plane, fighting for my life, and facing execution. Again.

I'd rather have just blown out some candles and got pissed.

"Hello? Is anybody there? Hello?"

"Lee? Oh thank God."

"Dad? Dad is that you? I can hardly hear you. Where are you?"

"Still in Basra, but we're shipping out soon. Listen, I don't know how much time I have. Is your mother there?"

"Er, yeah."

"Put her on, son."

I'd been scanning the terrain for about ten minutes, looking for a decent place to land, when small-arms fire raked the fuselage.

Stupid, careless idiot; I'd been flying in circles, just asking to be shot at.

The problem was that I couldn't find the airport. I could see the river snaking to the sea, the city straddling it and blending into desert at the edges. I could see the columns of smoke rising high off to the north, and the boats bobbing in the long abandoned harbour. But I couldn't see the bloody airport. So I had to get closer and look for somewhere to land.

I'd managed to fly thousands of miles, refuel twice without incident (if you didn't count that psycho in Cyprus, but he wasn't that much trouble) and make it to my destination unscathed. Then, on arrival, I descend to within shooting distance and wave my wings at anyone who fancies a potshot.

I bloody deserved to be shot down.

I pulled hard on the control column, trying to raise the plane's nose and climb out of range, but it didn't respond.

"Oh shit," I said.

I was at 500 feet and descending, nose first, towards a suburban street littered with abandoned cars and a single burned-out tank. I tried to shimmy the plane left or right, pumped the pedals, heaved and wrenched the control column, anything to get some fraction of control.

Nothing.

Too low to bail out, nothing to do but ride the plane into the ground and hope I was able to walk away.

My arrival in Iraq was going to be bumpy.

"Jesus Dad, what did you say to her? Dad, you still there?"

"Yeah, just... I, um... listen, Lee, there's something I have to tell you."

"Ok."

"The plague, from what we've been hearing here, it's sort of specific."

"Eh?"

"You only get it if you've got a particular blood type. No, that's not right. You don't get it if you've got a particular blood type.

Everyone who's O Negative is immune, that's what the doc here told us."

"And everyone else..."

"Is going to die."

I was coming in clean towards the road, lined up by pure chance. If the road had been clear, and if I could've got the nose up, I'd maybe have had a chance. But I was heading straight for the fucking tank, and no matter what I did the plane was just a hunk of unresponsive metal.

There was another burst of gunfire, and this time I could see the muzzle flash of the machine gun on a rooftop to my left. His aim was true and the plane shuddered as the bullets hit the tail, sending fragments of ailerons flying into the tailwind. I yelled something obscene, furious, defiant, then pulled the control column again, more in frustration than hope.

And, *hallelujah*, it responded. That second burst of fire must have knocked something loose. I never thought I'd be grateful that someone was shooting at me.

Of course, at twenty feet and however many knots, there wasn't that much I could actually do.

The nose came up a fraction, just enough to change the angle of attack from suicidal to survivable. Not enough to actually stop my descent, though.

I'm pretty sure I was yelling when the tail of the plane slammed into the turret of the tank, snapped off, and pitched the plane nose first into the hard-packed earth.

The world spun and tumbled as I screamed in tune with the crash and wrench of twisting metal. The plane somersaulted, over and over, down the road, bouncing off cars and buildings, losing its wings, being whittled away with every revolution, until it seemed there was just a ball of warped metal and shattered plastic cocooning me as it gouged the ground, ricocheting like some kind of fucked-up pinball.

Eventually, just as the darkness crept into my vision and I felt myself starting to black out, the world stopped spinning.

My head was swimming, there was blood in my mouth, I was upside down, the straps of my harness digging into my knotted shoulders, but I was alive.

"One more life used up, Nine Lives," whispered a familiar, sarcastic voice in my head. I told it to piss off.

Then I realised that I was wet. I reached up and wiped the slick liquid from my face. When my eyes could focus and my dizzy brain began to accept input, I realised that I was soaked from head to toe in fuel.

I heard gunfire in the distance, as someone started taking shots at what was left of my plane.

And I couldn't move.

"All of them?"

"All. Lee, you're O Neg. So am I."

"And mum? Dad, you there? I said what about Mum?"

"No."

"Oh. Right."

"Now listen, she might be safe if you can just quarantine yourselves. Don't leave the house, at all. For any reason."

"But what about food? The water's been switched off, we've got no power. There's these gangs going around attacking houses, Dad, they've got guns and knives and..."

"Lee calm down. Calm down. You mustn't panic, son. Breathe... You okay now?"

"Not really."

"I know. But you're going to be strong, Lee. For your mum."

"She's going to die isn't she... Dad?"

"Yes. Yes, she probably is."

"But there's no doctors, you know that right? The hospital's been closed for a week. They put these signs up saying to wait for the army to set up field hospitals, but they haven't shown up. They're not going to, are they?"

"No, I don't think so, not now. I know it's hard, but it's all up to you, son. You're going to have to nurse her. Until I can get there. I'm coming home, Lee. As fast as I can. You've got to hang on, understand?"

"But what if you're not fast enough? What if something goes wrong? What if I'm left here, alone, with... with... Oh God."

I reached across and unclasped my harness. It snapped free and I slumped, shoulder first, into a mess of tangled metal. I screamed as my left shoulder ground into a sharp metal edge. Something felt wrong about the way it was lying. I tried to move my left arm but all I felt was an awful grinding of flesh and bone.

It was dislocated.

Add that to the disorientation, which would probably give way to concussion, and the numerous possible wounds that I'd yet to discover, not to mention the chunk of my lower lip that I'd bitten out with what remained of my teeth...

Actually, I'd got off pretty lightly all things considered. If I could just avoid getting burned to death, this might even qualify as a good day. I squirmed in the wreckage, trying to find a gap through which I could wriggle, some way to gain purchase. It was agony; every move ground my shoulder joint against the slack, useless muscles, causing shooting pains so intense that they made my vision blur.

I could hear cries from nearby streets, and more gunfire, as men closed in on my position. I really needed to move.

Finding nothing that offered any chance of escape, I braced myself as best I could and pushed hard, using my full body strength to try and force my way out, like a bird kicking its way out of a metal egg. My spine cracked like a rifle, and my legs burned with effort. My shoulder joint minced the flesh that surrounded it, and I screamed in impotent fury until finally I felt something near my feet give ever so slightly. I redoubled my efforts, taking every ounce of strength I had in my small, wiry frame, and concentrating it in my feet. Oh so slowly, I forced a metal strut backwards and it groaned in protest.

Eventually it bent far enough to let in a small circle of sunlight. I squirmed again, rotating inside my shell, until my head and shoulder were positioned beneath the opening.

I gritted my teeth. This was really going to hurt. I closed my eyes, and pushed myself upwards, squeezing my agonised shoulder through the tiny gap. I felt something rip inside my arm and I screamed again. Once my shoulders were clear I was able to pull my right arm through and use it to push myself free.

Just as my feet emerged, the mass of wreckage beneath me shifted under my redistributed weight, pitching me forward. I lost my balance and tumbled to the ground.

I lay there on the hot, baked earth and I smiled through the pain.

This dirt was Basra.

I'd made it.

"Lee, focus, you've got things to do."

"Right. Yes. Okay."

"Now we're shipping out of here before the week's out."

"Back to England."

"Yeah."

"So, what, I should see you in ten days or so?"

"I'm afraid it's not quite that simple. They're not just letting us go home. I'm still a soldier and I still have to obey orders. If I try to just come home, I'll be shot as a deserter. They executed one of my mates yesterday. He wanted to stay here, got a local girlfriend, kid on the way. Tried to slip away, got caught. They shot him at dawn."

"Bloody hell."

"Apparently there's some big thing planned for when we all get home, but nobody's saying what."

"So what do I do?"

"You go back to school, to St Mark's."

Before I could gather my wits and rise to my feet, someone started kicking the crap out of me.

I tried to roll away from the kicks, raise my good arm to protect my head, find some space in between the blows to reach down and grab my Browning, which was tucked into my waistband. But with one arm useless, and my head woozy with shock and pain, I ended up just curling into a ball and letting the blows come. My attacker was shouting and firing his gun in the air, laughing as he kicked me to death. Luckily he was wearing trainers, not hobnail boots. So it was going to take him a while.

Then, what was left of the plane exploded. The shockwave actually rolled me along the ground a bit, like a balled-up hedgehog. My mouth and eyes filled with dust and sand. The kicking stopped. I cautiously removed my arm and saw my assailant sprawled on the floor beside me. There was a short metal stanchion protruding from his forehead. I uncurled myself, lurched upright, reached down and took the AK-47 from his still twitching hands.

He looked younger than me. Dreadful acne, dark skin, khaki combats, plain white t-shirt. He lay there on the sandy ground, staring sightlessly into the sky. My first victim of the day. I hoped he would be the last, but I didn't think it likely.

A yell from the far end of the street reminded me that he had friends. I had to move. I staggered as fast as I could in the opposite direction. I had no idea of the layout of this town, but it was their home turf. I was one wounded boy with a useless arm, a half-empty machine gun and pistol with a couple of clips; there were probably loads of them, armed to the teeth. I had salvaged no water from the crash, the midday sun was beating down on me hotter than anything I'd ever experienced before, I was losing blood, sweating as I ran, and had no idea how to come by safe drinking water.

I was so screwed.

I wished I had some of Matron's homebrew drugs on me. Just a shot of that had kept me fighting in the battle for St Mark's despite shattered teeth, a broken arm and more blows to the head than I could count. But I'd left without saying goodbye. I regretted that now; I'd almost certainly never see her again. Still, it seemed like the right thing to do at the time. I'd probably have ended up blubbing or, worse, trying to snog her, and that would have been excruciating.

A bullet pinged off a brittle brick wall next to my head as I dodged down an alleyway, weaving in between burned-out cars and abandoned barricades. This was pointless. If I could get far enough ahead of them I had a chance, but I just wasn't capable of any kind of speed. I'd never outrun them.

I had to go to ground.

"Back to school, seriously?"

"Listen, some of the teachers stayed behind didn't they? And some of the boys?"

"Yeah, but..."

"No buts. It's the only safe place I can think of. They've got weapons there, in that bloody armoury, haven't they?"

"Uh huh."

"Then get back there, join up with anyone who's left, arm yourselves and wait for me."

"You promise you'll come?"

"No matter what happens, Lee, I'll be there. It may take a while, that's all. If you're at St Mark's you'll be as safe as houses and I'll know where to find you. Promise me."

"I promise."

I emerged from the alleyway into a housing estate. Residential tower blocks rose up in front of me, some burnt out, some with great gaping holes punched in them by depleted uranium shells, one reduced to nothing but rubble. Their balconies were festooned with clothes, bedding and the occasional skeleton. This desolate, abandoned maze of passages, flats and stairwells was my best chance of eluding my pursuers.

I stumbled across the churned up paving stones, heading for the doorway of the block that seemed most intact. The sound of pursuit echoed eerily around the empty estate, making it impossible for me to know how many pursuers there were, or how close.

The blue metal door to the block lay half open. I shoved it, using my good shoulder. Something inside was blocking my way, so I had to shimmy through the narrow gap into the musty, foetid darkness of the stairwell. My foot sank into something soft and yielding. I felt something pop beneath my boot, and a pocket of evil smelling gas was released that made me gag and choke. I tried to free my foot, but it was caught on something hard. I looked down to find that I was ankle deep in a bloated corpse, my lace end snagged on a protruding edge of fractured ribcage.

After I'd dry heaved for a minute or two I slung the machine gun over my shoulder, reached down and gingerly unsnagged the lace, smearing my fingers in vile black ichor as I did so. I limped away from the unfortunate wretch, wiping my fingers on the wall as I went.

That man (had it been a man? I couldn't be sure) had been dead for some time, but he'd outlived the plague. He still had a gun in his hand, so I assumed he'd died fighting. On the evidence so far, it looked like Basra was still as violent and deadly a place as it had been before The Cull.

And I'd come here by choice. Bloody moron, Keegan.

The stairs were littered with junk. It was all the stuff I'd have expected: toys, prams, CDs, DVDs, clothes, a bike, some chairs, computers, TV sets. But the CDs and DVDs had Arabic titles and lurid cover pictures; the computer keyboard had a strange alphabet; the TV sets were old square cathode ray boxes, not widescreen or flat. The big picture was the same, but the details were different. It was disorientating.

This place had been taken to pieces, but it seemed like most of the stuff had just been thrown around for a laugh rather than salvaged and squirreled away.

I negotiated the wreckage and made it to the third floor without stumbling across any other recent casualties. I risked a glance through a shattered windowpane, and could see a group of three young men, machine guns at the ready, cautiously moving through the car park below. It wouldn't take much for them to realise I'd come into this block; one whiff of the doorway should do it.

I needed a hiding place, fast. I ran down the corridor, trying to decide which flat to hide in. Some still had their armour plated doors firmly locked shut from the inside, entombing anyone who'd sheltered there.

One door was decorated with a collection of human skulls, hanging from hooks in the shape of a love heart. I gave that one a miss. Eventually I just ducked inside a random door and pushed it closed behind me. I was about to slide the large metal bolts home when I realised that the bolt housings had been ripped from the wall when someone had kicked their way inside.

I turned to explore the flat, and found two long-dead bodies lying sprawled on the sofa. The one in the dress, with the long red hair, had a bullet hole in the middle of its skull. The other, presumably her boyfriend or husband, still held a pistol in his boney fingers, the muzzle clasped between yellow teeth. The flesh was long gone; all that remained were tattered clothes and bones, picked clean by rats that had long since moved elsewhere in search of food. I imagined that most of the locked doors in this block concealed similar tableaux.

It was the kind of thing I'd seen many times before, but again, the details were different. The sofa was a bright orange with the kind of swirling patterns that my gran used to like, and it was hard to tell which was more grotesque: the corpses or the wallpaper pattern. It was like some awful seventies throwback. But in the corner there was the first widescreen telly I'd seen here. New technology, old furniture; it was plain that Iraq had been changing when The Cull hit, caught between a brutal past and an uncertain future that at least promised shinier toys.

But Iraq hadn't moved forward into a bright new day of flatscreen HD tellies, democratic freedom and plush modern furnishings. It had bled out in a slow parade of mercy killings and suicide pacts.

Just like everywhere else.

"And Lee, listen, your mother..."

"Yes?"

"I've seen what this disease does. And I want..."

"No."

"Lee, I wouldn't ask..."

"Dad, no. Please. Don't ask me to do that."

"But..."

"No. I'm not like you. I couldn't do something like that. I just couldn't. I won't give up hope."

Right. First things first. I needed to sort out my shoulder. I took a quick walk through the flat but found only the abandoned fragments of other people's lives. I looked out the bedroom window at an expanse of sandy scrubland. It took me a minute to realise what I was looking at, but when I did it was all I could do to stop myself throwing up.

Lined up on the ground were three rows of impaled corpses. Maybe fifteen or more people, all with their hands tied behind their backs, lying with their faces skywards, sharpened wooden stakes protruding from their shattered ribcages. The stakes had been dug into the ground and then the victims must have been flung on to them. And pushed down. Recently, too; the flies were still buzzing.

I'd seen some pretty horrible deaths in recent months. I'd been responsible for a few of them. But this was far and away the most awful thing I'd seen.

I stood at the window for a minute or two, feeling the first stirrings of panic.

After all that had happened to me in the last hour, it took a field of impaled sacrifices to make me start panicking. That's a good indication of how fucked in the head I was at this point. Running, hiding, fighting for my life, killing people who were trying to kill me; all this had become part of an ordinary day. A year ago I'd have been a shuddering, stammering wreck. But now that stuff barely even touched the sides. I just got on with it.

A few weeks previously I'd stopped looking at myself in mirrors, started actively avoiding my own reflection, scared of what I'd see. I just kept telling myself to get on with it. Things to do. Sort it all out later. I think I imagined some sort of quiet solitude, a retreat or something, where I'd go and try to get my head straight once I'd got everything done, ticked the final item on my list of jobs (take out milk bottles, finish geography homework, defeat army of cannibals, iron shirts, fly to war zone and rescue Dad from enemy combatants who like impaling people).

I suspected that if I allowed myself too many moments of introspection I'd go mad.

I shook my head, impatient with myself.

Stop being maudlin.

Things to do.

Fix my shoulder. I was pretty sure it was only dislocated, not broken, and I knew how to sort that. You just grit your teeth and shove your shoulder really, really hard against a wall or something and it just snaps back in. Simple. I'd seen it in countless films.

It'd most likely hurt a lot, so I picked up a piece of wood from the floor, part of a smashed doorframe, and shoved it into my mouth. I didn't want any screams bringing my pursuers right to me. Then I stood before the bathroom wall and calmed my breathing, focused, and slammed my dislocated shoulder into the wall as hard as I possibly could.

The pain blinded me and I was unconscious before I hit the floor.

"All right, Lee. Look, I gotta go. Look after your mother. I love you."

"I love you too. And make sure you come find me, 'cause if you're not back in a year I'm going to come find you!"

"Don't joke. If I'm not back in a year, I'm–"

Click.

"Dad? Dad, you there? Dad?"

When you've been unconscious as many times as I have, you learn a few tricks. The most important is not to open your eyes until you're fully awake and have learned all you can about where you are and who's there with you.

I was bleeding, hungry and thirsty, and I ached all over from the crash and the kicking, but I was still alive.

The most obvious thing was that I wasn't lying on a tiled bathroom floor. I was sitting up, with cold metal cuffs binding my hands to the chair back. Someone had captured me, then. I'd probably screamed as I passed out and they found me where I dropped.

The second thing was that my shoulder hurt like hell and I still couldn't move my arm, so I hadn't managed to relocate it. Thanks a bunch, Hollywood.

The air was still and dry and there was no wind, so I was indoors. I listened carefully, but I couldn't hear anybody talking or breathing. I risked opening my eyes and found myself staring down the lens of a handy cam.

It took a minute for me to realise the implications. I craned around to look behind me, and saw that I was sitting in front of a blue sheet backdrop with Arabic script on it. That's when I really started to panic. Could I really have flown halfway round the world just to end up in a snuff video?

It took a lot of effort to regain my composure, but I calmed myself down, got my breathing under control, forced down the panic and concentrated on the details of the room. Dun, mud brick walls, sand floor. Single window, shuttered. Old, tatty blue sofa to my left, sideboard to my right. Lying on the sideboard was a big hunting knife, its razor sharp edge glinting at me like a promise. The handy cam was shiny and new, like it was fresh out of the box. Behind it there was a metal frame chair with canvas seat and back, the same as the one I now occupied. Next to that was an old coffee table on which were piled small video tapes. The last thing I noticed, which made the panic rise again, was the dark red stain on the floor, which formed a semi circle around my feet. There was a splash of the same stain across the floor in a straight line and on to the wall beside the sofa. That would be the first gush of arterial blood from the last poor bastard who'd sat in this chair.

I remembered the siege of St Mark's, two months earlier; walking into the Blood Hunters' camp, all cocky bravado, baiting the madman in his lair. I remembered the plan going horribly wrong, and the moment when they forced me to kill one of my own men. I remembered holding the knife as I slit Heathcote's throat, and felt the blood bubble and gush over my hands as I whispered pleas for forgiveness into the ear of my dying friend. I remembered the hollow ache that had sat in my stomach as I'd done that awful thing, the ache that had never left me, which still jolted me awake most nights, sweating and crying, reliving his murder over and over. He had not died easily or well. When the siege was over, and the school was a smoking ruin, I had found Heathcote's body in amongst the mass of slaughtered, and dug his grave myself. I had broken my arm so it took me two days, but I wouldn't let anyone else lift a shovel to help me.

It was as I placed the plain white cross on his grave that I realised I could not stay. All my decisions, all my plots and schemes and plans had just brought the school to ruin. It would be better for everyone if I left Matron in charge and gave the school a fresh start. I was cursed. I stayed long enough to heal the arm, and then I just walked away.

Dad hadn't shown up, and it had been nearly a year. Time for me to come good on my promise. Time to fly to Iraq and find out what had become of him. I had little expectation that he was still alive, but I had to try. I had to have something to keep going for, to stop me just ending it all. So I found myself a little Grob Tutor plane, the one I'd been taught to fly by the RAF contingent of the school's County Cadet Force, plotted a route via various RAF bases where I thought I'd be able to find fuel, and set off.

All that distance from Heathcote's grave, all that effort just to put myself in a place where I could suffer exactly the same fate. It seemed only fair. Inevitable, even.

"Poetic justice, Nine Lives," said the voice in my head. I couldn't really argue with that.

I heard footsteps approaching and low, murmuring voices. The door opened and two men stepped inside. They wore khaki jackets and trousers with tatty, worn out trainers. Both had their faces swathed in cloth, with only their dark eyes visible. They stopped talking and stood in the doorway for a moment, just staring at me. Not long ago I'd have wracked my brain for a quip or putdown, but there'd come a point some months back where I'd heard myself saying something flippant to a psychopath and I'd realised that it didn't make me cool; it just made me sound like an immature dick who'd seen too many bad action movies. So I just told the truth.

"I have no idea who you think I am," I said, trying to keep my voice level. "But I'm not your enemy."

They ignored me. The taller one moved to the handy cam and hunched over it, preparing to record. I wondered how he'd charged the battery. The shorter one checked the sheet behind me before picking up the knife and taking his place at my side, still and silent like a sentry.

"I'm just a boy from England looking for my dad," I went on hopelessly. "Just let me find him and I'll fuck off out of it, back home. I promise."

No response, just a red light on the handy cam, and the whirr of tiny motors as it opened to receive the tape.

Of course, it could be that they didn't even speak English.

"Look, there's no media any more anyway. There's no Internet or telly. So what's the point of cutting my head off on video? Who's going to see it?" I thought this was a pretty good point, but they didn't seem to care.

The cameraman slid the tape into place and snapped the handy cam closed. A moment's pause, then he nodded to his companion.

I tried to calm my nerves, tell myself that I'd been in situations like this before, that there was still a way out. But no-one knew I was here. There were no friends looking for me, no Matron to come riding to my rescue. I was thousands of miles from home, in a country where I couldn't make myself understood, and I was about to be executed as part of a war that was long since over.

I supposed it made as much sense as any other violent death.

I felt a tear trickle down my cheek, but I refused to give them the satisfaction of sobbing. The weird thing is, I wasn't sad for myself. I'd faced death many times, and I'd got to know this feeling pretty well. I was ready for it. I just felt guilty about my dad.

He'd never know what had happened to me after that phone call. I'd been looking forward to that conversation. I missed him.

The man standing beside me began to talk to the camera in Arabic. I made out occasional words (Yankee, martyr) but that was all. At one point I gabbled an explanation to the camera, drowning out his monologue. At least that way anyone watching it would know who I was. I had no idea where this video would end up so it was worth a shot, I supposed. Nothing else I could do.

"My name is Lee Keegan," I shouted. "It's my sixteenth birthday today, and I'm English. I flew here to find my dad, a Sergeant in the British Army, but my plane crashed and these guys found me. If anyone sees this, please let Jane Crowther know what happened to me. You can find her at Groombridge Place, in Kent, southern England. It's a school now. Tell her I'm sorry."

The guy with the knife punched me hard in the side of the head to shut me up. He finished his little speech and then there was silence, except for the soft whirr of tiny motors.

I stared straight into the camera lens, tears streaming down my face. I clenched my jaw, tried to look defiant. I probably looked like what I was: a weeping, terrified child.

I felt cold, sharp metal at my throat.

Then the guy behind the camera stood up straight, unwrapped his face and took off his jacket, revealing a t-shirt that read 'Code Monkey like you!'

"Hang on," he said. "Did you say your name was Keegan?"

And that's how I met Tariq.

CHAPTER TWO

I didn't follow the war in Iraq as closely as I should have.

You'd think that, with my dad on the front line, I'd have been watching and reading everything I could. But there was never any good news. It was all doom and gloom; insurgents, roadside bombs and body counts. It gave me nightmares to think of my dad in the middle of all that. So I stopped reading, listening and watching. I didn't want to know.

I knew the general details – Dad was in Basra, a coastal town important to oil supplies; things there weren't as bad as they were further north, where the Americans were in charge; the British troops didn't have the right equipment, or enough equipment, or any equipment at all, depending upon whether you watched the BBC, Sky News or Al Jazeera.

The only thing I knew for sure was that he was somewhere dangerous and there were people who wanted to kill him. Beyond that, I didn't ask.

But then, as Mum pointed out, that was his job. He was a

soldier. He put himself in harm's way to pay for our food and clothes, the roof over our heads and the education that would ensure I never had to risk my life the way he did.

I knew that her family paid for my schooling, not Dad, but I understood what she meant, so I just nodded. She knew how I felt, anyway; she was the daughter of a military man herself.

"John Keegan's son?"

He knew my dad. Oh God, maybe he'd already sat in this chair. Maybe that was his blood on the floor. My eyes went wide and I couldn't speak.

The young man stepped out from behind the camera. "Answer the question will you. Oh shit, he's going to..."

I leaned forward and threw up all over his sneakers. I wretched and wretched until I was dry heaving, snot and tears and puke sliming my face. He jumped backwards, but it was too late.

"Bloody hell, man," he said, grimacing at his vomit-coated sneakers. "Do you know how hard it is to get Chuck Jones out here? Fuck."

The guy with the knife laughed and said something to him in Arabic (is that what they spoke here? Or was it Iraqi? I'm ashamed to admit I didn't know). Sneaker man flipped him the bird, annoyed and sarcastic.

I sat back in the chair, feeling about as wretched and pathetic as it's possible to feel. I couldn't think of anything to say. My mind just kept replaying the image of my father sitting here, straining at his bonds as his throat was cut.

Sneaker man stepped forward, avoiding the puddle of puke. He reached into the back pocket of his jeans and pulled out a photo, which he held in front of me.

"My name is Tariq," he said. "Please, is this your father?"

It was Dad, in desert combats, smiling at the camera, holding a bottle of coke.

I nodded.

I wanted to scream "where did you get that? what have you done with him?" but experience back home taught me that people who enjoy slitting throats don't normally feel the need to explain themselves.

"Shit!" he said. "I thought you were one of the Yanks." Tariq shoved the knife man aside, grabbing his blade as he did so. He knelt down and began sawing at the rope that bound my wrists.

"If I'd known you were John's son, I'd never have done this."

The rope gave way and my hands were free. He shuffled around the front and began working on the rope that bound my feet.

"It's not like we were actually going to kill you. It's just a trick we use to make them talk. They think we're all Islamist nutters, so we play up to it. Works a treat."

Where the hell did his guy learn his English?

My feet came free and I sprang up, reached behind me and grabbed the chair with my good arm. In a moment I was standing in the corner, chair held up in front of me like a lion tamer.

"Honest, we weren't going to hurt you," he said, still crouching on the floor, discarded rope all around him. Then he rose to his feet, dropped the knife to the floor and kicked it over to me.

"We were just going to shit you up and make you talk."

"About what?"

He laughed. "You're going to love this."

"Try me."

"Well, we thought you could tell us where your father is."

Before I could answer, a young woman ran in. She was also wearing jeans and a t-shirt. What kind of radical Islamists were these? She spoke to Tariq quietly and with urgency, he replied briefly, then she ran from the room. Tariq reached around to the back of his trousers and pulled out an automatic, chambering a round. Another rush of adrenaline and fear; was he just going to shoot me?

"Your arrival attracted attention," he said. "We have to move. I do not have time to explain exactly what is happening here, but we are allies, you and I, and should be friends."

My disbelief must have been plain to see, because he sighed, stood up, ran his fingers through his thick black hair and said: "yes, I wouldn't believe me either. Okay, listen to me, Lee. We have to get away from this building quickly and quietly. If you make a noise or shout for help, then you will be killed. Do you understand? And later, when we are safe, I will explain everything and we will laugh about this."

"Right," I said. "If you say so."

He shook his head wearily and threw me the cloth that had bound his face. "Clean yourself."

I used my good arm to wipe my face clean. I finished with the cloth and dropped it to the floor. Jesus, I ached everywhere.

"We should fix your arm." Tariq reached forward and grabbed my useless limb. "Ready?" I nodded. "Don't scream."

He lifted, twisted and pushed, all at once. I felt the bone rotate and then snap back into its socket. I grunted, and my vision clouded for a moment, but I managed not to scream or pass out. He let go and I lifted my arm up. I could use it again, but it hurt like hell.

"Toseef is going to lead, you will go after him, I will follow you. Please, I beg you, don't do anything stupid. If you do, we will all die."

Then we were moving. We left that awful room and entered a living area with doorless frames and open windows. The girl was standing by the main door, rifle in hand, scanning the street outside. My three captors shared an urgent, whispered conference. It seemed the girl wanted to go out the front door and down the road; Tariq disagreed. Eventually he ended the discussion with a curt word of command, and we climbed out one of the side windows into a narrow, dusty alleyway that ran behind the houses on this street.

The sky was deep blue, not a cloud in sight, and the air was heavy and wet. I had expected Iraq to be dry, but Basra was a coastal town, humid and damp. It smelt different, the sandy tang of desert mixed with a dash of salt air from the sea. And something else, a hint of something thick and cloying; I would later learn that it was the smell of burning oil. As soon as I stepped out into that glaring sun I began sweating from every pore all at once. My t-shirt was patched with sweat before we'd even gone a hundred metres. I needed water. A whole great bathful, preferably, to wallow in for a week.

When we reached the end of the alley the girl motioned for us to flatten ourselves against the wall as she peered cautiously round the corner to see if the street was clear. She leaned back into cover and held up her hands to signal that there were two of whoever it was we were hiding from, to the right. She indicated that they were not looking our way.

Again there was a disagreement. The girl wanted to risk running across the road to the alley opposite; Tariq wanted to go back the way we had come. This time, she won the toss. She counted down from three with her fingers, and we broke cover. It was only a few metres to a burnt-out car, and we made it without the alarm being raised. We huddled behind it. She glanced down the road on my right, Tariq on my left. Stuck between them, with Toseef, I was unable to see who or what we were hiding from. All I could see was a tiny lizard, sunning itself on the rear bumper of the car, an inch from my nose. Lying there, frying itself alive on that scalding metal, it radiated warm contentment.

Toseef grabbed my bad arm to get my attention and I winced. He let go and gave me a look that said sorry. Tariq gave us a silent countdown and we all turned to face the other side of the road as the girl moved to my side, ready to run. There was no-one behind me. They all broke cover, scurrying for the other side of the road. But in the heat of the moment none of them tried to drag me with them; they were so focused on their own predicament they must have just assumed I'd follow suit. But I didn't. I let them run away and I stayed, crouched behind the car with my small, cold-blooded friend. They didn't realise I wasn't with them until they reached the safety of the opposite alleyway. Tariq turned, alarmed. I waved at him and smiled. He slapped Toseef around the head, annoyed, then urgently beckoned for me to follow them. I pretended to consider this for a moment, then shook my head, grinning. I didn't trust him an inch.

Of course, I hadn't exactly escaped, but I'd bought myself an opportunity. I turned away from his frantic gesticulations, and peered around the side of the car. About thirty metres down the road stood a humvee. Result! Through the heat haze I could just make out two soldiers standing either side of the vehicle, backs to me. I looked back at Tariq and I could tell he was about to come running back for me. Now or never.

I stood up and began walking towards the vehicle. I saw Tariq grasp the air in fury and frustration, so I gave him a jaunty wave and sauntered towards the soldiers. I was safe.

"Hey guys," I shouted when I was halfway between the burnt-out car and them. I had stopped walking and had my arms raised high and wide. Didn't want to give them an excuse to shoot.

They spun around, rifles raised to their shoulders, but they didn't fire. They hesitated, obviously surprised and suspicious.

"I'm British," I yelled. "I just arrived here. I'm looking for my dad. He's a squaddie like you."

That sounded as lame as it did unlikely, but it was the truth so it was all I had. I expected them to tell me to lie on the ground, hands behind my head, that sort of thing. But they didn't move. One of them reached for his radio and muttered something to someone, then his colleague shouted: "take off your shirt. Slowly."

It took me a second to work out what he'd said, and then another to work out why.

"Okay," I said. "But my shoulder's pretty torn up, so bear with me." Both rifles were sighted on my chest as I struggled out of my shirt. I let it drop to the ground. "All right? See, no bomb vest."

"Now your pants."

"Seriously?"

"Do it!"

So I unbuckled my belt and let my combats fall around my ankles. I considered making an inappropriate quip, something like "if you want me to take my boxers off, you'll have to buy me lunch first," but I thought better of it.

"On the ground, hands behind your head."

I sank to my knees and lay down on the ground as he'd instructed. The gritty dirt burnt my skin, and a sharp stone jammed itself between my ribs, but I didn't wriggle. I heard them walking towards me slowly, their heavy boots grinding the dust beneath them.

"Lie completely still," said the talkative one. "If you move a muscle my friend here will shoot you dead."

"Understood. Just be careful please, I dislocated my shoulder earlier and it hurts like fuck."

I heard him fumbling with something, and then a thin strip of cold plastic was looped around my wrists and pulled tight. Then he grabbed my bound wrists and hauled me upright, grinding my damaged shoulder horribly. I yelled in pain and anger.

"Sorry," he said sarcastically.

The talkative one pushed me ahead of him, back to the humvee, while his mate scanned the surrounding buildings for danger. I had so many questions I wanted to ask them, but I decided it would be best to keep quiet for now. These were frightened, frightening soldiers; anything could happen. Best wait 'til I was safe in their HQ talking to a senior officer. Shouldn't take long to sort everything out then.

And yet... I didn't tell them about Tariq and his friends, hiding in an alleyway behind us. I was probably concussed, certainly dehydrated, definitely scared, and it was only as they marched me back to the car with brisk military efficiency that it occurred to me, belatedly, that perhaps my judgement wasn't the finest right now. So I kept quiet about the Islamists who had nearly beheaded me, the ones who could even now be taking up positions in nearby buildings and sighting their rifles on us. I think that maybe, through all my confusion and adrenaline, I'd started to have an inkling that I'd jumped out of the frying pan into the fire.

They shoved me into the humvee roughly. My shin banged painfully against the metal lip of the door, making me curse. The quiet one stayed outside on guard, while the one who'd bound my wrists sat opposite me. He was a young man, about twenty; Hispanic, with a wispy, bumfluff moustache. But despite his youth he seemed confident, in control, self contained. His face was hard and cold, and gave nothing away. I suppose his accent could have told me which part of the States he was from, but apart from New York and the deep south I don't know my American accents well.

"Name, rank, serial number," barked Bumfluff.

"I'm not a soldier."

"You're British, right?"

"Yeah."

"Name, rank and serial number. That's all you Brits ever tell us."

"If we're soldiers. And it's the Second World War. And you're Nazis. But I'm not a soldier and you're not wearing jackboots."

So the Yanks and the Brits weren't working together. Maybe they were even enemies. Suddenly all my preconceptions came tumbling down. I'd assumed that the army would have retained some order and discipline in the face of The Cull, but sitting here, facing an American soldier who thought I was an enemy, that idea seemed wilfully naïve. They could have splintered into all sorts of warring factions. This led straight to the idea that maybe Tariq and his gang had not been all they seemed either, and I cursed my prejudices and my stupidity.

From the second I'd hit dirt I'd been reacting instinctively and without thought. I knew too well that that kind of thing gets you killed.

Engage your brain, Keegan.

"Tourist?" he asked.

"I flew here from England."

"Economy?"

"You must have seen my plane coming down, light aircraft, two seater. I've been unconscious but I think it was yesterday."

"Maybe."

"I was shot down."

"Not by us."

So should I tell him about Dad? I couldn't see why not. I had to ask someone, after all.

"Listen, I'm just looking for my father. He's a sergeant in the British Army. He never came home after The Cull. I flew here to find him."

"On your own?"

"Yes."

"And you're, what, fifteen?"

"Sixteen. Yesterday."

"Happy fucking birthday."

"Thanks. Do I get a cake?"

"I don't have time for your bull, kid. It'll be better for you if you just tell us the truth."

"My name is Lee Keegan, my father's name is John, he's a Sergeant in the British army and I just want to find out if he's okay. If you radio your base I'm sure they can just check their records and it'll all be sorted out in no time."

His eyes went wide with surprise and recognition. Obviously he knew my dad, or knew of him. So I'd been captured by two groups since touching down and both knew my dad. What were the odds? What the hell was going on here? Bumfluff was thinking hard. It looked like it hurt.

"John Keegan? Your father's name is John Keegan?"

"Yes. Know him?"

"Oh yeah. I know him. Our General is going to be very happy to see you."

Something in the way he said that convinced me that I wouldn't be so happy to be seen.

"Great," I said, cheerily. "But look, I'm not whoever you thought I was, right? I'm obviously not a threat, and I want to come with you. So can I please put my clothes on? I mean, I'm getting grit in places you don't want to grit to get, know what I'm saying? And I don't want to see my dad for the first time in two years just dressed in my boxers."

He considered me carefully and I gave him my most innocent, pleading grin.

"Please?"

He nodded slowly. "Reckon it can't hurt. Hey, Shane, go get the kid's clothes. We'll get him dressed then head back. We're going to get so much kudos for this." His friend looked at him quizzically. "This is Keegan's son." Shane gave a small whistle.

"Fuck me," he said, nodding in appreciation. "Score!" Then he walked off to get my clothes, gun raised, scanning the buildings as he went.

"My dad popular then, huh?" I asked, playing dumb.

"Oh yeah, kid. Everyone wants a piece of your dad." He chuckled. I chuckled with him. Good joke. He was now completely convinced that he had outsmarted me in some undefined way. If it came to a battle of wits, I didn't think this guy would be too much trouble. But the body armour, knife and guns did kind of give him the edge. I was going to need help whatever happened. Time to jump out of the fire and back into the frying pan; I just hoped Tariq and his crew were still watching, because despite what they'd put me through I felt they were more likely to be my allies than the musclebrain sitting before me.

Shane got back and threw my trousers and shirt on the ground outside the vehicle. Bumfluff indicated that I should step down, and I did so. I turned, holding out my bound hands for him to untie me.

"Don't try anything stupid," he said.

"Look I just want to see my dad. You're going to take me to him. Why would I cause trouble?"

He grunted and sliced open the plastic tie with his knife. "I'm gonna be standing right here. You so much as twitch and I'll stick you. Understand?"

I nodded. I shook the sand off my clothes and pulled them on. No point trying anything now; they were expecting me to. Once I was dressed I meekly turned around, put my wrists together behind my back, and let Bumfluff put on another wrist tie. Then he relaxed. Silly boy.

I struggled into the humvee and managed to sit back in my seat. Shane and Bumfluff took the opportunity to have a whispered conversation outside, and I undid my wrist tie.

Yes, I know, what kind of person travels around with a tiny scalpel blade gaffer taped to the inside of the back of their trouser waist band? All I can say is, when you've been tied up as often as I have you learn to take precautions, and it's the kind of little detail that a cursory pat down isn't going to uncover. I had one inside my right front pocket as well, just in case they tied my hands in front. And one in each of my shoes. And sewn into the hem of each trouser leg, in case they went for a hog tie approach. Back before The Cull it would have been crazy, now it was just part of life. Of surviving.

My life had brought me to the point where I took routine precautions against being hog tied. Jesus.

Now what to do? I could wait for them to get back in. One of them would sit in front of me and I could probably liberate his knife and improvise from there. But I'd be trapped in an enclosed space with two strong, armed men. Not an attractive proposition. Then an obvious approach occurred to me.

I reached forward, grabbed the door handle, and slammed it shut before they could react. I pressed down the lock and voila, I was safe inside an armoured cage.

I scrambled into the front as the two soldiers rattled the door handles, shouting and threatening me. I ignored them. The keys weren't in the ignition. I couldn't drive, but I figured I'd have been able to at least get the damn thing moving, but no luck. I needed another plan; assuming the glass wasn't bullet proof it wouldn't be long before they just shot me. I scanned the controls for inspiration as I rifled through the glove compartments hoping to find a spare firearm. Nothing. I saw a radio clipped on to the dashboard, but who would I call? Then I noticed a tiny button next to it that said 'loudspeaker'.

I grabbed the radio, flipped the switch and shouted "Okay Tariq, I trust you. Come get me."

The two soldiers immediately shifted their attention from me to the surrounding buildings, raising their rifles to their shoulders, eyes going wide with sudden fear. It didn't help them. There was a single crisp rifle shot and Shane's back slammed against the side of the car. He left a red stain on the window as he slid down to the ground. Bumfluff started running for the street corner. I thought he was going to make it, and I was almost rooting for him, but then there was another crack and his head jerked sideways and blossomed with red. He fell to the ground and didn't move again.

Two more deaths on my conscience. And what would happen when I opened the door? What if they decided to just shoot me too? I didn't fancy the odds, but I'd made my choice and I had to live with it. What option did I have?

So I unlocked the door, jumped down, grabbed the rifle from Shane's cooling corpse, and stood there waiting.

Tariq burst out of the side alley on his own and came haring towards me, shouting.

"Keys, get the keys."

I didn't move, keeping my rifle trained on him as he ran.

His face was a mix of frustration and fury as he skidded to a halt beside me.

"Fine, I'll do it." He fell to his knees and rummaged through Shane's pockets until he found the keys then he ran around to the driver's side and leapt in. "Coming?"

I heard the sound of an engine echoing down the street; someone was coming, probably more soldiers. I jumped into the passenger seat and slammed the door. Tariq didn't hesitate. He turned the ignition, revved the humvee, and we took off at full speed in a cloud of sand and dust.

"Where are the others?" I asked.

"Lying low. We've got to draw the soldiers away from them. We'll meet up with them later."

"If we escape."

"If we escape." He wrenched the wheel and we careened around a corner. "What changed your mind?"

"Call it a hunch," I said

"Good call."

"I'm still not so sure about that. Did you really need to kill them? You couldn't have just fired some warning shots or something?"

He cursed in Arabic; obviously my stupidity was annoying him. "You told them your name, yeah?"

"Yeah."

"But they didn't radio it in, did they?"

"No."

"If they had, we'd be in a lot of trouble."

An armoured car appeared in the distance ahead of us. I was flung sideways as Tariq swerved into an alleyway littered with abandoned cars. We smashed our way through the obstacles, sending the hollow metal wrecks spinning and rolling as we slalomed our way between them.

"More trouble than this?"

"Fuck yeah."

One car braced itself against another and they dug into the

ground as we hit them. The humvee's nose wrenched itself upwards and we rolled over the vehicles, bouncing madly, my head
crashing against the roof. Tariq was yelling, but it was hard to tell
whether it was in excitement or terror. Then we hit dirt again and
the alley cleared ahead of us. Left on to another main road and
that was that, we didn't see another car until we pulled up at the
dock ten minutes later.

Tariq hit the brakes and the humvee skidded to a halt just inches
from the water.

"Out," he barked.

I didn't need telling twice. I clambered down, bruised and shak-
en, holding the rifle tight.

"Now help me," he said, leaning forward and pushing with all
his strength. I didn't bother asking why, I just took up the strain
on my side. Together we pushed the humvee into the water and
watched it sink. Then Tariq turned and walked away. I stood and
watched him for a minute then I shouted after him.

"Should I come with you, or what?"

"I don't really care," he replied, without glancing back or slowing down. "If Toseef or Anna are dead because of your fucking
stupidity, I'll kill you myself when we get back to base. But if
they're fine, you're better off with me. Your call."

He rounded a corner and was gone.

I thought about it for a moment then I shrugged and ran after
him.

At the near-derelict building that Tariq's group used as an HQ,
an American deserter called Brett gave me anti-inflammatories for
my shoulder, and patched and dressed my various wounds.

When he'd finished, Tariq apologised for being so harsh by
referring to yet another online personality I'd never heard of –
"sorry, I was a dick. Wil Wheaton would not be impressed" – then
spent a couple of hours telling me his story. We sat on a flat, warm
roof looking out over the city as the dusk turned to darkness and
he laid it all out for me. It was a lot to take in, and it raised almost as many questions as it gave answers, but I mostly let him

talk without interruption. When he had finished we sat in silence for a while, and then I told him my story in return. By the time I finished I felt that we had reached an understanding; after all, our experiences weren't that different when you got to the root of it.

Then he told me his plan and my role in it.

Then he gave me food and water and showed me where I could bed down for the night. I slept well, woke with the dawn and went looking for Tariq. I found him on the roof, exactly where I'd left him the night before.

"Well?" he asked.

"Your plan is insane."

He shrugged as if to say 'what can you do?' I laughed and shook my head ruefully.

"Our chances of success are..." I didn't have a word for that amount of small.

Again he shrugged and smiled.

I looked out over Basra. The squat white buildings of the centre, the tower blocks in the distance, the docks full of abandoned boats. And on the horizon the columns of rising smoke as the oil burned out of the wells. I was so very far from home. I'd come here on a very personal mission, tired of having the weight of everybody's expectations hanging on me, weary of making decisions that determined which of my friends would live and die. I'd figured that either I'd find my dad or I'd die trying. Either way, the only person paying for my mistakes would be me.

Now here I was, in Basra only a day, and a guy I barely knew was asking me to take on a huge responsibility. It almost seemed like fate was laughing at me. No matter how far I flew, I seemed to end up at the centre of things. I might as well just get used to it. I shrugged and held out my hand.

"It's a stupid plan, but okay," I said. "I'm in."

So an hour later, unarmed and on my own, I walked up the main gate of Saddam's palace and surrendered myself to the American Army.

CHAPTER THREE

It took my eyes a minute to adjust to the darkness.

The cell, deep underneath the palace complex, smelt of sweat and bad breath, fear and urine. The silence was absolute once the footsteps of the American soldier who'd thrown me in here had faded away; no whirr of air conditioning, no echoes from the long corridor outside, no snatches of distant conversation. Which is how I could hear the soft breath of the cell's other occupant.

I stayed just inside the door until I began to make out shapes.

Thin chinks of light filtered in through the square holes in the metal window shutter, picking out the concrete walls, the bucket in the corner beside me with the cloth over it to mask the stench, the filthy mattress on the floor and the man lying upon it, knees pulled up, arms around his legs, foetal. It was hard to make out details but he seemed wounded; something about the hunch of his shoulders, the way his head was buried in his lap, spoke of pain and endurance.

My stomach felt empty and hollow, my head swam. I think I was more scared at that moment than I had ever been. It wasn't the fear of combat or imminent death; that fear was half adrenaline. This was deeper, stronger; the fear of loss, fear born of love.

My mouth was dry as chalk so my first attempt to speak came out as a strangled croak. I bit my cheeks, squeezed out a drop of saliva to moisten my tongue and tried again.

"Dad?"

I remember the excitement I always felt when I knew Dad was coming home. I'd run to meet him in the driveway where he'd pick me up, swing me around and hug me so tight I couldn't catch my breath. The house smelt different when he was home, of Lynx deodorant and shaving cream, boot polish and Brasso (which, trust me, doesn't really make pigeons explode). We'd go see football matches, take trips to the cinema, he'd teach me to swim or ride my bike and it would be glorious. And then he'd be gone again, for months at a time, just phone calls and letters and Mum putting a brave face on it.

We never lived on station, in barracks or Army housing. Mum's family had money, and Dad insisted that I shouldn't grow up an Army brat. He'd always been so determined to keep me as far away from the trappings of the military as possible, absolutely insisted that I should never pick up a gun.

I wondered how he'd react when I finally found him, when he saw what The Cull had made of me. But it never occurred to me to wonder what The Cull would have made of him. He'd become this fixed point in my mind. My dad. Solid, reliable, capable, wounded inside but getting on with things as if he weren't. He couldn't change.

How naïve of me.

The foetal figure didn't stir. I spoke again.

"Dad, is that you?"

He let out a low mumble. I couldn't make it out.

"Dad, it's me. It's Lee." I took a step forward, tentatively.

Again he mumbled, this time a little louder.

"Go away," he growled.

Once, when Dad was home on leave from his Kosovo posting, I came running into the bedroom to find him fast asleep, taking a crafty afternoon nap. I had something I wanted to show him. I can't remember what it was any more, but I was five and it was super mega important that I show my dad this amazingly cool thing.

Anyway, I ran in, grabbed his arm and shook him awake.

One of the stupidest things I've ever done.

I don't remember the movement clearly, but he was instantly in motion. Before I could utter another syllable I was in a head-lock and he was squeezing my windpipe tightly. I remember that his right hand went to my temple and braced. I realise now that he was about to snap my neck.

He came to just in time, got his bearings, woke up properly. Then he sprang back across the bed, pushing me away from him with a cry of terror and alarm. He curled up into a ball then, too, shaking, the horror of what he'd almost done sending him into a near catatonic state of shock. I sat on the floor, mouth open, stunned. I definitely remember thinking that my dad really needed me not to cry, so I tried very hard and managed to stop my lower lip trembling.

After a minute or so I calmed myself down and I climbed on to the bed, where I put my arms around him and gave him a cuddle. We stayed like that for a long time as he muttered, over and over again "I'm so sorry, so sorry", and I said it was okay, everything was okay.

From that day on, if I ever had to wake Dad for any reason, I always talked to him at a normal volume from beyond arm's reach until he awoke. Nothing like that ever happened again, but I had learned, at five years old, that my dad, my brilliant, wonderful, funny, teach me cycling, football kicking, fish and chip supper Dad was in some fundamental way broken. And he never told me why.

I sat in the corner of the cell, opposite the bucket, at the foot of the mattress, and just started to talk.

"I waited for you. At school. I waited a whole year for you to come and get me. But you didn't show up, so I figured I'd better keep my promise and come get you. I stole a plane, mapped out a route, selected RAF bases for refuelling and here I am.

"Remember how annoyed you were when I joined the cadets? Even though it wasn't the army cadets, you were still furious. 'I don't care if you get to fly, you still have to handle a gun and I won't allow it,' you said. But I argued and argued, and Mum backed me up. Wow, I remember that row. But hey, they taught me to fly, which is all I really wanted. I didn't care about the guns and the uniform and the drill. It was just an excuse for the really crappy teachers to shout at us a bit more and make themselves feel important. Anyway, I hate guns. Always have. Still do. But I can't deny that training came in useful.

"So here I am and it's all the RAF's fault. So I'm glad I stood my ground, 'cause otherwise I might never have found you. And that would have been terrible.

"I got shot down on approach though. I couldn't find the airport and I was circling the city trying to make it out, navigating by the river. I flew God knows how many thousand miles in a straight line, found and landed at three different RAF bases, then I get to my destination without a hitch and can't find an international bloody airport! Pathetic, really.

"Anyway, I crash landed, threw out my shoulder, and got chased halfway across town by a bunch of local nutjobs who kept taking pot shots at me. But eventually I got lucky, found this place. I thought I was safe.

"So much for that."

The man on the mattress slowly began to unfold himself as I wittered. I caught my breath and my monologue petered out. Gradually he levered himself upright and I could see his face.

He was unshaven, his hairline had receded a bit and there was a lot more grey there. His eyes were deep pools of black. But it was Dad.

"Lee?" His voice was little more than a whisper.

"Yes."

"Oh God, Lee?"

He raised his hands to his face and a flash of white bandage caught the scarce light. His right arm ended in a mass of bandages.

Someone had cut off two of his fingers.

I gulped the coke gratefully but soon remembered why it was a drink for sipping; the bubbles burned my parched throat and I let out a mighty belch.

"I'm sorry," said Brett after he'd massaged my damaged shoulder more securely back into its socket. "We've got no painkillers left. It's just going to have to heal at its own pace. You'll have restricted movement for a while."

I laughed. "I broke my other arm about six weeks ago and I still can't quite use it one hundred per cent. I'm going to look like Frankenstein's monster." I tried to lift both my arms straight in front of me, but it hurt too much. "Maybe not."

Brett smiled and went back downstairs. I remained on the roof with Tariq, sprawled on a tatty old sofa that had been dumped up here, enjoying the soft, shapeless, smelly cushions; after a week in the cockpit of a light aircraft it felt like the Ritz.

Tariq looked at me thoughtfully. Nineteen or twenty, the Iraqi was about five seven, with short black hair, dark skin and brown eyes. His geeky T-Shirt ("what, you don't know Jonathan Coulton?" he said, amazed, when I asked about it), Converse sneakers and jeans, not to mention his improbably white teeth, brilliant colloquial English, and the shoulder holster with sidearm nestled snugly beneath his left arm, sent out a confusing mass of signals that I couldn't quite decipher.

"So Brett's a Yank," I said, "but you and your friends are fighting the Yanks?"

He nodded.

"And even though the Yanks and the Brits were allies, my dad has been fighting with you?"

Tariq nodded again.

"And you're not Islamic fundamentalists?"

Tariq shook his head, grinning.

"What are you then?"

Tariq thought about this for a moment then he shrugged and said: "Brett is a hockey fan from Iowa, Toseef has a thing for thrash metal, and I'm a celebrity blogger." My confusion must have been obvious. Tariq laughed. "We're a family," he said simply.

I thought of Norton and Rowles, the dinner lady and Matron, and all my friends back at the school. I nodded. I understood that. "And the guy who attacked me? The one who died?"

He shook his head sadly. "Jamail. Good kid but hotheaded. A shoot first, ask questions later kind of boy. He was hard to control, and he made me crazy. But he would have grown into a fine man. He was the one who shot you down, even though I ordered him not to."

"I didn't kill him, you know. The plane exploded, there was shrapnel." It suddenly occurred to me that word was way too obscure, so I added: "that's metal that goes flying around after a big bang."

He looked at me like I was an idiot. "I know what shrapnel is."

"Sorry. Of course you do."

"I've lived in a fucking war zone the last eight years."

"Of course, I'm sorry. It's just that it's not a word we use every day in England." I suddenly felt very embarrassed. "Your English is really good," I added, lamely.

He beamed, his face transformed into a mask of boyish glee. "I know. I studied very hard. I wanted to go to university in England. Your father was going to help me with my applications."

"You knew him before The Cull, then?"

"Everyone knew your dad. Most people kept their distance. It was not wise to be too friendly with the occupying forces. But it was his job to make friends with local people, and I decided to become his friend. I was a liaison. I got good books and DVDs that way. And these sneakers which you fucking well threw up on."

"Sorry. But you did tie me to a chair and threaten to decapitate me."

"It's a traditional Iraqi greeting." He was so stony faced as he said this that, for a moment, I didn't realise he was joking.

"Very funny," I said. Only the tiniest twinkle in his eye betrayed his amusement. A big, gun-carrying geek with a desert-dry sense of humour.

"My name's Lee," I said, holding out my hand. "I think we're going to be friends."

"I would like that," he replied, taking my hand.

"I don't have any DVDs though."

"Oh. Sod off then."

In the fetid darkness of the cell, I looked at him. And he looked at me. And neither of us knew who we were looking at.

"But..." Dad shook his head and blinked his eyes as if he couldn't believe what was happening.

"Your time was up," I said. "I told you I'd come and get you if you didn't come home within a year. So here I am." I laughed and gestured at the dry concrete walls. "I've come to rescue you."

His shoulders hunched and he gritted his teeth.

"You think this is funny?"

"No, I..."

"You think this is a fucking joke?"

"Dad, listen..."

"You were safe! I told you to go to school and stay there. You were safe! Christ. Everything I've been through, everything I've done here, the one thing, the one thing I held on to as my friends were dying, was that at least you were out of it, at least you were safe. What the hell are you doing here, Lee? Why couldn't you just do as you were told, eh? Just this fucking once, why couldn't you do what I told you?"

My stomach tied itself in knots as he shouted at me, just as it always had. When you hero worship your dad, the last thing you want to do is let him down, make him angry, give him a reason to shout at you.

It had been a long time since I'd felt the shame of a child who's let down a parent, and it took me by surprise.

"Safe? Jesus, Dad, I'm safer here!" I protested.

"Do you have any idea what's going on here?" He shouted. "What you've come running in to the middle of?" Then suddenly the anger just drained out of him. His shoulders slumped as he closed his eyes and bowed his head. "Oh God, Lee," he whispered. "What have you done? What have you done?"

I felt the shame slowly change and build into the kind of self-righteous anger unique to teenage boys having a fight with their dads.

"What have I done?" I hissed. "I'll tell you what I've done. I've shot and killed my history teacher, shoved a knife into the heart of a prefect, shot three others, slit the throat of one of my friends, watched my best friend murdered right in front of me. I've been complicit in torture, executions and gang rape. I've been shot, stabbed, strangled, blown up and hanged. I've seen battles and massacres and all of it's on me. My fault, my doing. All the bloodshed, all the death, all of it on me. And through all of it, all the shit, all the killing, all I kept telling myself, over and over again, was 'Dad'll be here soon, he'll sort this out'. But you never came. You left me on my own in a fucking nightmare and you promised, you swore you'd come and find me. Where were you, Dad? Where the fuck were you?"

Hot, furious tears were streaming down my cheeks as I shouted terrible things at the person I loved most in the world.

"You left me, you bastard" I shouted. "You fucking left me!"

My anger gave way to impotent sobbing. And then he was holding me, like I'd held him on the bed all those years before, and he was saying softly: "It's okay, I'm here, everything's okay now."

And despite everything, it was. It really was.

"Your dad was on the last plane out," Tariq explained. "Part of his job was to liaise with local people, and he stayed as long as he could, trying to see that everyone he knew was taken care of. I lost count of how many people he helped when things got bad; bringing food and medicine, persuading the army doctors to visit the sick, even looking after some people himself when the withdrawal began.

"That's why he was on the last plane out, because he stayed to help. But someone shot the plane down. We don't know who or why. Cowardly thing to do, shooting down the last retreating plane. It was a Hercules, full of troops. It crashed over by the river and only your father and two other men survived. He is very lucky to be alive. Assuming he is still alive."

"He's alive," I said, trying to persuade myself.

Tariq looked at me curiously. "What was it like in England?"

I sighed. "I heard it was chaos in the cities. Fires and mobs and mass graves. But where I was, in the countryside, it was kind of civilised. Lots of old ladies locking themselves away, desperate not to be a bother to anybody. The odd farmer started shooting anyone they saw on their land, but that was about as bad as it got. The trouble only really started after the plague burnt itself out."

"It was not like that here," said Tariq, shaking his head wearily. "Exactly the opposite. The British got orders to pull out and leave us to die. There was talk of a big operation back home."

That triggered a memory: a dead man, tied to a chair screaming.

"Operation Motherland?"

"Yes, that was it. Your father never told me what it was, but the army just packed up and left. The Medhi army tried to take control for a while. There were some massacres, lots of fighting. It was horrible. But then Sadr died of the plague and eventually there weren't enough of them left and it just sort of dribbled away.

"For us, the plague ended the fighting. The big armies were gone and there was more than enough room for all the religious and racial groups to stay out of each other's way. The Kurds have their own homeland now, in the north. The Shi'ites and the Sunnis have their own towns and holy places and they leave each other alone. And although there are only a few hundred of them left, it's the first time in living memory that no-one's been trying to wipe out the marsh Arabs up in Maysan.

"The Cull was the best thing that ever happened to Iraq. It achieved what no army ever could: it brought peace."

I couldn't help but laugh. The irony that so much death could end the killing.

"So what went wrong?" I asked.

"After the British had gone, the Americans came to Basra."

"What was so bad about that?"

Tariq looked at me in amazement, as if I'd just asked the stupidest question of all time.

"Did you not see the pictures from Abu Ghraib? Hear about the murders in Haditha?"

"Of course, but you're not going to tell me that all American soldiers are like that. I mean, those were isolated incidents. Bad apples."

Tariq inclined his head, as if to say "maybe".

"You may be right. We have Brett with us, and there were others who deserted rather than follow the orders they were given. Brett is American and he has saved my life more than once."

"Well then."

"But what they did here, Lee. It was awful."

"Then tell me."

He thought for a second and then shook his head.

"No," he said. "I will show you."

"Start at the beginning," said Dad. "And tell me everything."

So I did. From the moment I arrived at the school gates, to the explosion that levelled the place. I left nothing out. All the decisions I'd made, the consequences of those choices, the lives I'd ended or destroyed. The blood and the guilt. When I finished he just sat there and stared at me, tears rolling down his face. It took him a long time to find his voice.

"I don't..." he whispered. "I'm so sorry."

I shrugged. "Not your fault."

We sat there in silence for a few moments, neither of us knowing what to say.

"Remember all those arguments you and Mum used to have about Grandad?" I asked, forcing a grin, changing the subject.

He smiled and nodded, wiping his eyes.

"He thought the army was the only place for a young man," he said.

"'Just look at your father,'" I said, imitating Grandad's round, fruity, upper class vowels. "'It made a man out of him.'"

"And the way he said that, so you knew that he meant 'and he was just a bloody guttersnipe'."

"Never liked you much, did he?"

"Oh, he was all right I s'pose. He could have been a lot worse, believe me. It's just, well, he was a bloody General and he thought his little girl married beneath her. She should have married an officer, but she ended up with a Black Country grunt for a son-in-law and he didn't really know how to talk to me. He had this idea that if you joined up you'd go straight to Sandhurst and the Officer's Club, and at least the next generation would sort of get things back on track. He could pull some strings, make sure you'd never end up a squaddie. Not like me."

"You used to get so angry when he started banging on about me joining the army, especially when Mum didn't tell him to stop."

"I never wanted you to become a soldier," said dad, seriously.

"Well, look at me. That's what I am now, Dad. Sorry. At least Grandad would be proud of me."

He started, looked surprised, made to say something, but I cut him off.

"He died early," I said. "Him and Gran. First wave."

"I know, your Mum told me on the phone."

There was an awkward silence, then he said: "About your mother."

"I don't really want to talk about it."

"But it must have been..."

"It was what it was."

I avoided his eyes as he searched my face for clues. Eventually he nodded, accepting my refusal to talk about her death. I was grateful for that.

"So the school was destroyed and you just, what, stole a plane and flew here on your own?"

I nodded. He whistled through his teeth.

"Nowhere else for me to go," I said.

"You could have stayed there. Gone with them to the new place. They're your friends, surely you'd have been welcome?"

I didn't feel like explaining myself any more, so I just shrugged.

He gestured to the cell walls. "And how...?"

"I surrendered. Thought they'd know where you were. Which, as it turns out, they did."

"Oh Lee, you shouldn't have come here. You really shouldn't."

"Why are you a prisoner?" I asked.

But I knew damn well why.

There were skeletons everywhere, picked clean by predators and bleached by the sun. Charred, tattered clothing still hung off most of them.

The low stands of the rickety football stadium were mostly free of bodies. A few people who'd tried to escape were sprawled across the wooden benches, but the majority of the dead lay in piles on the pitch itself. They were grouped in tens and twenties, as if neighbours and families had huddled together when the shooting started.

"The adults tried to protect the children," said Tariq, following my gaze. "Used their bodies to shield them from the bullets. Told them to play dead. Didn't work. The soldiers went through the bodies, finishing off survivors. Then they poured petrol over them and set them alight. One man had been missed by the sweep but he ran, screaming and burning out of the bodies and was shot. That's him, there." He pointed to a small heap of disarticulated bones.

In the face of such a sight all I could manage was the obvious question.

"Why?"

"Orders. Secure the town, evict the survivors, kill anyone who wouldn't leave willingly. All these people wanted was to be left alone, to rebuild their town."

But in spite of the evidence I still couldn't believe that the Americans had done this. Dad used to call them cowboys, insisted their army wasn't as well disciplined or trained as ours, but they were still the good guys. No matter how bad things got I couldn't believe that the American army would do such a thing. A few loose cannons losing the plot at a checkpoint and killing some civilians, yes. But cold-bloodedly massacring a hundred people? Surely not.

Then I remembered something Grandad told me once: "An army is only as good as the orders it receives."

So who was giving the orders?

"It was a SAM that brought us down," said Dad. God knows who fired it. We never found out. There were about seventy of us on board. I've never been so certain I was going to die. But somehow I walked away. I was sitting right at the back, just got lucky. I wasn't the only one, mind. There were two others, Jonno and Jim. Good lads. Quite a double act, they were."

"What happened to them?" I asked.

"They're dead now. It took us two days to get back to HQ. We figured it was the safest place. But when we got here we found the Yanks had moved in. I tell you, I'd never been so happy to see a white star in my life. So we come rolling up to them, waving and smiling, and they welcome us with open arms. Then they throw us in here and start interrogating us."

"About what?"

"About home. England. The army. Something called Operation Motherland."

"What's that?"

He shrugged. "Search me. I know it's what we were supposed

to be doing when we got back to England. But no-one briefed us before we left. And fuck knows why the Yanks here are so bothered what we're doing back home. Makes no sense."

I started to ask Dad how he got free but I was just able to stop myself. I remembered what Tariq had told me; the Yanks would be listening to us and they mustn't know I'd had contact with them. Which meant I had to mislead Dad as well, at least for now.

"So how did you... cope with being tortured then? I mean, you must have been locked up for, what, eight or nine months?"

It was lame. My hesitation was too obvious, the substituted question too stupid. Dad looked at me askance for a second but I just about carried it off. I hoped whoever was listening to us was as easily fooled.

"Nah, we broke out," he said. "Well, we were helped. The guy in charge here, General Blythe, he started doing some strange things; running the survivors out of town, harassing the ones who wanted to stay. Quite a lot of the lads here started to get antsy about the orders he was giving. So they decided to do a bunk. And they broke us out on the way. There was a fight, Jonno didn't make it, but Jim and I did, and eight Yank kids. And we were on our own then."

"What did you do?"

Now it was Dad's turn to play his cards close to his chest. He knew we were being overheard as well.

"Met some locals, formed a resistance movement, did a bit of asymmetric warfare."

"What's that?"

"We blew stuff up a lot."

"Oh."

"And then I got captured again a few days back."

"What happened?"

"We were betrayed." Tariq shrugged. "Blythe wanted your father. Badly. It was only when he took charge of us that we became a proper resistance. A little army. Your dad is a good soldier, he led us well. You should be proud of him.

"There were more of them, and they had better equipment; night goggles, heat sensors, helicopters. And they hunted us. But we know this town, where to hide, how to move unseen. We fought well. Killed many of them. But we could not prevent what happened at the football ground. And after that we were more visible. There 'were no local people to shelter us, no market crowds for us to hide in. Things became more difficult. And there was nobody left for us to fight for. So we decided to leave, find somewhere else to go. I thought maybe I would like to grow vegetables and tend goats. Something simple, you know? I mean, there's no-one left to read my blog even if there was an Internet to post it on!

"But then they attacked us at night, as we slept. Only six of us escaped and they captured the rest. Fifteen of them."

It took me a minute to realize, and then I gasped.

"Oh Jesus," I said. "The people on stakes."

Tariq nodded.

"Blythe wanted your father to surrender. He sent out humvees with loudspeakers, telling him to give himself up. But of course your dad was planning a rescue.

"Anyway, Blythe gathered his prisoners in that courtyard and had his men fix big wooden stakes into the ground. Then he tied them up, stood each one in front of a stake, and told your father to surrender or they would be impaled.

"We just didn't believe he would do it. But Blythe killed Jim himself. Grabbed his shoulders and pushed him down, looking into his eyes as he did it. When he stood up his face was splashed with blood. Your dad immediately put down his gun and walked out there, hands in the air.

"The Yanks tied him up, forced him to sit on the ground and made him watch as they impaled the rest of the prisoners anyway. Just because they could. The one who betrayed us, an American called Matt – barely nineteen, always scared – he begged and screamed. But Blythe showed him no mercy. Then they left. That was two days ago."

"They've been questioning me ever since. Nothing I can't handle."

Dad shrugged, trying to make light of it, not going into detail so he wouldn't terrify me. But I looked at his sunken, haunted eyes and I felt more anger than I've ever felt. It was amazing; I didn't know I could want to hurt someone so much. I hadn't even wanted to kill Mac as much as I wanted to take a knife and shove it into the hearts of the men who'd tortured my dad.

"They want me to betray my friends," he said. "The ones who are still free. I won't do that. They can't make me. I'll die first."

I let that lie there for a moment and then I said what we were both thinking.

"But now they have me."

The look on his face said it all.

We heard footsteps in the corridor outside, then the cell door slammed open.

"Get up kid," said the soldier silhouetted in the doorway. "General Blythe wants a word."

CHAPTER FOUR

"Have a seat, son."

The general's voice was deep and warm, and his tone was friendly. He sat in a plush, red leather chair, the kind you expect to see in front of roaring fires in the libraries of grand houses. It looked out of place behind the huge black marble desk. But then, this whole place was absurd.

I'd been brought out of the filthy underground cells, up into the great entrance hall with its amber mosaics, gold lined ceiling dome and intricate pine balconies. It seemed like something Disney would have built. I was marched up the sweeping staircase, where the enormous windows gave stunning views of the Shatt-Al-Arab waterway as it meandered through the various mansions and gardens that made up Saddam's old palace complex. White stone bridges arched across the slow flowing water. It looked like paradise outside, and all I wanted was to lie in the shade beside the cool water and feel the wind on my face.

Matron would have loved it here, I thought. She liked lying

on the soft earth and closing her eyes. But I was glad she wasn't with me in this cold stone building; it wasn't a friendly place.

The general had set up camp in a cavernous, empty ballroom on the first floor. His desk sat in front of double doors that led out to a balcony. The doors stood open, and white gauze curtains billowed into the room, bringing the scents of jasmine and orange blossom from the gardens below. Beside the desk was a huge flatscreen telly on a big stand, hooked up to some sort of computer equipment with wires snaking out the back of it; they ran outside through the balcony doors, presumably to a generator.

He was about 50, at a guess. His black skin was lined and weathered, and his close cut hair almost entirely grey. Barrel-chested and broad shouldered he gave an impression of contained physical power, and his voice reflected that. He was exactly what I would have expected an American general to be; all he needed was to start chomping on a cigar and the picture would be complete.

I shuddered as I imagined that weighty frame leaning into me, pushing me down on to a sharp wooden stake.

He gestured to a metal and canvas chair on my side of the desk, and I sat down.

"Dismissed," he said. My escort saluted crisply, turned on his heels with a squeak of rubber, and stomped away. The tall doors, made of elaborately carved dark wood, slowly swung shut behind him. We were alone.

General Blythe regarded me curiously and I could see the muscles in his jaw clenching and unclenching as he did so. I met his gaze and held it. Not too defiant, but trying to seem confident. I'd looked into the eyes of madmen before. There's a feral quality they have which, once seen, is impossible to forget. I searched the general's eyes for signs of madness.

He narrowed his eyes and smiled.

"Yes, I think I believe you, son," he said.

"I'm not your son."

"Well, we'll come to that in a minute. I believe your story, though. That you flew here from the UK looking for your dad.

Gutsy thing to do."

"Didn't have a choice."

"We always have a choice, son. You could have left him behind, grown up on your own, become your own man."

"Is that what you did?"

He laughed. "I'm asking the questions." There was a flash of warning in his eyes that hinted at all sorts of unpleasantness. "Drink?"

He reached across the desk and poured me a beaker of water from a tall glass jug that was frosted with condensation. I took it and swallowed it at once.

"Thank you," I gasped, wanting more but not willing to ask.

"You're welcome. So what's it like in Britain now?"

"Chaos, what else?"

He considered this and then said: "But you've got the arms, right? I mean to say, when our British allies pulled out of Iraq they had a plan to restore law and order. Must have started to work by now."

"Not in my part of the country."

"Fancy that. And what part of the country would that be?"

I don't know why I lied, it was just instinct I suppose. But I didn't want to tell this guy a single true thing.

"East Anglia. Ipswich."

He nodded. I couldn't decide which was odder: his interest in British internal affairs, or the fact that he'd heard of Ipswich.

"And that's where you flew from?"

"Yes."

"Hell of a thing, kid your age. But you've got plenty of scars, I can see that. Fresh too. You ever killed anybody, son?"

"If you were listening to my conversation with my dad, then you already know the answer to that question."

He nodded, conceding the point.

"You knew I was listening from the start, didn't you?" he said with a smile.

"No."

"Liar. Otherwise you'd have told your old man about meeting up with his buddies."

"I don't know what you're talking about."

The playful smile vanished from his face and he became impassive, his eyes dead and cold.

"Let me put you straight on a few things," he said. "Prisoners have rights. Many checks and balances exist to ensure those rights are protected. You are not a prisoner because you don't exist. Ain't nobody looking out for you. I could kill you now with my bare hands and nobody but your daddy would give a damn."

"You forgot to say 'in this place, I am the law!'"

"It goes without saying."

"Why?"

He seemed surprised by the question. "Excuse me?"

"Why? To what end? For what purpose?"

"There has to be law, son. Chain of command is the only way I know of running anything, and this place needs running."

"But why?" I pressed him. "I mean, shouldn't you be back in the US, shooting looters on Capitol Hill or something? Why are you here?"

"Capitol Hill ain't there anymore. Nuked."

"Okay, so New York, LA, Boston, Buttfuck Idaho, I dunno. Since The Cull the world's been full of tinpot dictators throwing their weight around. I've met a couple of them. You're not like that. I'm looking you in the eye and you're not insane, and you don't strike me as power crazy. So why are you still here?"

"I got my orders."

"From whom? Who can possibly..."

I didn't get any further because this huge granite man sitting opposite me suddenly moved faster than I've ever seen anybody move in my life, pulling a gun out of nowhere and firing a round over my head so close it ruffled my hair.

"Next one goes between your eyes. Understand?"

Fuck, yeah.

"I have no beef with you, boy. Your daddy's a dead man, but if you tell me what I want to know you can still walk out of here. Hell, I'll give you a lift back to Ipswich myself. But if you don't answer my questions now, while I'm still of a mind to be civil,

I'll start asking a lot less nicely. Clear?"

"Crystal."

I gritted my teeth. This was my last chance to back out of Tariq's plan. If I said the wrong thing now, I was dead.

"Good. Question one, and make sure I like your answer: two of my men were shot and killed yesterday. Before they were shot they radioed that they had captured a British deserter. Was that you?"

"No," I replied. "It was Captain Britain."

He didn't like that answer.

I hate bullies.

They're worse than madmen, psychopaths, dictators or power mad religious cultists; at least they all have either an excuse or an objective. Bullies are just cruel to make themselves feel cool.

I was bullied when I started school. Once.

I was six years old and had only just started at St Mark's prep. The bully in question, Jasper Jason, was a year older than me. He was a snotty-nosed prick with a little coterie of fawning acolytes who laughed at his cruelty. They tortured cats, that sort of thing.

Anyway, one day, who knows why, he decided that I was going to be his victim. He came over to me in the playground, grabbed my Gameboy and started taunting me with it, threatening to break it, promising to make me cry and so on.

I punched him as hard as I could and broke his nose.

I was suspended from school for a week. Dad was at home that summer, and I remember him coming to collect me. I was terrified of his reaction, but when the circumstances were explained to him he just laughed at the teachers. Then he took me out for MacDonalds and told me he was proud of me.

Nobody ever bullied me again.

As the hood was pulled over my face, I tried to remember how I felt in that playground.

As the ties were fastened around my wrists and ankles, I tried to find that sense of mocking superiority I felt when I realised that Jason was just an insecure little shit who could only feel good about himself by picking on weaker kids.

As I was laid on the thin wooden board and trussed like a chicken so that the board and I moved as one unit, I recalled the satisfaction of feeling his nose crunch and the realisation that I wasn't scared of him.

As the towels were laid gently across my hooded face, I drew on all the anger, resentment and hatred I felt for bullies and I projected it on to the men who were about to drown me. How insecure they must be to torture a child. I laughed at them.

As they began to pour the water on to the towels, I felt myself tilt backwards. The liquid dribbled up my nose and I felt the hard pressure of a finger in my solar plexus, testing whether I was timing my breaths to coincide with the dowsings. I felt the purest resolve I had ever felt in my life.

I was stronger than this. I was The Boy Who Was Never Bullied. I knew they weren't going to kill me, so all I needed to do was be strong. I could do this.

And then I had to exhale, unable to hold my breath for another second.

And then I was drowning, the thick cotton towels moulding themselves to my mouth and nostrils, gagging me, choking me, sealing me in a dark, wet, airless nightmare.

I felt the board tip up, a momentary respite, the towels loosened, I dragged in a ragged gasp of air, and then tilted again, more water, more choking, flooding, drowning in the unstoppable water as it probed every orifice, relentless, drawn by simple gravity, pushing its way inside me.

There was liquid somewhere else, but I couldn't tell where, my senses were so scrambled. Only later did I realise that I'd wet myself.

And my resolve vanished, my strength disappeared, time elongated and claustrophobic terror took its place. Before I knew I was doing it, I was begging for release, promising to tell them everything they needed to know. Anything to make it stop.

So they did it once more, just to be sure. This time I lost my mind. I may have screamed and begged, I don't know. But in my head I was with Matron. She was at Groombridge, I was in the gardens outside the room where I was dying, yet we still lay side by side, holding hands with our eyes closed, feeling the Earth turn beneath us, breathing slow, steady meditative breaths as the darkness closed in.

It seemed like a lifetime, but the whole ordeal probably only lasted thirty seconds.

When I regained consciousness I was lying on the floor in a puddle. It was better than being tied to a chair, I supposed.

They had untied me and dumped me on the hard marble floor I was foetal, with my hands, now untied, near my ankles. I kept my breathing shallow, pretending to still be asleep, and I listened, trying to work out how many of the men who had waterboarded me were still in the room. I heard someone clear their throat, but that was it. Just the one, then.

The question was: where was he looking? I cracked one eye ever so slightly and I saw him standing near a window with his back to me. Either he was a rank amateur, which I doubted, or he had underestimated me.

"Oh yeah," said the sarcastic voice in my head. "Can't imagine why he underestimated you. You proved how gnarly you are with all the begging and pissing."

I forced myself not to think about what I'd just gone through. Banished it to the back of my mind; something to deal with later. There was no lasting physical damage, and a resumption of torture didn't seem imminent. Any psychological wounds could be cauterised later.

I had things to do.

I slowly moved my right hand to the hem of my left trouser leg and searched along it until I felt a tiny bit of resistance. Then I grasped it with my finger and thumb and pushed the thin metal down, slicing open the bottom of my trousers and slipping the razor blade out and into my palm.

I was not in the dungeon, as I'd assumed. Instead I was in a large empty room, perhaps an antechamber of the ballroom the general was using. It seemed incongruous that somewhere so light and opulent could be used as a place of torture. But with the bag over my head I hadn't known where I was, so it hadn't made any difference to me. I supposed the guys here just liked doing their job in the nicest available office.

I decided my best bet was to pick up where I'd left off.

I pretended to jerk awake with a yell. I breathed as hard and fast as I could, widened my eyes in panic, then sat up and scrambled backwards 'til my back was against a wall. I pulled my knees up tight to my chest, buried my face in my lap, and began begging for them not to hurt me any more, rocking slightly as I did so.

The torturer turned away from the window and walked over to me. He crouched down, reached forward and grabbed my chin, forcing my head up, getting right in my face.

"Start at the begin..."

The word lapsed into a strangled gargle, half rasp, half choke. I swiped the blade across his windpipe again, harder. And again, and again, feeling my fingers slip into the slick wet wound as they sliced deeper and deeper into his neck. I had grabbed his head with my left hand, holding him in place, preventing him from tumbling backwards and escaping. By the time he twitched free of my grasp he was unable to cry for help. He clawed across the floor leaving a thick red smear behind him.

I got to my feet, stepped over him, turned and looked down at one of the men who had tortured me. I looked into his despairing eyes as he gazed up at me, grasping at the air, and I felt not one shred of pity or remorse.

"I hate bullies," I said. Then I jumped and landed with both feet on the back of his neck. There was a sharp crack and I felt his body crumple and grind beneath my heels.

Strangely, it still wasn't quite as satisfying as breaking Jason's nose all those years ago. I suppose you just feel things that bit more intensely when you're a child.

I rolled the cooling corpse on to its back, intending to take his trousers, but he'd wet himself too, and more besides, so I left them.

I frisked him, looking for a gun or knife, but he wasn't armed;

probably hadn't thought it necessary. There was bound to be a man on guard outside, but the thick wooden doors had masked any noise, so I reckoned I had a few minutes at least. I ran to the window, but there was no balcony or convenient ledge I could climb out onto. The door it was. I looked around the room for some kind of weapon.

In the centre of the room stood two wooden chairs with the board laid across them. The hood, towels, bucket and ties were lying discarded on the floor beside it. I walked over to the apparatus, lifted the board and placed it on the floor. Then I picked up one of the chairs and smashed it into the wall as hard as I could, snapping one of the legs off. Voila: one genuine vampire-slaying stake.

I ran over to the door and banged on it, and then I crouched down, holding the stake in both hands against my chest, pointing out and up. The door cracked open. In normal circumstances a well trained soldier would have drawn his weapon and pushed the door open at arm's length, but these doors were so weighty that the soldier outside had to lean his full weight against it, and even then they moved slowly.

He was so focused on pushing the door open that he didn't notice me, crouched down below his eyeline, until it was too late.

I sprang up and drove the stake with all my strength into his belly and up under his ribcage into his heart, lifting him off the ground with the force of my attack, pushing a spout of blood out through his mouth. I couldn't hold his weight, and he fell backwards, crashing to the floor in a dead heap.

Was a time I would have felt bad about doing something like that, but I thought of all those people left to rot in the town with huge shafts of wood sticking out of their shattered ribcages, and any remorse I might have felt evaporated.

The general's desk stood alone at the centre of the vast room, but there was no-one else there. I grabbed a gun and some magazines from the impaled soldier and ran to the main doors, familiarising myself with the weapon as I ran. It was some variant of an M16; not a weapon I was familiar with. All I knew is that you load it by pulling the charging handle back and letting it go.

Simplicity itself. Other than that I'd have to hope it wasn't too different to the guns I knew. I found the safety and switched it off.

The problem with these huge bloody doors was that you couldn't hear a thing through them. Probably useful if you wanted to stage a little private torturing, or a discreet orgy, but fuck all use if you wanted to sneak around the place undetected. I pressed my ear to one of the doors but there was no way of knowing what was happening on the other side. I was about to climb out the balcony when I noticed something slightly askew in one of the wall patterns in the far corner; a tiny line that didn't quite fit the design. I ran across to it and found a concealed door with a metal ring flush to the wall. I popped it out and pulled, revealing a narrow, gloomy back staircase, presumably installed for the servants.

I stepped inside, pulled the door closed behind me and made my way downstairs, gun at the ready.

I passed one exit, which I gently cracked open. It led into a large kitchen on the ground floor. There was no-one inside, so I took the opportunity to slip out and find a couple of good knives which I slipped into my waistband. I then returned to the staircase and continued my descent. Eventually the stairs ended at another door, beyond which lay the damp concrete corridor and the cells. I crept along the corridor to the point where it met the cell block at a kind of T-junction. Back to the wall, I risked a quick glimpse into the prison run and saw only one guard, sitting reading near the main entrance. He was facing me, about fifty metres away. No way to take him out silently. I was just going to have to hope for the best.

I shouldered the M16, took a deep breath, and steeped into his line of sight. He didn't look up; too engrossed in Tom Clancy. I walked towards him, gun sighted square on his chest as I did so. I was half way to him when he turned the page, and in that instant he registered my presence. He looked up at me in surprise and opened his mouth to challenge me. I squeezed the trigger softly and sent a round spinning straight at his chest.

And missed.

I'm not accustomed to missing, but I'd never fired an M16 be-fore so I was unfamiliar with its quirks. The gun pulled upwards much more than I'd expected. The bullet hit the wall beside his shoulder, sending out a puff of white plaster. My surprise at missing caused me to hesitate, and in the instant before I could resight and fire again my target said: "Jesus, Lee, what the hell are you doing?"

Which was unexpected.

Ten minutes later, with a knife at my throat and my right arm pinioned behind my back, I was led out of the palace into the dark orange of sunset. The palace looked oddly unimpressive from outside. Partly this was because it had been shot to shit more than once, partly it was that all the opulence inside wasn't reflected in the blocky, uninspired exterior. The effect was that of walking out of a cinema into the street; glamour and colour replaced by dullness and dust.

The man with the knife – the man who I'd failed to shoot – marched me straight ahead, past the wonderful gardens and on to a paved path that led from the main palace building to a smaller, but still very large outbuilding (a palacette, perhaps, or a palacini?) There were a few of them dotted around inside the thick stone walls that ringed the enormous compound. There were fields too, scrubby and untended with a few lonely trees, probably once intended as orchards but never irrigated properly and now ignored.

It was a grim place. Badly planned, hardly finished, aban-doned, fought over and now occupied, baking in the relentless heat. But that garden somehow seemed to have survived. Perhaps it was because I was so nervous, but I fixated on the garden as I walked away from it, daydreaming about its pools and arches. But I wasn't going to somewhere calm and cool and green. I was going to be executed.

There were two other soldiers escorting me, and two more at the open doors of the building ahead. We entered a large reception hall, lit by the amber light that flooded through an enormous lattice window. Blythe was there, seated on a seventies style sofa; polyester covered foam squares on a basic metal frame, all in a garish swirling pattern of green and brown. My father sat beside him, hands cuffed to the frame. In front of them stood something that came up to my shoulders, covered in a white sheet out of which snaked thick cables that coiled across the mosaic floor and out of the door we had just entered by.

"Thank you, Major," said Blythe. "You can release the prisoner."

The knife was removed and my arm freed. The man who'd been steering me stepped back into the lengthening shadows.

"You all right, Lee?"

"Yeah Dad, I'm fine."

"You are anything but fine, son," said Blythe.

"He's not your son," spat my father.

"I told him that, Dad, but he wouldn't listen. Maybe he wants to adopt me."

"I already have a son, Sergeant Keegan," replied Blythe. "One more than you, in a few minutes."

"If you touch one hair..."

"Soldier," barked Blythe.

The nearest of his troops yelled "Sir!" in reponse.

"If Sergeant Keegan utters another threat you will shoot him dead."

"Sir, yes, Sir!" The soldier raised his rifle and stepped forward, keeping the muzzle a few inches from my dad's head. Blythe glanced at the soldier and said witheringly: "Not there, you'll cover me in brains. Stand behind him."

"Sir, yes, Sir!"

I looked into Dad's eyes and I could see him willing me to be strong and calm. I could also see his panic. I smiled at him.

"Lee, you surprise me, you really do," said the general, turning his attention back to me. "I thought you were going to be the answer to my prayers. Instead you kill two of my men in what I can only call very creative ways, and you almost manage to make it three. I'm impressed."

The look on Dad's face was a picture; a mixture of horror,

disbelief and pride. He mouthed 'really?' and I nodded, matter of fact.

"I don't like being bullied, General," I said.

"I can tell. Anyway, here's what we're going to do. You're going to tell me where your father's band of merry men is hiding or I am going to kill you."

"You're going to kill me anyway."

He laughed at that, a rich, warm laugh that contained no humour whatsoever.

"I surely am," he said. "But I can make it quick or slow, and given how long you lasted on the waterboard I'm thinking you don't have the stomach for slow."

He wasn't wrong.

I considered my options and the general waited for my response, studying my face closely as I did so.

"What constitutes quick?" I asked.

"I like to give people a choice."

"A choice?"

"Yes. You can be shot, hanged, electrocuted or given a lethal injection. Your call."

Again I considered. Again he watched me do so.

"Well, I've been shot, and I've been hanged, and I really don't like needles, so I reckon I'll go for the electric chair please."

As soon as I said it I realised I'd made a mistake – he hadn't mentioned a chair. Dad noticed too, and his eyes narrowed as he cocked his head at me curiously, trying to work out what was going on.

Blythe, however, missed it.

"All right, the chair it is. It is a classic, after all. But first..."

"They're in the souk. It's a courtyard behind a carpet shop with a green sign with red letters on it. I know they're planning to stay there until tomorrow night. That's the best I can tell you."

Blythe nodded, satisfied.

"And why did you give yourself up?" he asked. "They must have told you about me, you must have known what would happen. Did you really think you could rescue your dad single handed? Can you possibly be that naïve?"

I shrugged. "What can I say? I have this thing about walking into the compounds of my enemies and baiting them. It worked once before, I figured why not try it again."

Blythe stood up and walked over to me, leaning close into my face and studying me.

"I know you're lying," he said softly. "You're not that stupid. And I'm curious, but not that curious. You are a footnote, son, and I don't have time to waste on you. I've got a major operation to stage and this sideshow is holding me up."

He turned back to face my dad.

"I had intended to torture your boy, make you beg me to stop, break you, force you to tell me everything you knew and then kill him in front of you," said the general. "But events have moved more quickly than I'd anticipated. I have new orders, and that's no longer necessary."

Then he stepped to his left, reached out, and pulled the sheet away with a theatrical flourish to reveal an electric chair.

"So I'm going to skip to the end."

The sun was half hidden by the horizon now. In a few minutes darkness would fall. The shadow of the electric chair stretched long across the marble. It was a curious thing, home made and jerry rigged. It was an ornate, tall backed ebony chair that probably once sat at the head of a grand dining table. Who knows, it may have been Saddam's. Thick metal wire had been wrapped around the arms and legs, leading to a plain metal bowl, once intended for eating out of, now pressed into service as the head contact. The four other contacts – two for the feet, two for the hands – were made of gold, some relic of Ba'athist luxury beaten with hammers and flattened into something far less elegant. It made sense, though; gold's the best conductor there is. Thick straps festooned the framework, ready to secure my body and limbs and ensure that contact was not lost when I thrashed and jerked as the current hit me.

"Please, I beg you, don't do this," cried Dad. "He's my son. Please, God, no."

I tried to catch Dad's eye, tell him to stay calm, but it was getting too dark, and anyway it sounded like his eyes would be too full of tears to see clearly. The sound of my father begging for my life was the purest despair I'd ever heard. I wanted so much to tell him everything was all right, but I couldn't. The truth was, I was probably about to die, and he was going to have to watch it happen.

"Power up the generator," shouted the general, and the man who'd brought me here emerged from the shadows and stepped outside. A moment later there was the sound of a large engine spluttering into life, faltering momentarily, then finding its rhythm and settling into its work.

"Strap him in."

I felt strong hands grab me and force me towards the chair. I tried to resist, I screamed my furious defiance, but they were too strong and too many. One of them punched me hard across the face and my senses reeled. Then I was sitting in the chair, and my arms were forced down and strapped in place. My shirt was cut off and my boots removed. Then the straps were fastened across my chest, forehead and legs. My hands and feet rested on solid gold as I felt someone taking an electric shaver to my head, shaving off all my hair and smearing my raw scalp with conducting gel.

The sun was gone now, and twilight was fading fast. I heard someone pull a switch, and arc lights burst into life, flooding the room with cold white brilliance. My father, able to see me again, let out a feral cry of agony and screamed his fury into the echoing dome above us, where it reverberated and rebounded, briefly amplifying his defiance before fading away into hopeless, beaten sobbing.

The general stepped in front of me and said: "any last words, son?"

"I am not your fucking son."

"So be it."

Then he crouched down beside a junction box and pulled a big red lever, releasing the current to fry me alive.

CHAPTER FIVE

"He gives them a choice," Tariq had said, as we sat on the roof the night before.

"A choice?"

"Of execution."

"You have got to be kidding me."

"No. You can be shot, hung..."

"Hanged."

"What?"

"Sorry, it's hanged, not hung."

"Oh. Your father said hung."

"Yeah, well. Hanged. I got this scar on my neck when I was hanged. I like to be grammatically correct about the forms of execution I survive. I'm a pedant. Sue me."

"Okay," said Tariq, rolling his eyes. "Anyway, you can be shot, hanged, injected, or he's got this electric chair he's made."

"Made?"

"Yeah, out of a big generator, a dining chair, some wires and a lot of gold."

"Shit."

"Your dad is going to be executed tomorrow. Blythe has decided he won't break, so he gave him the choice."

"Shot," I said immediately.

"Um, yeah, how did you know?"

"Dunno, just seems like the one he'd choose."

"But we have a plan to rescue him and it depends on him changing his mind and sitting in the chair. Unfortunately our inside man can't get a message to him and tell him to change his mind."

"So your plan is, what, I get captured and tell Dad to change his mind?"

"Perhaps. But I think it will not be so easy. Blythe will try and use you to get your father to break. So you may have to improvise."

"Okay. No, wait, hang on. Your plan is that I get captured and then give Blythe an excuse to kill me – but not there and then, later, at his leisure – and I choose the chair?"

"Yes." He saw the look on my face. "I know."

"That is a fucking useless plan."

"I know, I know."

"And who is your inside man?"

"Oh, that's the best bit..."

As the lever slammed home, the arc lights dimmed and flickered.

My back went rigid, I gritted my teeth as my eyes bulged out of my head. The veins in my temples strained to bursting point and the muscles in my neck stood out like ropes. I shook uncontrollably in the grip of the current.

Then I turned my head to General Blythe, smiled, winked, and said "gotcha!"

The lights went out and darkness fell, but not for long.

The chain of high explosives that ringed the walls of the compound exploded one by one, like a string of enormous firecrackers, lighting the room with a blinding orange strobe.

I saw the man who'd turned on the generator run into the room, pistol raised. In his early twenties, dark skinned, of medium height and build, he was nothing to look at. Just another shaven haired grunt made anonymous by the shapeless uniform and regimented body language. But his face was a terrible mixture of fury and pain.

He picked off the guards one by one, calm and efficient, his gunshots timed exactly with the explosions, so it took the guards – those not already dead – a few moments to realise what was happening. And a few moments was all it took.

When the explosions finally ended, he and Blythe were the only men standing in the room, cast into sharp relief by the flickering fires that now raged outside.

"Put down the gun, son," said the general.

"I'm not your son," said the man with the gun.

"Yes, David, you are and you will do as I say."

"Screw you, Dad."

"And who the fuck are you?" I asked the guard with the book.

"David Blythe," he said. "I'm the one..."

"I know who you are. I thought you couldn't get a message to my dad, so what are you doing here guarding him?"

"He's been moved. My dad's taking one last pop at him."

"Where?"

"It wouldn't do any good. Too many of them. You'd just get yourself killed."

"I thought that was the whole idea," I said drily.

"How the heck did you get down here?"

"Scratch two of your dad's goons."

"Holy... well, at least that should have sealed the deal. If you let me take you in, I reckon Dad'll give you the choice."

"Why should I trust you?"

"Tariq trusts me."

"I'm still not entirely sure I trust Tariq."

"Look, I've spent three days setting this up, at great risk," he told me. "Sooner or later someone's going to notice that I've been rewiring things. We get one shot at this. And Dad's been talking about new orders, hinting that we're moving out soon. If we wait too long, he may be too busy to waste time with games; he might just shoot you both in the head. We have to do this now."

"I do not like this plan."

"Complain about it if you survive. Now give me the gun. Thank you."

The crisp chatter of automatic weapons fire drifted across the darkened compound as Tariq and the others fought their way in. All they had to do was create a diversion for a few minutes and allow Dad, David and myself time to escape.

"Ser'nt Keegan, untie him," yelled David.

Dad was already working at the straps that bound me, but it was slow going with only one useable hand.

"What is going on, son?" Blythe sounded calm and reasonable, even indulgent, as if this was all just some little misunderstanding that could be sorted out with milk, cookies and a moral homily from Papa.

"You're not my father. Not any more."

"I assure you, I am."

"My dad's a soldier, not a butcher. The man who raised me doesn't massacre civilians, impale people for fun, strap kids into electric chairs. My father was a man of honour and principle, proud to serve his country. You're just a madman."

My head and chest were free.

"David, I'm just following orders," said the general. "Same as I've ever done."

"Bullcrap. What orders? Who the heck is there left to give you orders? And even if there were, these orders are illegal."

The general shook his head. "That's not my judgement to make." Was that regret I could detect in his voice?

"You told me once that a soldier's greatest duty is to protect the people from their rulers," shouted his son. "Refusing to obey an illegal order is a soldier's highest duty. That's what you told me. Remember that, Dad?"

My right hand came free and I started loosening the strap on my left.

"I surely do," said the general. "But the world has changed, son. New laws, new rules."

"I don't accept that."

"That would make you a fool, and I didn't raise a fool."

With both hands free I got to work on my feet.

"Weapons," I said, and Dad nodded, moving away to salvage guns and knives from the corpses of the guards.

There was a huge explosion somewhere nearby. The room shook and my eyes were dazzled by a flash of pure white light. When my vision returned, the general had gone.

"Shit, where'd he go?" I yelled.

David just stood there, gun still raised, dazed by the enormity of his betrayal.

"He just vanished," shouted the young man, surprised. But I'd seen how fast his father could move. I was amazed he'd chosen to run rather than fight.

We urgently needed to be anywhere else.

As the last strap came free I leapt out of that awful chair. I held out my hands for a gun, but Dad dropped the weapons to the floor and grabbed me, holding me in a tight, choking embrace and kissing my head.

He muttered over and over: "thank God, thank God."

I squirmed free, embarrassed and annoyed by his show of emotion; we didn't have time for this. I held his good hand in both of mine.

"We have to go," I said.

"So you're giving the orders now, huh?" he said, shaking his head in wonder.

I wanted to say "can we bond later, yeah? When there's less chance of sudden, bloody death? That okay with you?" But I decided to go with the more laconic "looks that way."

I bent down and picked up an M16, cocking it as I stood. I handed a sidearm to Dad.

"You still able..."

"Oh yes."

"Then let's get the fuck out of here."

At that moment Tariq came haring through the door, bullets churning the ground behind him, and yelled: "RUN!"

He ran right through us and kept going, so we turned and followed him, scattering the chunks of plaster that had been knocked free from the ceiling and walls by the earth shattering explosions. At the rear of the entrance hall was a sweeping marble staircase and Tariq made to climb it. David shouted at him not to, and he took the lead, dodging right and taking us to ornate double doors behind the stairs. These led into a kind of sitting room, empty except for one painting of Saddam on to which someone had felt-tipped a noose, and a large cock and balls squirting into the dead dictator's face.

David held one door open as we all ran through it, and then raked the hall behind us with fire to discourage pursuit.

"Where?" shouted Dad.

"This way," replied David breathlessly, and ran to the corner of the room. In the half light I would never have noticed the door ring, but David had planned this well, and he went straight to the hidden door, pulled it open and ushered us through into a dark passage.

I was last through, and as I passed the threshold I heard a metallic clatter from behind me which, although new to me, I instantly realized was the sound of grenades bouncing across marble. I grabbed the door and pulled it closed just in time. A deafening roar, amplified by the cold stone acoustics of the enormous, empty room, filled my senses and flung me backwards.

The door held.

David reached across me and slid a bolt home, locking it behind us. Then he leant down, helped me to my feet, and dragged me away into the depths of the unlit passageway.

"Lee!" hissed Dad urgently.

"I'm all right," I replied.

"Ahead thirty metres, then turn left and up the stairs," said David loudly. I dimly heard Tariq give a grunt of acknowledgement somewhere ahead of us.

We made our way forward in the pitch darkness as quickly as we could.

"Thank you," I said. "You saved my life."

David said nothing. I wondered which he was regretting most – betraying his father, or not shooting him when he had the chance.

We soon reached a door, and huddled together, lit by the chink of light that gleamed through the tiny crack that outlined its frame.

"This leads into a private bedchamber," whispered David. "Uday would bring his whores here in secret. It should be unoccupied, but you never know. Once I open the door we run to the balcony. It looks out over the river, and over the wall. There's a ladder under the bed. I'll get it; we lay it across the gap, walk over the wall and drop down. Clear?"

"And if the room is occupied?"

"Then, Sergeant, we have fight on our hands. Everyone ready?"

There was the sound of four guns being cocked and then David counted down from three. We burst into the room, guns waving.

"Clear," said Dad. I got to the balcony first, and looked out into the night. I couldn't see much because the balcony looked out of the compound across the waterway. There was less gunfire than before. It was coming in sporadic bursts now, somewhere off to my right, from a building that stood close to where one of the bombs had exploded. I could see the riverside wall was ablaze, flames licking out of the empty window frames. Tariq had only a few people left to him after last week's massacre. The plan was that they would stay outside and lay down covering fire at the points where the wall was breached, that way the Yanks wouldn't know which breach we planned to exit by. We would go across the wall here and then we and the rest of the gang would simply melt away into the darkness. It was a good plan, but it had one fatal flaw.

"Where is it?" hissed Tariq urgently, behind me. I turned to see the three of them standing by the bed. No ladder.

"I don't know," said David. "It was here this morning. Someone must have taken it."

"Fuck," said Tariq, succinctly. "Fuck fuck fuck fuck fuck. What now?"

"Can we jump it?" asked Dad.

I shook my head. "It would be suicide. Options? David, you know the layout of this place. Where's the nearest breach in the wall and how do we get there?"

"Two hundred metres east. I set a charge near the swimming pool."

"Okay then," said Dad, looking for the door. "Hang on. Where's the door?"

"There isn't one," replied David. "Secret bedroom, remember? The passage is the only way in or out."

"Jesus," I said. "Who the fuck builds a secret chamber with only one entrance?"

"The Ba'ath party," said Tariq, "never could do a damn thing properly."

"So you mean we're trapped?" asked Dad, incredulous.

"Yeah," said David.

"And how long before someone figures out where we are?" I asked.

"Not long."

"Then we have to go out the window."

"You said it was too high," protested the Iraqi.

"He didn't say anything about jumping," said Dad, smiling. Weird, but that moment, when he read my mind before the others, made me feel closer to him than all the hugging and wailing a few minutes earlier.

"We climb," I said.

One of the good things about the palace compound is that the buildings were as ornate as they could possibly be. It wasn't hard to climb up on to the roof using all the elaborate cornices, cupolas and jutty-out bits. Tariq went first, then me. Then David gave Dad a boost while Tariq and I pulled him up. David was still outside on the wall, perched on the ledge above the balcony, reaching for the lip of the roof when Uday Hussein's secret fuck pad was blown to shit by grenades.

The shockwave dislodged him and he began to topple backwards. I leaned out and grabbed his flailing right hand, pulling him back in. He scrambled up, flinging himself on to the roof. Almost immediately we heard someone run out on to the balcony and shout "clear!" I silently mouthed "close". David nodded and mimed back "thank you". I smiled and patted his shoulder.

The flat roof was littered with discarded bits of stone, half cut rolls of waterproof tar stuff and other assorted junk left behind by the builders responsible for this architectural abortion. We moved away from the edge so we couldn't be seen from below.

"Now they're going to be confused," whispered Tariq grinning.

"I hope so," replied Dad. "Because if they figure out where we are, they'll just blow up the building, or worse, set a fire and leave us up here to burn."

That shut us all up for a moment, and in the silence we all realized the same thing; the gunfire had stopped. Tariq's forces had fled, been captured or killed.

We were on our own, trapped on a roof in the middle of a compound swarming with people who wanted to kill us.

"I told you I hated this plan," I said.

There was little we could do but wait.

From our vantage point we could see that the area was heavily patrolled, plus there was a team sorting out David's creative rewiring of the backup generator, so the building was a hive of activity. Come daylight, things would start to return to normal. This part of the compound was usually pretty quiet, said David; the main activity was all focused on the barracks, supply dump and vehicle store, about half a mile away on the compound's northern side.

"It may sound counter-intuitive," he said, "but we've got a better chance of sneaking out in broad daylight tomorrow than we do now."

And so we decided to get some sleep. I was just clearing a space to lie down when Dad came over to me and sat beside me.

"I'll take first watch, keep an eye out," he said.

"Okay," I replied.

There was an awkward silence. I don't think either of us knew what to say to each other.

"When I last saw you, you were a just a schoolboy. It was all *Doctor Who*, *Grand Theft Auto* and wondering if you were going to snog that girl from the High School, Michelle, wasn't it?"

"Yeah," I muttered.

"Did you?"

I looked at him, incredulous. This is what he wanted to talk about?

"She's dead, Dad."

He looked down at his feet. "Yeah, of course she is."

Another silence.

"So you're going to take watch, yeah?"

"Um, yeah," he said, lifting his eyes and regarding me curiously, as if he had no idea who I was. "You get some sleep."

"Wake me when it's my turn."

"Will do."

I lay down and turned away from him, resting my head on my folded arms and closing my eyes.

"And Lee, thank you," he said softly.

I said nothing. A moment later I heard him moving away.

Of course he didn't wake me. A distant secondary explosion jolted me awake; the fires must have reached an old fuel tank or gas cylinder in one of the other buildings. It was still dark, but I checked my watch and saw I'd been asleep for four hours. I lay there for a moment looking up at the stars, so clear and bright now, without electric light bleeding into the sky to hide them. I pulled my jacket tighter around me as protection from the cold, even though I knew it was still hot by English standards.

I looked around and saw that Tariq was on watch now; my dad was asleep over to my left, and David was sitting balled up in the middle of the roof, head rested on his knees, staring blankly into space. I didn't think he'd welcome it if I approached him.

I could tell I wasn't going to get any more rest, so I got up and went to sit next to Tariq.

"Anything happening?" I asked.

"Not really. They've fixed the generator and gone away, but they are still searching all the buildings. It's the third sweep they've done, but Blythe must think we're still here so he's getting them to do it over and over. Just pray he gives up soon. I don't want to starve to death up here." He gave a quiet, sardonic laugh.

"Back when I first met you, you told me you were a celebrity blogger," I said.

Tariq nodded. "I used to blog about life in Basra under the occupation. I had two hundred thousand readers. Some of it was printed in a British paper and a publishing company wanted to do a book. A few other bloggers did it, made big bucks. I'd just signed the bloody deal when everyone started dying. Just my luck."

"So how..."

"Did I become a soldier? My knowledge of covert stuff made me a natural, I suppose."

I was confused. "But how does a blogger become an expert in covert stuff? I mean, why would you need it?"

"You really know nothing about what life here was like, do you," he said, shaking his head in wonder. He wasn't annoyed at my ignorance, merely resigned, as if he expected the rest of the world to be blind, stupid and uninterested.

"Enlighten me."

"Bloggers were targets. If I dared to criticize one of the militias, there was a very good chance they would find me and kill me. And that's just for writing about how hard it was to buy bread in their district."

"People would try and kill you just for blogging?"

"And I did more than that. I investigated. I chased stories, played the journalist, tried to find the truth about certain things."

"Like?"

"Kidnappings, massacres, bombings. It wasn't hard. Basra was not a huge city, the grapevine was very good. And all the time I had to keep my identity secret. If anyone ever connected me with my blog, I was dead."

"And did anybody ever realize it was you?"

"No, but they laid a trap for me. I thought I was so careful, but they threatened the family of one of my contacts and lured me into an ambush. I was looking into the looting of the stores outside town. My contact told me he knew a British soldier who was helping the looters. But the militia was waiting for me at the rendezvous. Luckily a routine patrol came past, and I was able to just walk away. One in a million chance.

"But after that they knew who I was, so I could never go home again. I had to go into hiding, which is why I ended up working with your dad. I was lucky. Some of my friends, fellow bloggers here and in Baghdad, they were not so lucky."

"And now you lead the resistance."

"What's left of it. Anyway, I've got nothing better to do; my laptop's run out of batteries. If only I had an XO, with wireless mesh networking and some good cantennas we could have a local network up and running in no time."

"Stop," I laughed. "I have no idea what you're saying. I can use computers but I have no idea how they work"

"So what were you going to be, huh?" asked Tariq. "Before The Cull turned you into soldier boy. You were going to university to study?"

"I have no idea. I wasn't a failure at school, but I didn't exactly get the greatest grades either. I'd probably have ended up doing English at some crappy university, assuming I got in. After that, God knows.

"All my life I've had my dad telling me what he didn't want me to be – a soldier. I never had a clue what I wanted to be. Rich, I suppose. Irresistibly attractive to women. I dunno. I was fourteen when The Cull hit. I hadn't even chosen my GCSEs yet, although I had one meeting with a careers advisor to help me choose."

"Careers advisor? Someone who tells you what jobs you'd be good at, yeah?"

"Yeah, something like that."

"What did they recommend for you?"

"Promise not to laugh?"

"I swear on the grave of Warren Ellis."

"They said I should go into banking."

"Ha!"

"Yeah, that was my reaction too."

He fell silent, and I could see he was trying to frame a question.

"What you did," he said eventually, "was insane. You know that, right?"

"Which bit? Flying here, giving myself up to Blythe, trying to escape, letting him strap me into an electric chair?"

"All of it. Fucking insane. I mean, I know a lot of it was my idea, but honestly, if someone had tried to persuade me to do what you did I'd have told them to go fuck themselves."

"He's my dad."

"Is that all, though? I wonder if maybe you do not have a death wish."

"Don't be daft," I said, but he didn't seem convinced.

He pressed on. "You would not be the first. Many of the people who survived The Cull took their own lives. Those who could not do that looked for people to do it for them."

I felt a sudden surge of anger. "Well that's not me, right?"

He just looked at me, head cocked slightly to one side, his face asking silently "are you sure?"

"Fuck you, Tariq," I hissed and made to rise. He grabbed my arm and I shook it off angrily before walking back to my clear patch of roof and lying back down.

I lay there seething. How fucking dare he!

"Why so angry, Nine Lives?" said the voice in my head. "Touch a nerve, did he?"

I lay there a long time watching the night turn to grey twilight before the soft glow of morning bled across the skyline. David didn't move a muscle in all that time. Tariq, on the other hand, was restless and unsettled. He moved from one side of the roof to another, checking the area, keeping his head low to avoid being spotted. He must have been worried sick about his friends.

Dad slept like a log, proving that he was the only real soldier amongst us; he once told me that the ability to fall asleep anywhere, at any time, is one of the best tricks a combat soldier can learn.

He woke with the sun and we gathered in the centre of the roof. No-one would make eye contact with me.

"Sitrep?" asked Dad.

"They've stopped searching, and the generator's fixed," said Tariq. "I think we can go now."

No sooner had he said that than there was a hum of power, a screech of feedback, and Blythe's voice echoed across the compound.

"Good morning," he said.

"Oh crap," said David.

None of us moved, waiting to hear what the general had to say.

"I hope you slept well," said the echoey tannoy voice. "I know you're still inside the walls. Your chances of getting out of here alive are not that great."

"How the fuck..." began Tariq, but David shushed him urgently and ran to the edge of the roof, looking north. He gestured us to come and see. Blythe was standing on a clear patch of ground off in the distance, with a small group of men. It was too far to make out details, but I assumed he had a mic headset on, patched into the speakers which I now saw were hanging from every lamppost. But we were close enough to make out the detail that mattered. Five stakes driven into the ground, each with a person kneeling beside them, their hands bound behind their back.

I heard Tariq gasp in horror. My dad put his arm around him and hugged him tightly. It was a comradely, even paternal gesture and I felt an unexpected pang of jealousy.

"Is that all of them?" I asked.

Tariq nodded.

"I have with me," the general continued, "five of your friends. I am going to kill them whether you give yourselves up or not.

But you have a choice."

"Always a bloody choice," said Dad.

"If you surrender now," said the general, "I will kill you all quickly and painlessly. You have my word."

"And if we don't?" muttered Dad.

"If you don't surrender now," Blythe went on, as if he could hear us, "I will impale your friends one by one and leave them to die slow, painful deaths. My soldiers will then lay fires in every building in this compound and burn them to the ground. All the gun towers are manned, there's no way to escape. Wherever you're hiding, we'll smoke you out. And if you survive the fire, then you'll join your friends on a stake. Quick and easy; slow and painful. Your choice. You have two minutes to make your position known."

We moved back from the edge. Tariq was in shock, David looked furious, Dad's face gave nothing away; he was busy calculating the odds.

"Okay," said Dad, "here's what we do..."

"Pardon me Sar'nt, but I think I'd better handle this," interrupted David. "I can get us out of here."

Dad looked skeptical.

"How?" I asked.

"I'm Special Forces, Mr Keegan. I'm trained for this kind of thing. Just before deployment I completed a SERE course."

"Seriously?" asked Dad. "You're like, what, twenty?"

"When you've got a father like mine, Sir, you don't have much choice but to be the best. He started preparing me for Special Forces the day I finished potty training. I'm the youngest soldier ever recruited to my unit, and trust me, I did it all on my own."

"Your father must have been very proud," I said, sarcastically.

"I no longer have a father," he replied, matter of fact.

"What's SERE?" Tariq asked.

"Survival, evasion, resistance, escape," he replied. "I can get in and out of anywhere."

"Then we have to stop him," said Tariq, finally. "I can't watch this happen again."

He looked at us desperately, but none of us could meet his gaze.

"We can't leave them! We can't!" he said urgently. "If you won't help me, I'll do it myself."

"Sit down, T," said Dad.

"John, I won't let this happen," said Tariq, almost shouting now. "They're going to die because they followed my orders. Orders I gave trying to save your life. We can't abandon them."

But his face, the tears in his eyes, betrayed the truth. Tariq knew it was hopeless.

Dad put his arm on Tariq's shoulder and gripped it tightly, leaning forward and resting his forehead against the distraught Iraqi's. "They're dead already, T. It's over."

"So what, we just run?" said Tariq, crying now. "We let him kill our friends and we walk away? Then what the fuck has this all been for? What's it all been for?"

"Oh no, we don't walk away," said Dad. "Not now. Not after all this." He turned his attention to David. "You know this camp, right?"

David nodded.

"You can help us move through it undetected?"

"If you do exactly as I say and keep your heads, I believe I can, Sir."

"Then here's what we're going to do," said Dad, and I could see the resolve harden in his eyes as he spoke, seeing my father the soldier fully apparent in front of me for the first time. Suddenly I could see why he'd commanded the respect of the resistance. When he turned to us and outlined his plan, the force of his determination was impossible to resist.

Ever since I'd arrived in Iraq he'd been on the back foot, imprisoned, reacting to events, frightened for me. But now he was in a position to take direct action again. I realized there was a whole side to my father I'd never seen before. And it echoed in me. I learned as much about myself as I did about him in that moment, and I felt proud.

"We're going to hunt and kill General Blythe before the hour is out," said Dad, calmly. "And anyone who gets in our way dies. Everyone with me?"

All eyes were on the son of the man we were proposing to kill.

An awful, gut wrenching scream of pure terror and agony erupted from a hundred tiny speakers.

"I believe that is an achievable objective, Sir," said David.

CHAPTER SIX

Dad took me to one side as we prepared to leave.

"I want you to stay here, Lee."

"What? Why?"

"We're going to into combat against a vastly superior force of men who want to kill us. It's no place for a boy. I couldn't live with myself if I got you killed. You sit tight, wait 'til dark and then try to slip out on your own. You'll have more of a chance that way. We'll rendezvous at the football ground tomorrow morning. Okay?"

I didn't know where to start, but I felt the anger welling up in me and tried to choose my words carefully. I failed.

"Fuck that. And fuck you," I spat. "I'm the one who rescued you, remember? No place for a boy, my arse." I clenched my jaw and stared him down, full of defiance.

I could tell he wanted to get into it, shout me down, ground me, even give me a slap. But I could see the uncertainty in his eyes, no longer sure which, if any, approach would work with me. He was right to hesitate.

Eventually he just nodded.

As the dying screams of Brett, Toseef and Anna echoed around the buildings and gardens, we moved through the compound like ghosts.

We stole the uniforms off the first four soldiers we encountered, and took their weapons too. Viewed from a distance we would now look like a normal patrol. But we only broke cover when needed, preferring to move through the buildings and shadows.

David was terrifying; silent, focused, seemingly without fear, and totally in control. My dad and Tariq followed his every move and gesture like the practiced guerrilla fighters they were. I just tagged along behind them, trying not to give the game away with a careless move.

When we encountered guards or patrols David would take the lead, sidling up to them with the grace of a dancer, silencing them so quietly he almost seemed gentle. He would wrap his arm around their throat, compress their carotid artery and squeeze until they passed out. Then he would lay them on the floor, take hold of their hair and slit their throats.

When two or more stumbled across our path Dad would take the second, and Tariq would take the third. Although neither of them were as poised and fluid as David, they each held their own.

Tariq favoured a slow, delicate, tiptoe approach until just out of striking range, and then he would suddenly leap forward with his arms raised and snap the neck of his prey with a flourish, and let them collapse to the ground at his feet as his arms went wide as if to take a bow.

My father, on the other hand, was more straightforward. I was shocked by the calm precision with which he killed.

He would walk casually up behind his intended victim with his knife drawn, looking like he was going to pat the guy cheerily on the back and suggest a quick beer. He would then wrap one arm around the man's mouth as he slid the knife in between their ribs, as matter of fact as slicing open an envelope.

We hid the bodies as best we could, but we knew we had to move quickly. Sooner or later someone's absence would be noted, or a patrol would not radio in on time, and they would begin to zero in on us.

It probably only took us fifteen minutes to make our way to the main palace, but it felt like a lifetime. I didn't need to kill anyone during the journey, and I was grateful. I didn't want Dad to see me get blood on my hands. Not yet, anyway.

I was worried that he'd see my face as I took a life and he'd realize the truth about me.

The first time I murdered someone – not the first time I took a life, that was earlier – I was out of my head on drugs. I remember the actions but not how it felt.

The second time I took a life it was more by luck than judgement, scrabbling around on the floor, slick with blood, struggling to free myself from a man who was throttling me. I was stabbing his leg as I passed out; he died before I woke up. But I remember how sickeningly tactile it was. Here I was sharing – causing! – the most important moment in this person's life, more intimate even than sex, and I didn't know anything about him. Not his name, his sexual orientation, footy team, nothing at all. His entire existence culminated in a meeting with me, and yet we were strangers.

After that my killing became more focused and deliberate, even clinical. I saw the confusion and pain on my next victim's face as my knife penetrated his heart. I knew him, so his death was more than just meaningless slaughter; I was aware who and what I was snuffing out. It made me feel unbearably sad and guilty.

And powerful.

Then there were those that I killed in the heat of battle, gone in a flash. They were barely even people, just objects, like cars, which I had to stop in order to prevent collision. Yet each of them was unique, identifiable, and known to someone, just not to me, their killer. I had complete power over them, but they never even saw my face.

That feeling of power grew in me with each death, like a sickness I couldn't control and wasn't sure I wanted to. Until Mac, who I didn't even kill.

It shames me more than I can say, but when I stood in front of Mac, preparing to put a bullet in his head, I felt a thrill of anticipation and excitement that transported me. It was only because I lingered in order to savour the moment that Green was able to shoot him instead.

Let me be clear: I didn't hesitate because I wanted to be merciful; I hesitated because I wanted the moment to last. I even got a hard on. I can't stand to think what that says about me.

And now I was watching another killer, one I had thought I knew better than anybody still living, plying his trade with cool efficiency, and I thought: "Is that what I look like? Is that what I've become?"

Even with all that blood on my hands, the smooth, practised ease of my father's emotionless murdering shocked me. It shouldn't have. He was a soldier, after all. I knew he'd been in combat, I knew he'd killed people, just as he'd been trained to do. I knew who he was and what he did.

But seeing those hands, the ones that used to tickle me, throw me up in the air, lift me on to his shoulders on sunny country walks, coolly sliding a blade into the back of a man whose face he'd never seen, was a revelation. I realised three things in quick succession.

He was much better at this than me.

I had no idea who he really was.

And finally, if I got to know my murderous father, maybe it would help me understand his murderous son.

Our point of entry to the palace was the cell block. There were no prisoners in there any more, so it was unguarded. Then we were into the servants' passageway and safe in the dark, forgotten staircase. We soon came to the hidden door I had used to escape from my torturers the day before. On the other side was the vast room the general had taken as his office. The only problem was that we had no way of knowing who was in there.

There was nothing for it but to take the plunge, so David gently cracked the door open and peered through the tiny opening. There was nobody there, so he pushed the door open and ran, soft footed, to the main doors of the room. They stood ajar, and he looked through the gap then waved us out; there was nobody around. Everyone was too busy scouring the compound for us. This was the last place they'd be looking.

He gestured for me to watch the stairs, and waved Dad and Tariq across to search the room where I'd been tortured. There was a pool of congealed blood by the door, a memento of my most recent kill. There was a wide smear running to the balcony where the body had been dragged away and tossed over the railing to the ground below.

Tariq indicated that the room was clear. Dad went to the balcony to scan the area. David was already at the desk, hard at work placing the small block of C4 that he'd appropriated from stores on our journey here. I heard footsteps echoing through the hallway below and hissed at them to hurry. But David continued to work. The footsteps reached the stairs, and I hissed again, but David still stayed put. I ran across to him and grabbed his shoulder but he shrugged me off. I looked up at Dad, frantic, what do we do?

Dad ran around, grabbed my shoulder and dragged me towards the torture room. We ran inside and Tariq pushed the door almost closed behind us. Through the crack we could see David finish his handiwork and stand up, turning as if to leave. But then the main doors opened and there was his father, framed in the doorway.

"Ha," said the general. "You got balls, son."

David said nothing. I could see he held the detonator in his left hand, his thumb on the small, shiny switch.

The general turned, said "stay outside" to the men who had been escorting him, and closed the main doors behind him.

Father and son stood face to face for a minute before the elder man spoke.

"Bet you ten bucks I can put a bullet in your head before you press that button," he said in a pally way, as if referring to an old shared joke.

"Bet you ten bucks you can't," said David, with a wry smile.

But neither of them moved a muscle.

I went to push the door open, but my dad's hand on my shoulder stopped me.

"Let it play out," he whispered. "David can handle himself."

I nodded, but Dad kept his hand on my shoulder as a gentle reminder of who was in charge.

"I remember the day you were born..." began the general.

"No," interrupted David, shaking his head.

The general considered for a moment and then nodded, abandoning that approach.

"I agree," he said. "It's gone too far for that, hasn't it?"

"Yes, it has."

The general shook his head in weary disbelief.

"Was it always going to end like this, do you think?"

"No. If things had stayed the way they were, we'd be eating Thanksgiving dinner with Mom and Sarah, fighting over the gravy."

"But things didn't stay the same, did they?"

"No, they didn't. They never do."

"I reckon that's true. I love you, son."

I expected David to respond with "I'm not your son" again, but this time he replied: "I love you too, Dad."

There was a brief pause, and then a blur of movement and sudden violence that I couldn't even process. There was a single shot and David was lying on the floor, his head at a terrible angle, glassy eyed, his limbs in spasm, a thick pool of blood spreading out from the back of his shattered skull.

My dad gasped, his fingers crushing my shoulder (thankfully not the one I'd recently dislocated, or I'd have yelped). I placed my hand over his and squeezed back.

General Blythe stood over the body of his dead son for a minute, silent, shoulders hunched. But there were no tears, not even a single sob. Eventually he drew himself back up to his full height and walked to the doors, pulling them open and gesturing wordlessly for a soldier to remove David's corpse.

When the mess was cleared away, the general was once again alone in his room with the doors closed. He sat heavily in his chair and swiveled to stare out at the rising sun.

Tariq and I both looked at Dad, guns tight in our grips. Dad nodded and we began to push open the door. Suddenly there was a shrill alarm. I felt a rush of adrenaline. Had we triggered it somehow?

But the general spun his chair so he had his back to us and the large flatscreen telly buzzed into life. That was where the sound had come from. Dad grabbed my shoulder and dragged me back, pulling the door almost closed again. I shrugged his hand off me, full of resentment, but resumed my previous position, watching the general as he began to talk to the man who had appeared on screen.

It was clearly a live feed, so some satellites must still be functioning up there somewhere. The man on the screen was old; seventy at least, with a liver spotted face, pallid, ghostly skin and a thin ring of white hair around his shiny bald pate. He was wearing a black suit, white shirt and dark blue tie, all immaculately pressed, and he was sitting in front of the stars and stripes. He was obviously indoors, but well lit, as if in a TV studio about to present the news. Wherever he was he had lots of power to burn.

"Good evening, General," said the man. His voice was thin and reedy.

Even with all the clues the screen offered me, nothing prepared me for what the general said next.

"Good evening, Mr President."

"Fuck," whispered Dad under his breath.

"Progress report?" wheezed the old man.

"We've eliminated all local resistance, as ordered."

"And the English soldier, Keegan?"

"Dead." So the general wasn't above lying to his Commander-in-Chief. Interesting.

The old man smiled a little at this news. It was not a pleasant sight. "Good. About time. Did he give you anything useful before he died?"

"No. He didn't break."

The old man gave a harrumph of displeasure. "Pity. We'll just have to make do with the satellite images. Did you receive them?"

"Yes, Sir. Are you sure about the choice of target, Sir? I still believe that it might be better to take out the Tsar now, before his power base grows even more."

"We considered it, General, but we've decided that a strong Russia is actually to our advantage at this point. Let the Tsar continue his rise to power. He cannot threaten us. We predict that he will control most of Russia within two or three years, and that suits us. We have long term plans in that respect."

"In that case, Sir, we've prepared flight plans and fuelled the planes. We're ready to go whenever you give the order."

"Good, good. No time like the present, General. In your own time, proceed with the plan. Destroy Operation Motherland and take control of their arsenal at your earliest convenience. Establish marshal law in as wide an area as you can. Put the techniques you've honed in Basra to good use. Terrorise the population, bring them to heel, by any means necessary. They shouldn't be too much trouble now they've been disarmed."

The main doors cracked open and a soldier poked his head in. The general waved him to enter, and a group of four heavily armed men silently filed into the room and stood waiting. It looked like there was now no chance for us to kill the general without sacrificing ourselves.

"I'd like to initiate a secondary operation, if you'll permit it, Sir," said the general.

"Explain."

"I've received intelligence about an armed camp. It's outside our target area, but I believe that a show of force there could send a strong message that our operations are not confined inside our perimeter."

"Where is this camp?"

"Somewhere called Groombridge Place, Mr President. I believe it's the base of operation for a group of Special Forces, a training school for new recruits. One of them came here to retrieve Keegan and killed some good men. We dealt with him, but I think it would be wise to shut the facility down."

"Do I detect a lust for revenge, General?"

"Just doing my job, Mr President."

"Very well, proceed as you see fit."

"You can count on me, Mr President. By this time next week, England will be in American hands and we can proceed to the next phase."

"Don't let me down, General."

The screen went black, there was a momentary burst of static, and then silence.

The general rose and barked "follow me" at the soldiers who'd waited patiently during his teleconference. They filed out of the room and we were alone again.

My mind was whirling with the implications of everything I'd just heard. But one awful image was inescapable: me on a video screen, tied up in front of a blue sheet, yelling for someone to find the school and tell Matron about my death.

They must have found the tape.

Oh God, what had I done?

Jane.

PART TWO

Jane

CHAPTER SEVEN

Work hard, keep your nose clean, own your house. That was the advice Kate's gran always gave her.

"It's not difficult, dear," she'd say. "Just follow those simple rules and you can end up like me and your granddad." Of course, when Kate was seventeen that was the last thing in the world she wanted. But she loved her gran, so she'd nod and smile, and say "Yes, Gran."

On one hand I was glad that her gran died before The Cull, as it spared her all this horror. On the other, she'd have been magnificent, riding out the apocalypse on a wave of warm, milky tea and allotment carrots. It was at moments like this that I missed her most.

But Kate and her gran were gone now.

Rowles strained at his leash, trying to pull away from me. I cuffed him around the head.

"Don't mess me about," I growled.

He whimpered.

The guard in front of us smiled a gruesome, black-toothed grin.

"Can I come in and trade these kids or what?" I said. "Olly's expecting me."

The guard ran his slimy tongue along his lower lip, considering us carefully, then sucked his disgusting teeth and nodded. Lee once told me he used to give people descriptive names to help him keep track of them in his head. It was something that helped him focus when he was under pressure. So I christened the door guard.

"S'pose," said Blackteeth. "Come on in, love."

He turned and waved to the man on the wall behind him, who shouted something to someone in the courtyard. The huge doors swung inwards with a shriek of rusty metal. The guard leered at me and mock-bowed, sweeping his right arm towards the doors, inviting us to enter.

I remembered Kate willingly walking into danger – a heavy, steel-reinforced door, a cold, dark warehouse, and a man standing there with a machine gun strapped across his chest, saying exactly the same thing to her. "Come on in, love." And Cooper's voice in her ear had whispered: "we're right here, don't be afraid."

Eight years ago.

I shook my head and dismissed the memory. If Lee were here he'd tell me to stay focused on my objective.

I so wished Lee were here.

I flashed the guard a disgusted look. "About time."

Drawing myself up to my full height – I'm 5'3" and I was wearing flats, but it's all about posture – I strolled through those gates with all the dignity and attitude I could manage. As I passed the guard he goosed me.

I stopped dead, turned towards him slowly, gave him my most seductive smile and slapped him hard across the face.

"Touch me again, sunshine, and I'll rip your balls off and feed them to you."

I heard Kate's gran saying "Now, now dear, don't be a potty mouth". I had to bite back the urge to giggle. It's something I do when I'm scared.

The guard laughed.

Caroline sobbed involuntarily. I tugged her chain hard and aimed a half hearted kick at her shin. She looked up at me, chin wobbling, wide eyes full of tears.

"Button it, you," I said.

"Third stable on the right, darlin'," said Blackteeth. "Tell you what, when you're done you come find me. I've got a bottle of real wine in my bunk. Been saving it for a special occasion."

I turned my back on him and walked towards the stables, tugging the kids behind me. Rowles slipped and fell on his face. I didn't look back or break my stride; I just dragged him through the mud until he regained his footing and staggered after me. I imagined his collar was really chafing by now.

The courtyard ahead of me was deserted. I knew there were at least three guards behind me at the gates, but I didn't turn to see if there were more. The main farmhouse stood at the far end, three storeys high. Tattered curtains hung from dusty windows, some of which were shattered. The kitchen door was open and I got an impression of movement inside. To my left was a large derelict barn, its roof fallen in; to my right stood a row of brick stables. A large truck was parked awkwardly in the far left corner, its engine idling, the exhaust fumes misting in the chill morning air. That was a statement in itself – who had enough fuel to waste it warming up a lorry cab, even on a morning this cold? I knew exactly what its cargo would be, but after long weeks of investigation I still had no idea where it was going.

I thought about knocking but decided I'd make an entrance, so I walked into the stable, dragging the children behind me. The man behind the desk jumped slightly and reached for the pistol that lay in front of him, but relaxed when he saw that it was only me. He leaned back in his chair, his great blubbery weight threatening to topple him backwards at any second. This was Olly.

"What bloody kept you?" he asked as he returned his attention to the thick rare steak he was eating, held in a piece of old newspaper.

"Ask your guards. More interested in flirting than doing business." I looped the chain and the rope around a hook on the wall, and shoved the two children to the floor. I sat in the chair facing Olly and put my feet up on his desk.

Careful, I thought. Don't overdo it.

"The reason I want to do business with you, Olly, is 'cause you're such a class act," I said.

It took him a moment to realise what I meant, and then he laughed, his thick lips parting in a strangled wheeze, revealing half-chewed raw meat. He thrust the steak towards me.

"Want some?" he offered. "Fresh kill."

"Thanks, but no thanks."

"Suit yourself. Talking of fresh meat, what do we have here?" He levered himself out of his chair and waddled around the desk towards Rowles and Caroline. Both of them cowered against the wall, a pathetic sight in their tattered, muddy rags.

"The boy's eleven, been living rough," I said. "Girl's twelve. Untouched, if you can believe that. They're a bit scrawny but they're healthy as far as I can tell."

Rowles put his arm around Caroline's shoulder as Olly leered at them.

"Don't worry, C," Rowles whispered. "I won't let him hurt you."

Olly leaned down and grabbed Rowles' chin in his greasy fingers. He got very close indeed and hissed into the boy's face: "Of course I'm not going to hurt her. I'm most gentle, me. Break her in all carefully, I will. You too, if you're good."

Rowles spat in Olly's eye as Caroline sobbed and buried her face in his shoulder. Olly snarled and raised his ugly paw, ready to strike the boy, but I leapt up and grabbed the man's wrist. It was so thick I couldn't even get my fingers around it.

"You don't lay a finger on either of them till I get my payment, fat man," I said.

He turned to me, teeth bared. But his raw meat snarl changed into a grin, he wheezed his laugh again and lowered his hand.

"There's no hurry, is there?" He looked down at the pair. "I'll have plenty of quality time with these two when you've gone, won't I? No need to rush."

I let go of his arm and he moved back to his side of the desk and sat down again. I followed suit. He took another bite of steak, tearing the flesh off and chewing sloppily.

"Price is fixed, as discussed," he said. "Go see Jonny in the big house, he'll sort you out. If you make a habit of bringing me good stock like this I'll make it worth your while. Any more where these came from?"

"Plenty, but I can only take them one or two at a time. Don't want to get caught. The villagers might not take kindly to me pinching their kiddies."

"Can't imagine why, little runts."

"But you'll be moving them soon, won't you? 'Cause they might come looking for these two." I tried to sound conversational, barely interested, but I knew immediately that I'd made a mistake. He looked across at me, suspicious and threatening.

"What do you care?" he demanded.

I pretended to think about this, then shrugged and rose to my feet. "I don't. Just curious. Jonny, yeah?"

"Jonny. Yeah."

"See you around, Olly." I didn't look back at the two children as I left.

I crossed to the farmhouse door, which was still hanging open, and casually glanced back at the gates. The high brick wall was solid, so they felt secure in here. Apart from Blackteeth who was outside the metal doors, now closed, there was a guy on a ramshackle scaffold inside, looking out over the flood plain to the south. He had a shotgun over his shoulder. A third man lounged on a damp sofa inside the doors reading Oliver Twist. He also had a shotgun, but his was sawn off.

Two inside the doors, one outside. Then Olly in the stable and Jonny in the house. Might be more, though. But where?

I walked into the farmhouse kitchen. The smell was appalling. In the centre of the large flagstone floor was a wooden table, around it six children of varying ages. All of them had ropes looped around their necks, binding them together in one long chain. They sat there, eyes dead, faces white, most with black eyes or thick lips, dressed in clothes either too big or small, mechanically eating porridge from bowls. I doubted any of them had seen soap and water for at least a month.

Again, Kate's gran came to mind. I had a sudden flash of her cooing "Poor dears", spitting on to her hankie, and wiping all their faces clean with saliva. Kate used to hate it when she did that. God, she used to squirm. Looking back, it seems like the gentlest act of kindness imaginable. Small acts of kindness, that was what the world was missing these days.

I forced my attention back to my situation. I was distancing myself from it, retreating into my head, rambling. It's a trick I learned the first time things got bad, back before The Cull. It had come in handy once or twice since.

But I couldn't afford to absent myself now. I needed to stay sharp. Anyway, I wasn't the one in danger, not really. I wondered where these children had gone to in their heads. I was pretty certain none of them were entirely present any more. I looked into their eyes and I thought that this was how I must look when I zone out. Like a victim. That made me sad and angry to my core. I held on to the anger, focused it, concentrated, brought myself back.

I am nobody's victim. Not any more.

An interior door swung open and a scrawny teenage boy walked in. His face was a battlefield of acne and bum fluff and he dragged a young blonde girl behind him on a rope. Thirteen at the oldest, her face was streaked with tears and snot. His belt was still unbuckled.

I didn't give him time to react to my presence. I was around the table and my arm was around his neck so quickly he didn't know what was happening. He was unconscious before he had a chance to open his mouth. It took all my willpower to relax my grip – it was so tempting to squeeze the life out of the sorry bastard. I wanted to kill him, I felt justified in killing him, even righteous.

But I hadn't let the horror overwhelm me, so I wouldn't let the fury take me either. If I succumbed to either I'd lose myself, and there were children here who needed me.

The boy stopped struggling and his eyes rolled back in their sockets. I relaxed my grip and gently laid his head on the floor. I ran back around the crowded table and closed the door into the courtyard. No-one had raised the alarm, so the struggle hadn't been seen.

I turned back and found six pairs of eyes staring at me with distant curiosity. One boy was still eating, so far gone that he didn't even register what was happening around him. The young girl who had just entered was staring down at the boy who lay unconscious at her feet. I opened my mouth to speak but before I could utter a sound the girl raised her foot and stamped it down, as hard as she could, on the boy's neck. There was a dreadful crunch, the boy spasmed and twitched, gasped, sighed, then lay still. A trickle of blood leaked from his mouth. The girl looked up at me and wiped the back of her hand across her face, smearing away the tears and snot. Then she cocked her head to one side, and said: "Now what?" She spoke primly, with the self-possession of monied privilege.

It took me a few seconds to respond.

"Is there anybody else in here with you?" I asked.

"Just Tim," said the girl. "He's upstairs. He's sick."

"No more guards?"

She shook her head.

"All right. Can you open the front door for me? Walk outside and wave. My friends will see you."

She looped the rope over her neck and let it drop to the floor, then she nodded, turned and left.

I looked down at the seated children. One boy seemed more present than the others. He looked about ten. I leant down so we were eye to eye.

"When my friends arrive can you show them where Tim is and help them get everyone out the front door?"

He nodded solemnly.

"Thank you. Now, could you all just keep quiet for a moment? I have one more thing to do then we can get you out of here."

A few small nods. One girl went back to her porridge.

I avoided looking at the dead teenager, closed my eyes, took a deep breath, fixed a smile on my face and opened the door to the courtyard again. I strode out confidently, but I was painfully aware that I was unarmed. It wouldn't have helped anyway; my hands were shaking too much to use a gun even if I'd had one. I couldn't tell you whether they shook from fear or fury – probably an equal measure of both. I took a deep breath and tried to relax; I'd need steady hands for the next bit.

As I walked past the stables, I saw Rowles and Caroline, still sitting on the floor in Olly's office. I caught Rowles' eye and inclined my head. He nodded back and rose to his feet. I kept walking past the doorway, towards the bookworm. He lay his book aside as I approached, carefully inserting a bookmark to keep his place.

"I thought you were getting paid?" he asked as he swung his legs over the side of the sofa.

The plan had been to find a bag and fill it with stuff, make it look like I'd been paid. I'd been distracted, lost my concentration, and forgotten. Stupid mistake.

"Nothing left," I improvised. "Jonny told me to come back tomorrow. He reckons you'll be flush once you've offloaded this consignment."

The man looked confused.

"Yeah, we will be. But we won't be back for a week."

So wherever they took the children was much further away than I'd thought.

The guard smiled. "Jonny probably just wants you to come and visit him while we're away. Dirty bastard."

The gun was on the sofa beside him. Bookworm stood up and walked past me to yell at the farmhouse. "Oi! Jonny! You dirty fucker. Your dick making you tell porkies again?"

He obviously expected a comeback. But Jonny wasn't saying anything. He stood there, smiling, waiting for a sarcastic reply. Then the smile gradually changed to puzzlement. "Oi! Jonny! You in there?" He took another step forwards. Suddenly he realised something was wrong, and he spun around to face me. I couldn't go for his gun because the guard at the top of the scaffolding was watching us. He'd have picked me off if I'd made a move. But I was standing between the bookworm and his sofa, blocking access to his gun. I silently urged everyone to get a move on.

"Last I saw Jonny, he was dragging some girl upstairs by a rope," I said, shrugging.

Bookworm eyed me suspiciously.

"Probably can't hear you for her groans of ecstasy," I added. Then I flashed my eyes at him knowingly, pretending to be one of the lads, laughing at the teenage rapist.

I felt sick.

"So not tomorrow, next week, yeah?" I asked.

"Yeah," he said thoughtfully.

We stood there facing each other as he see-sawed between amusement and suspicion. Amusement eventually won.

"He's a dirty little bastard, Jonny," he laughed. "You want to watch him."

"Will do. See you next week then?"

He nodded and walked to the gate, unshackling the chains and pulling hard. The guard on the tower returned his attention to the flood plain as the door swung open. I leaned down and grabbed the sawn-off shotgun from the sofa, and walked up behind Bookworm. I buried the muzzle in the small of his back. He stiffened and froze. I pushed him forward so that the metal door shielded us from the man on the scaffolding.

The guard outside the door looked puzzled for an instant and then raised his gun to his hip.

"Drop it," I whispered to the black-toothed lech. "Or the bookworm dies."

He considered this for a moment.

"I don't really like him that much," he replied.

"Fred!" protested Bookworm.

"Shut up you speccy twat," said Blackteeth. "Always got your nose buried in a book. Think you're better than the rest of us. Threatening him ain't gonna stop me, love. Oi, Mike, we've got a situation down here. Wanna lend a hand or you just gonna sit up there staring into space all afternoon?"

I heard the metal clang of the other guard climbing down the scaffolding.

All the plan required was that I disarm the door guards. It should have been easy. Instead I had two barrels ready to fire, two armed men coming at me from two sides, and one unarmed but still dangerous guy stuck in the middle with me. Lee would have known what to do.

I just had to stall. What was keeping everyone?

"What about you, Mike?" I shouted. "You want to see your mate's guts blown out?" I had my free hand on Bookworm's shoulder, and I began backing us away from Blackteeth, back inside the courtyard, towards the sofa. When Mike finally hit the ground and rounded the gate we were far enough back that I could see him and Blackteeth without dividing my attention. At least I'd avoided being caught between the two of them – now they were all in front of me.

"Not really," said Mike. He was tall and lean, bald, about forty. He wore a Barbour jacket, blue jeans and green wellies, and he had the shotgun held up to his shoulder, aimed steadily at us. Something about his poise made me very nervous. He wasn't a thug like Blackteeth, or a novice like Bookworm – he was experienced and deliberate. He was the real threat here.

I remembered the briefing that morning. "Nobody gets hurt," I'd insisted. "Whatever happens, no-one gets killed. All right?" I looked pointedly at Rowles as I said this. He smirked, then nodded. "Yes, Matron."

One dumb teenage bastard was already going cold twenty metres to my right. I didn't want anyone else to join him. Not even these guys.

"Olly!" Mike shouted. "Get out here, boss."

"Olly's not available right now," came the reply. "Can I help at all?" It was Rowles; all five foot nothing of him. He was standing outside the stables, muddy and bedraggled, legs apart, arms raised, with a pistol in his hands. His face and hair dripped fresh blood.

"Dammit Rowles," I shouted. "I told you not to kill him."

"He's not dead Matron," replied the boy quietly. "I can't guarantee he'll ever be the same again, but he's not dead."

Mike's aim didn't waver for a second, but his eyes widened as he calculated the odds. He was square in Rowles' sights.

"Fuck me," said Blackteeth.

"It's just a kid, Fred," said Mike. "Get a grip."

"Caroline, you got a minute?" said Rowles.

Caroline walked out of the stable to join him. Taller than Rowles, one year older, solidly built, her ginger hair cut brutally short, Caroline also held a pistol. She bit her lip thoughtfully, concentrating, as she took careful aim at Blackteeth.

"Actually, he is dead," she said, quite matter of fact. Rowles looked at her, surprised.

"Really?"

"You hit him over the head with an iron bar. Twice. Of course he's dead. Idiot." She said 'idiot' indulgently, with love, as if talking to a silly toddler or sullen boyfriend. My very own pre-pubescent Bonnie and Clyde.

"Oh," said Rowles, nonplussed. "Sorry, Matron." He blinked back his surprise and refocused his attention on Mike.

"Shall we shoot them, Jane?" asked Caroline.

Mike looked into my eyes as I pretended to consider Caroline's question. That made his mind up. He began backing away slowly, heading for the gate.

"I think we'll be leaving," he said. "Coming, Fred?"

Blackteeth nodded and joined his mate, walking backwards, gun raised. As soon as they were clear of the wall they ran left, out of sight.

The farm was ours.

The children were safe.

We were too late to help Tim. He had pneumonia and didn't survive the day.

I had Rowles bury Olly, Jonny and Tim as punishment for his overzealous retribution. He didn't complain. He might go over-board at times, but he had never once questioned any order I'd given him, which is partly why I relied on him so much.

A team of older boys and girls from the school joined us, and we loaded the rescued children into the back of the lorry then set out for home. We left Rowles burying the dead. He could walk back to the school. That was another part of his punishment. It was only ten miles, and I wasn't worried about him. I was far more afraid for anyone that tried to cross him.

Bookworm came with us, too. I reassured him that no harm would come to him, but I still tied him up and put a sack over his head. I had questions I wanted to ask.

Half an hour later I swung the lorry into the driveway of the school and hit the brakes as hard as I could. The lorry skidded and ended up diagonally across the tarmac. I heard protests from the cabin behind me, but I couldn't worry about that now.

There was a roadblock ahead of us, flanked by armed men in combat uniforms.

I reached down, grasped the sidearm that I'd taken from Caroline, and considered what to do. One of the men was approaching the lorry, rifle raised. He didn't look like the usual rabble. None of the local wannabe soldiers wore uniform that convincing.

I thought about throwing the lorry into reverse and running, but it would require a three-point turn, and he'd be here long before we could escape. If he opened fire the children could be hit. I wouldn't put them at risk.

Charge the checkpoint, then? I seriously considered it for a moment, but eventually decided against it. I had to follow the rules I'd set down for myself: never shoot first and prepare for the worst but assume friendly intent until proven wrong.

I kept the engine running and the lorry in first, with my foot on the clutch. I had no idea who this guy was or which group he represented. They could be friendlies. I forced myself to stay calm and wait for him to show his hand.

But he and his mates had obviously taken control of the school. My school. That made me angry. I tried not to imagine what could be going on in there right now.

I cocked the pistol and rested it on my lap, then I rolled down the window.

The man stopped about ten metres from me, rifle raised.

"Are you armed?" he shouted.

"Yes, thanks," I replied, politely.

"Throw down your weapon and step out of the cab. Keep your hands where I can see them."

"Why?"

"Because I'm asking nicely, ma'am. I don't want to shoot you."

"That's good. I don't want you to shoot me either. We have something in common. Now do you mind telling me who the fuck you are and what you're doing in my school?"

"Not your school any more, ma'am, I'm afraid. You'd be Jane Crowther, yes?"

"That's right."

"Then it's my duty to inform you that in accordance with emergency provisions, and Royal decree, this estate is now under the control of the British Army. And you are under arrest for looting, kidnap and suspected murder."

CHAPTER EIGHT

Kate's brother had a thing for soldiers.

If I close my eyes and concentrate I can almost see those bright eyes, that cheeky grin, and hear him saying: "Imagine, all that time in uniform, being butch, sharing showers and never even copping a snog. I mean, talk about repressed. I tell you, Sis, a closeted soldier on a night out is my idea of heaven. So gloriously dirty!" Then he'd tell that unrepeatable anecdote about a captain from Aldershot, a rubber hose and a camcorder, and Kate and her friends would all be wetting themselves by the time he got to the bit where the lube tube exploded.

"Something funny, miss?"

I put my hand over my mouth and forced myself to concentrate. "No, Captain, nothing at all. Just... wind."

I was sitting in my office on the ground floor at Groombridge Place, but I was on the wrong side of the old mahogany desk. I loved that desk. It's amazing the sense of power and confidence just sitting behind a big desk can give you. Props like that help when you're making it all up as you go along, like I'd been. But today I was sat on a hard plastic chair with my hands cuffed behind my back while the man who had introduced himself as Captain Jim Jones sat in my comfy leather swivel chair, facing me across my desk. He pouted sourly and rubbed the back of his neck. He kept doing that. As nervous tics go it wasn't the worst, but it was starting to irritate me.

The captain was thirtyish, six feet tall, slightly built, with thin sandy hair and big teeth that looked like they were trying to escape from his face. Pretty rather than attractive. He seemed comfortable in his uniform, though, and when I'd been brought in here his men had followed his orders efficiently and without question. Command came easily to him, it seemed. Whoever these guys were, they were well disciplined.

He narrowed his blue eyes warily, as if daring me to give my assessment out loud.

"Well then Miss, as I was saying before your breakfast interrupted me, we've taken control of this establishment following a report that you were involved in the trafficking of children."

There was something about the way he said 'Miss' that made me want to kick him in the shins. I suppose I should have stayed calm and pliant, played the innocent, but he was in my chair and he was patronising me. I wasn't in the mood to be patient.

"Okay," I replied. "Let's deal with that first, before we get to the question of who you are and by what authority you've taken control of my school. What report? From who?"

"We have certain assets in play, Miss," he said. Smug git.

"Right," I snapped, irritably. "In English we say 'spies'. You've got a spy or spies in the trafficking network that I've been negotiating with."

I paused for a second and ran through everyone I'd come into contact with since I'd started negotiations with Olly a few weeks ago.

"There was only one person in that organisation who knew where I came from, except Olly," I said. "The spotty one, Smith. He wasn't there this morning. Reporting in, was he?"

Jones was wrong-footed by that and almost stammered.

"I can't discuss ongoing operations," he said curtly.

"Right, so Smith told you I was selling children to Olly, and instead of shutting that scumbag down you waited 'til I'd gone to do business, seized the school, presumably to protect the kids, and then waited for me to get back. That way you leave Smith in place, which means you don't know where the kids end up yet. That about it?"

The captain rubbed his neck.

"Thought so," I said. "Only two problems there, Captain.

"One: I'm not trafficking children, I'm rescuing them. If you talk to the kids from the back of the truck I was driving when you arrested me – kids, by the way, who need medical attention, which is what I should be doing now rather than explaining myself to you – if you talk to them, they'll confirm what I'm saying.

Two: Olly is dead, as is one of his goons. The other two ran away and the final one is the sod with the bag over his head. I was going to interrogate him and find out where the kids end up, but if you really are the British Army and not just a bunch of roleplaying inadequates, then I'm sure your interrogation techniques will be far more effective than mine. I don't enjoy inflicting pain."

Captain Jim was not used to people talking back to him. I could see that it was taking a lot of effort for him to stay calm. He was used to unquestioning obedience; maybe I could use that.

"If what you say is true, we'll have it sorted out in no time, Miss."

This was not the reasonable, measured answer I wanted. And he'd called me Miss again.

"And while we're at it," I said, "who the sweet holy fuck do you think you are to come walking into my school at gunpoint and start tossing orders about?"

"As I've explained, Miss, we are the British Army." He was getting testy. I wondered what would happen if I really pushed him.

"My big fat arse you are."

"I can assure you..."

"If you're the army then where were you after The Cull burnt itself out? Where were you when martial law fell to pieces? Where were you when the rape gangs and cannibals and the England-for-the-English death squads started running things? Where were you when I had to lead an army of children into battle, for fuck's sake? We could've used you! What, were you too busy putting 'assets' in place to actually fucking help? And how many of you are there, eh? Seriously, are there even enough of you to be an army? Even if you are all soldiers you're just another militia now. And as for that Royal Decree bollocks, Christ, don't make me laugh. That bunch of parasites bled out and died just like everyone else. Who's left? Fergie? Is that it? Are you Fergie's Forces? God help us. Or is it Harry? He likes a good uniform, that one; just make sure it's not got a swastika on it."

I was red in the face, breathing hard, and I'd stood up half way through my rant, trying to assert some measure of control over the situation, impose myself on him a bit.

The captain just sat there, placid, letting me get it out of my system.

"Finished?" he asked.

I'd misjudged him. He'd been annoyed by my niggling jibes and insubordination, but a full temper tantrum just brought back his sense of superiority and condescension.

I nodded and sat back down. So much for that idea.

"Well?" I asked.

He spoke calmly and with control. If he was angry he was determined not to let me see it.

"I can assure you, Miss, that I am a member of His Majesty's Armed Forces. At present the UK has no civilian administration, but the emergency provisions laid down by the government at the start of the crisis still hold. Martial law remains in effect. However, we do not have enough troops to enforce it. Instead, we are engaged in an operation designed to restore some level of order and security."

I waited for more information, but he said nothing else. "Is that it?"

"I am not authorised to tell you more," he said smugly. "We

are not in the habit of revealing top secret plans to school teachers."

"I'm a matron, not a teacher, and if you think you're going to restore order by wearing a uniform, looking pleased with yourself and being vague at people then the best of luck to you."

He smiled thinly and for the first time I suspected that Captain Jim could be quite ruthless if the circumstances demanded it.

"You misunderstand, Miss. I have more than a uniform." He reached down and I heard the soft metallic click of a button being undone, then he laid a browning semi-automatic pistol on the desk in front of him. "I have my standard issue browning sidearm."

I was about to make some sarcastic rejoinder when he reached down and produced the handgun I'd been carrying when I was detained. He gently placed it alongside his own.

"The curious thing," he said, "is that you do, too. And you're no soldier. Which raises some interesting questions, don't you think?"

Before I could reply there was a sharp knock at the door and the captain barked "Come!"

A young female soldier entered, snapped to attention and saluted.

"We found what we were looking for, Sir."

"Thank you, Private," replied the captain, getting to his feet and holstering his gun. "Bring her," he said, and left without giving me a second glance.

I felt the squaddie grip my shoulder, so I stood up and was led out of the room and into the main reception hall of the old house. The double front doors were to my right, the main staircase with its plush red carpet was to my left, and a series of doors led to rooms off the hall. Normally this space would be full of life – running kids, play fights, all sorts of wonderful commotion. Now there was just a young man in uniform with a machine gun nestled in the crook of his arm, indicating to the captain that he should walk past the staircase and into what would once have been the servant's area. I followed, receiving a sneer of contempt from him as I passed. Like I cared.

We went through a small door beside the staircase into a narrow corridor that led to the scullery, pantry and kitchen. But it turned out that our destination was the cellar. As I got to the cellar door I caught a glimpse of the courtyard through a small window. I saw all the children and staff of my school, lined up, stood to attention, being watched by three soldiers whose guns were trained on them. My first instinct was to raise hell, but I'd realised what was coming, so I bit back my anger and followed Captain Jones down the stairs into the armoury. The female squaddie remained in the corridor above.

A single naked bulb lit the cool, damp, barrel-vaulted chamber where we kept our guns and ammunition. It was not that different to the armoury back at St Mark's, out of which we'd hauled as many boxes as possible while Mac's time bomb counted down. The captain was standing by a box of SA-80 machine guns, inspecting them closely. He lifted one out, felt its heft, and assured himself it was the genuine article and not a replica or a toy. Then he scanned the room, found the ammunition, checked that too, and slammed the magazine into place. Satisfied, he shoved the muzzle hard into my abdomen and looked me in the eye.

"I'm authorised to shoot looters," he said quietly. "In fact my C.O. positively encourages it. But lucky for you I like to get my facts straight before I start shooting. So I'm going to give you one chance to explain to me how a young nurse and a house full of children happen to be in possession of enough army property to wage a small war. And you'd better make it good, Miss Crowther, because the serial number on that box tells me that this ordnance came from a Territorial installation about ten miles from here, and the men who were guarding it were found tied up and murdered last month. As you can imagine, we take a dim view of people who kill our colleagues."

I took a deep breath and maintained eye contact. Such pretty blue eyes, but they were hard and cold. I didn't doubt he'd shoot me if I said the wrong thing.

"I thought," I said, "that you were here to stop me trafficking children?"

"I am. And I'll do as you ask – talk to the children from the truck, interrogate your prisoner, check on Olly and see if he's as dead as you say. It's easy to check a few facts and find out if you're lying. But this," he gestured to the crates, "is another matter. And I'm still waiting."

There was nothing to do but tell the truth.

"I took control of this school a few months ago," I explained. "Before that it was briefly run by a man called Sean MacKillick – a ruthless, violent psychopath. He was setting himself up as some kind of tribal leader until he was betrayed and killed by the children he was attempting to lead. Then I stepped in and took his place. These children were – are – horribly traumatised. I'm trying to look after them and keep them safe. It was MacKillick who raided your base, killed those men and took the guns. I just sort of inherited them."

His eyes were sharp and calculating as he considered what I'd just said. I stood there underneath the light bulb, with my back to the staircase, waiting for his decision, knowing that I might only find out what it was when a bullet hit my spine.

Looking back at that moment, I think he believed me. I fancy that I saw the change in his eyes, the instant he chose trust over fear. But I may be wrong. I'll never know. Because at that precise moment the young woman soldier from upstairs was thrown down the cellar stairs. I looked down and to my left and saw her eyes blink once in surprise before she died. Her throat had been slit and there was arterial blood still pumping from the gash.

"Drop the gun," said a familiar voice behind me.

Oh no.

Captain Jim still had the machine gun jammed into my stomach but he was looking over my shoulder at the boy coming down the stairs. Then he looked back to me and held my gaze. I suppose that's one of the things about soldiers – they're trained to stay cool even when awful things happen out of the blue. I could see the captain calculating the odds, weighing his chances, not sparing a second thought for the poor dead girl lying next to me on the floor.

"I said drop it," barked Rowles as he came down the stairs. I couldn't see him, but I presumed he had a gun aimed at the captain's head.

I needed to try and defuse this situation.

"I thought you were walking back, Rowles," I said, maintaining eye contact with the captain, telling him with my eyes that he shouldn't do anything hasty.

"They had horses. I nicked one. Who are these bastards?" asked the boy.

"They say they're the British Army."

"Ha. And who are they really? More traffickers? Militia? What?"

"Thing is Rowles, I think they might be telling the truth. I think they may actually be the army."

The captain inclined his head slightly, acknowledging what I was doing, giving me leave to continue

"So why have they got everyone lined up outside like they're about to start shooting?" asked Rowles.

"He's got a point, you know," I said to the captain. "You go around kidnapping people at gunpoint with no explanation, they're going to assume you're just another bunch of thugs. They're not going to think 'hang on, maybe they're here to help, maybe they're lining us up against a wall for our own good'. They're going to think 'oh look, another shower of bastards with big guns', and they're going to start a fight. You can't blame them for that. After a year of fighting for our lives against all sorts of gun toting, uniform wearing bully boys, why would anyone give you the benefit of the doubt if this is the way you do business?"

Don't do anything stupid, Captain, please don't shoot the boy.

He considered what I'd said, his gun muzzle still nestled in my tummy, Rowles' gun still pointing at his head.

"We're the army, Miss," he said. "We don't have to explain ourselves."

"And that's the kind of arrogant bullshit that gets people killed," I replied angrily. "Of course you have to explain yourselves. Anyone can get army guns and uniforms these days, they're just lying there. The point of the army is to be better than that. You're supposed to protect us from the thugs, not act like them. That girl on the floor, what was her name?"

"Julie, Julie Noble."

"Well Julie Noble would still be alive if you'd just knocked on the door and introduced yourselves instead of waving guns around and lining up children like cattle."

"These days people have a tendency to shoot first and ask questions later," he said. "We've lost a lot of good soldiers trying your approach. It's proven more efficient to seize control and then explain later. Saves lives."

"Army lives. But how many innocent people have been killed resisting you before they knew what was going on?"

He shrugged. "A few."

"Even one is too many. Your job is to risk your lives to keep them safe, but you're risking their lives to keep yourselves safe. And if you do that you lose what little authority that uniform gives you. The boy behind me is eleven. Look what this world has driven him to. Look what you're driving him to. Someone is going to die here in a moment – you, me or a eleven-year-old boy – if you don't start acting like a proper soldier. And I'd really, really like it if no-one else died today. So be a dear, Jim, and put the bloody gun down."

"Him first," he said.

I rolled my eyes. It was hard to know who was the bigger child, the soldier or the schoolboy.

I glared at him and said: "Rowles, lower your gun please."

"But what if he shoots you, Matron?"

"He won't."

"I can take him, Matron. Just say the word."

A momentary flash of disbelief crossed the captain's face.

"Oh, he's not lying, Captain," I said.

"Listen, son," said the soldier.

"No no no!" I interrupted, frantically signalling him to stop. "Don't do that. Don't."

There was a long pause and then Rowles said: "I don't like people in uniforms telling me what to do." The emotionless calm in his voice told the captain everything he needed to know about Rowles' state of mind and why it would be a really bad idea to patronise him.

"Rowles," I said firmly. "you've never disobeyed a direct order from me, or moaned once if you don't like an order I've given. As long as I let you say your piece before I make up my mind you let me make the call. Right?"

"You listen and you're fair. I trust you."

"Trust me now and put down the gun. That's an order."

After a moment's hesitation I heard the sound of his gun being uncocked. That was half the battle. Now which way would the captain jump?

"He's eleven years old," I said quietly. "You've invaded his home and kidnapped his friends at gunpoint. He's done nothing wrong, nothing you wouldn't have done in the same situation. This is your fault, Captain. Your actions led us here. And your actions will determine whether this ends peacefully or not. I don't think you want the blood of children on your hands, do you?"

The captain was staring at the floor, at poor dead Julie, his jaw clenched, furious and armed and eager to avenge the death of a soldier under his command.

"No, I don't," he said eventually. But it was an effort, I could tell.

"Good," I said. "Then here's what we're going to do. Rowles, throw your gun over here."

He did so.

"Captain, lower your gun and uncuff me. Then we'll walk out of here, brew up a nice cup of tea, have some of Mrs Atkins' flapjack and sort this out like civilised adults."

The captain half laughed, a mixture of amusement and warning. Then he nodded.

I breathed a sigh of relief as he withdrew his gun from my stomach.

But I was a fool.

Quick as a flash he stepped sideways and opened fire at the staircase behind me. The noise was unbearably loud in that enclosed chamber. I whirled to see what was happening and felt something hot and sharp hit my left ear. I caught a glimpse of

Rowles diving to his right, gun in hand, muzzle flaring. The light bulb was shot out and we were plunged into darkness, lit only by strobe flashes of gunfire.

I should have dived for cover, but I was frozen in place. I should have shouted for them to stop, but my teeth were too tightly clenched.

I don't know how many rounds were fired, but I heard the captain give a low grunt and the gunfire stopped. All that was left was the ringing in my ears and the soft thud as someone hit the floor.

"Matron!" shouted Rowles in the darkness. It wasn't a cry for help, he was desperate to know that I was okay, which meant that it was the captain lying on the ground.

"I'm here, I'm fine. Quick, find the keys to the cuffs, they're in his top right breast pocket."

"Okay." I heard him fumbling about in the dark. There was no point shouting at him now, but something was going to have to be done about that boy. He was leaving far too many corpses in his wake. I worried what he'd be like without me to keep him in check.

I heard the jingle of keys and Rowles began feeling around for my wrists.

"Oi! Hands!"

"Sorry Matron."

"Do you always carry two guns?" I asked as he unlocked the cuffs.

"Three. One for show, one in my boot, one in my pants."

I crouched, found the captain, and took his pulse. He was alive, just about. I grabbed his gun and stood up.

"How many?" I asked.

"Two in the courtyard, one at the front door."

"I meant, how many did you kill?"

"Oh, um." There was silence as he did a little bit of mental arithmetic. "Five, including this one."

"Jesus, five!? How the hell did you manage that?"

"There were three of them on the perimeter, in the woods," he sounded confused. Why was I asking such a pointless question?

"I did them one at a time. Quietly. Then the girl, then him."

"We're going to have a very long, very serious talk about this when we're done, young man."

"Yes, Matron."

"But for now, options?"

"You've got one option," said a voice from the hall upstairs. "And that's to walk up these stairs with your hands above your heads and surrender. Or I toss a grenade down there and blow you to pieces."

I held the scalpel in my hand and looked at the mess in front of me.

The captain had taken two bullets to the chest and there was massive damage. His breath was just a soft, raspy whisper, laboured and painful. I knew there was nothing I could do to save this man's life. He was dead already.

I didn't have any of the equipment I needed to try and stabilise him, but at least I had a blood donor – Green, the school's senior boy and an avowed pacifist who never touched a gun, had volunteered.

I stood in the enormous kitchen and looked across the operating table, which was really just a big wooden kitchen table that I'd washed with alcohol and spread a clean sheet over. The sharp tang of the alcohol mixed with the iron smell of the captain's blood and burnt my nostrils. The only light came from the window but the sun had come out and was streaming through the old mottled glass.

Green was lying on a couch that we'd dragged to the far side of the table, a tube coming out of his arm snaking its way into the captain's. Beyond him, in front of the Aga, stood the young soldier who'd assumed command after his C.O. had been shot. His eyes were wild with shock, and his face was pale. He was only a kid, barely in his twenties, and he was nervous and twitchy. But he had Rowles kneeling on the cold floor tiles, with his hands handcuffed to a radiator, and a gun aimed at the back of his head. Rowles seemed only mildly concerned, as if this was a minor inconvenience rather than the last minute of his life.

"I mean it," shouted the soldier, barely in control of himself, his thick Bradford accent sounding strangely out of place. "You said you were a doctor. You save the captain or I execute the boy right here. Then you. If he dies, you die."

There was nothing I could do. I needed to buy some time, think of a way out of this. So I raised the scalpel and made the first incision.

And with a low groan, the captain died.

CHAPTER NINE

I remember the day Kate decided to become a doctor. She was nine years old.

It was a cold, wet Sunday morning and her gran had taken her to the local swimming pool. It was a grotty, run down place with cracked tiles and graffiti on the doors of the changing cubicles, but she loved it there. There was a girl from her school called April, and they would meet there and splash around every week. I remember that they were always giggling. Their shrill little voices must have echoed around that pool and driven all the adults nuts, but they didn't know or care. Kate's gran just sat there watching them with an indulgent smile.

The pool attendant was supposed to stop anyone running on the slick, wet tiles, but he couldn't be bothered. He was too busy chatting up bored mums. That morning he was nowhere to be seen.

Anyway, that Sunday, April and Kate were having a splash fight in the shallow end. It wasn't that busy, there were about ten or fifteen people in the pool and a collection of parents reading the Sunday papers on the hard wooden benches. There was one guy swimming lengths. He was fast and energetic, obviously there for exercise rather than fun. He was bald and slightly pudgy, and he was red in the face as he swam past them, gasping for air.

I remember Kate doing an impression of him – rolling her eyes up, pouting like a guppy and turning her face puce – and making April laugh. Then suddenly the man was thrashing about in the water, gurgling and trying to shout for help. Kate didn't know what was going on, but April surprised her by shouting loudly: "Help! Someone get a doctor!"

Kate's GP was Doctor Cox, a small sweaty man who smelt of boiled sweets. She neither liked nor disliked him, he was just a fact of life – the guy who gave her injections and took her temperature when she had flu. Kate couldn't imagine how he'd be able help a drowning man.

Then this mumsy woman with short blonde hair came running out of the pool attendant's changing room wearing only her bra and pants, and dived cleanly into the water. She swam to the man and wrestled him to the side, keeping his head above water. By the time she'd got him to the edge the attendant had joined her, pulling on his t-shirt as he ran. Together they heaved the man on to the side and the woman knelt down beside him. A little gaggle of curious bystanders gathered to watch.

"Give me room," shouted the woman. "I'm a doctor."

The man was blue by now, but she was calm and efficient as she took his pulse, massaged his chest and administered CPR.

"Call 999, this man's having a heart attack," she said. The attendant hurried away.

As she worked, the colour gradually returned to the man's face and he seemed to stabilise. By the time the ambulance arrived it looked like he was going to be okay. The doctor kept working on him until he was stretchered away. And then, when they were gone, she was just a bedraggled middle-aged woman standing by a grotty pool in soggy, see-through undies.

But she was the coolest, most heroic person Kate ever seen.

April sniggered and said: "Her tits are all saggy."

"I want to be just like her," Kate said. Then she turned her back on April and swam away.

"He's having a heart attack," I shouted, dropping the scalpel on to the table.

The squaddie snarled at me through gritted teeth: "Fix it or the boy dies."

He was serious, but Rowles didn't look worried as he knelt there with a gun to his head, waiting to die. He just looked bored.

"I need help," I said desperately.

"Get him to do it," replied the squaddie, gesturing to Green, who sat beside the captain, auto transfusing to try and maintain his blood pressure.

"If I disconnect him, the captain will die. Now come here!" My tone of command worked.

Stressed and panicky, the soldier stepped to the opposite side of the table and laid his gun alongside his stricken C.O.

"All right, what do I do?"

Over his shoulder I saw Rowles, handcuffed to a radiator, miming to Green that he should tackle our captor. But Green just shook his head and stayed where he was. Rowles cast his eyes skywards, looked at me and shrugged. Green also looked at me, apologetically.

Green was a gentle boy, sensitive and artistic, but during MacKillick's reign at the school he had been forced to do the most awful things. In the end he'd snapped and shot his tormentor to death, emptying an entire clip into him. Since then he'd been passive and withdrawn, totally refusing to take part in any of the patrols that defended the school. He looked at the gun on the table, within easy reach, but I knew he'd never make a grab for it.

So it was down to me.

But the soldier was on the opposite side of the table.

I started to massage the captain's chest, pushing down rhythmically, one two three, making it look good. I considered the young man in the uniform. He couldn't be more than twenty, so he'd probably only just joined the army when The Cull hit. His manner didn't exactly scream high intellect. He was an uneducated, inexperienced, scared young man. Just the kind of person my school was intended to help. But he had a gun, a twitchy trigger finger and he was threatening my children. I didn't think I could talk him down or overpower him. Which didn't leave me many options.

"We need to shock him," I gasped.

"With what?"

"I dunno, Sherlock. Improvise!"

"But there's no fucking power, is there!" He looked around the room, frantic.

I pointed at a large battery-powered torch on the sideboard. "Get that," I said.

He reached over and got it. If only it had been a little further away I'd have made a grab for the gun, but there wasn't time.

"Now smash the bulb," I instructed, "switch it on and when I say so, shove it into his chest."

"But it'll cut him."

"For fuck's sake," I yelled, "do you want him to die or not?"

"Okay, okay."

He cracked the glass on the table side and stood there, poised, with the torch in his hands, ready to save his captain's life.

"No," I said, leaning across the table and moving his hands so that the torch was over the captains's left breast. "There."

He nodded as I leant back over to my side of the table.

It took him a second to realise that I'd stopped working on the captain. Another half a second to notice the sticky wetness at his throat. Then he saw the scalpel in my hand.

"Torches don't work like that," I said softly. "I'm sorry."

"But..."

"You left me no choice."

He stepped back and dropped the torch to the floor.

"But..."

"He's already dead, I'm afraid."

The young soldier reached up to his throat and his hands came away covered in blood.

"Benefits of medical training," I said sadly. "It only takes the tiniest cut in the right place."

He looked confused and upset, as if I'd said something that had really hurt his feelings. His face crumpled.

"I couldn't let you hurt my children," I explained.

His legs gave way and he crashed to the floor.

I walked around the table, knelt down, lifted his head and cradled it in my lap, stroking his hair.

"It's all right," I said. "Everything's ok now. Don't be afraid. You're fine."

"Really?" He sounded hopeful and relieved. "That's good."

His eyes glazed over, he wheezed, and he was gone.

There I was in my surgery, the place where I was supposed to mend broken people, with blood on my hands for all the wrong reasons.

And I wasn't finished yet.

I stepped into the courtyard with my hands in my pockets.

It sits on the west, with the house on one side, stables on another, mews buildings on the third, and a wall with large wooden gates on the fourth. The floor was cobbled and muddy. In the centre of the courtyard stood all the children and staff of my school, lined up and standing to attention with their hands on their heads, watched over by two soldiers who kept their machine guns trained on them at all times.

There was Mrs Atkins, the dinner lady. With her florid face, ample bosom and floury apron she looked like a character from a *Carry On* film, but she was cunning and determined when she needed to be. The boys adored her unconditionally.

Beside her stood her husband Justin, a tall, stick-thin man with thick grey hair and a hawk-like nose. Quiet and soft spoken, I didn't know much about him except that he used to be a customer service manager for BT, had lost a wife and two children in The Cull, and he made Mrs Atkins' hair curl (her words).

Then there was Caroline, Rowles' partner in crime. I'd never seen them hold hands or kiss, so I wasn't sure if they were what you'd call boyfriend and girlfriend, but they were inseparable and she was almost as scary as he was. Almost.

There were also twenty-one surviving boys from the original St Mark's, fifteen girls who'd joined me when I'd been hiding from MacKillick, the strays we'd rescued that morning, plus three teaching staff who'd joined us from the nearby community of Hildenborough.

These were my people, my responsibility, my family. I'd killed to protect them before and I'd do it again.

The two soldiers guarding them were young – a man about the same age as the one lying dead on the surgery floor, and an older woman, about twenty-five. I'd describe them, but in their uniforms and helmets, in that gloomy brick-lined square, I'm ashamed to say that nothing leapt out at me. They were just soldiers, that's all.

Maybe I deliberately didn't look too closely.

Mrs Atkins smiled at me as I entered, but her smile quickly faded when she saw how much blood had soaked into my clothes.

The female soldier saw me then and brought her gun to bear. She was to my left, about eight or nine metres away, at eleven o'clock. Her male colleague was hidden behind the hostages but I knew he was to my right at about one o'clock, in the far corner.

"Don't move," yelled the woman.

I stopped moving.

"Where's Rich?" she asked.

"Do you mean the young man who took charge?"

"Where is he?"

"Dead. Your C.O. too. Sorry." I meant the apology, but I can see how that wouldn't have mattered to her.

"Why you..." She took one step forward. There was a sharp echoing crack and one of the cobbles at her feet splintered into flying shards. She froze.

Nice shot, Rowles.

There was another shot and I heard a cry of "Fuck!" from the other soldier. Green making his presence felt – under the circumstances he'd agreed to use the gun, but had sworn he wouldn't shoot anybody. I hoped it wouldn't come to that.

"Do I have your attention?" I asked.

The woman nodded.

"Yeah," came the nervous reply from one o'clock.

"Would everybody except the soldiers please sit down."

Silently, all the children and adults sank to the floor. Not much protection if bullets started flying, but it was something. I could see both soldiers clearly now, above everyone's heads. Time for my big speech.

"I woke up this morning feeling nervous," I began. "I planned to take two of these children into a hostile, dangerous situation and put their lives at risk. Mine too. I had a plan and I was determined that no-one would get killed. But I should know by now that plans rarely work. As soon as you start waving guns around somebody dies. Somebody always dies.

"But I thought I was doing the right thing. There were children who needed rescuing from bad people, and I decided it was my job to do that. You might think that was arrogant and reckless of me, but no-one else was going to rescue them. Not the police, not the army.

"Anyway, the decision to take action was mine alone. And we rescued those kids. But two people died. Two vicious, evil bastards, but people all the same. And I'm a doctor. It's my job to save lives, not take them. But you two are the sixth and seventh people today to aim guns at me and I'm sick to the back fucking teeth of it. So here's where things stand.

"Your C.O. is dead. His second-in-command is dead. Every one of your colleagues is dead. You two are the only surviving members of your team and both of you are in the crosshairs of the telescopic sights of sniper rifles. If I give the word your heads will be blown off. Then we'll take your corpses to the farm we raided this morning, pile you up outside it, pour petrol over you and set you on fire.

"When your friends come looking for you they'll find evidence of a firefight and they'll think you died fighting vicious child traffickers. And when they come here we'll be ready for them. With tea and cake. Then maybe second time round things will go a little better for everyone.

"To be honest, we'd probably be better off if I killed you now. But I'm sick of killing and I'd really like to go to bed tonight without any more blood on my hands.

"So put your guns down and I promise that you won't be hurt."

I had the guy at "I woke up", his face told me that. But the woman was a different story. Even as she laid her gun on the ground I knew what was coming. I opened my mouth to tell Rowles to shoot, but I was too late. She crouched to lay the gun down and then sprang forward like a sprinter off a starting block, a large knife suddenly in her hand.

Rowles managed a shot but she was too fast. She was on me before I could get out of her way. She led with the knife, going straight for my heart. I managed to turn just in time and the blade nicked one of my ribs and bounced off again. I was wearing a green t-shirt and the blade didn't snag at all, which told me how sharp it was. I didn't feel the pain of the cut for a few seconds, just the glancing impact, and by the time I felt the sting I was too busy to scream.

As the knife carried on past me she lowered her shoulder and took me in the midriff, winding me and sending me flying backwards on to the cold, hard cobbles. I went down hard, with her on top of me. My right shoulder smashed into the stones and I was unable to stop my head bouncing off a cobble, which left me briefly dazed.

Some of my old training was still in there, even all these years later, and I heard Cooper telling me to rush a gun and flee a knife. Which was perhaps not the best advice for my subconscious to offer me at that precise moment. The other thing I remembered Coop teaching me was that if you find yourself in a knife fight, the most important thing is to never, ever lose track of your opponent's blade.

I must have reacted automatically, because when my head stopped spinning I was lying flat on my back with the soldier astride me, both my hands wrapped around her wrist, trying to stop the knife coming down. She was snarling and furious, but controlled. I'd been in fights before, but if this woman really was army trained then I was in serious trouble; she'd know moves I'd never even heard of, and she wouldn't hesitate to kill me.

I saw Caroline out of the corner of my eye, moving to get up and come to my aid. I shouted at her to stay where she was as I suddenly stopped blocking the knife and instead pushed left with all my strength, shoving the knife aside for a split second and bringing the soldier's head and shoulders closer. Then I sat bolt upright and smashed my forehead into the bridge of her nose. There was a sharp crack and a crunch then she reeled backwards, blood spurting everywhere, still with her knees keeping me on the ground.

I let go of her wrist and hit her as hard as I could, pushing her broken nose into her face with the heel of my hand, releasing a small explosion of blood and making her scream.

Before I could press my advantage her left elbow slammed into the side of my head and then I felt something swipe past my face. The knife. As it swung out on its arc, trailing blood from my cheek, I brought both arms to my chest and shoved up and forwards with all my strength, knocking her backwards. Then I pulled my legs in, toppling her on to the cobbles.

There was a shot and I felt something tug my shirt. My attacker grunted as Rowles' bullet hit the ground an inch from her head.

"That nearly hit me!" I yelled.

"Sorry," he shouted back from the roof of the main building where he was lying safely at the roof's edge. "Just trying to help."

"Do me a favour and don't."

But the distraction had enabled the soldier to regain her footing as well.

The shining blade formed the centre of a circle as we sidled around each other looking for an opening. Then she took me by surprise, darting sideways to grab a girl by the hair, pushing the point of the knife into her throat.

The girl's name was Lucy. She was ten and had long red hair and freckles. She wore thick specs and had buck teeth, but she sang like an angel and was nobody's fool. She went rigid with fear as the soldier threatened to slit her throat.

"Up," said the soldier. Nervously, Lucy rose to her feet. The soldier wrapped herself around the girl, keeping her as a human shield between herself and Rowles.

"Anybody follows us, the girl dies," she snarled.

I nodded.

"Barker, get your gun, we're leaving," she said.

The male soldier slowly took his hands off his head.

"Don't move, Barker," I said. He stopped, unsure which way to jump.

The woman pressed the knife just a bit harder and Lucy whelped.

"I fucking mean it, bitch," growled the woman.

"The second she dies my boy on the roof will end you," I said, then I walked, as casually as I could given that I was shaking like a leaf, over to Barker the squaddie. Our eyes locked as I reached out and removed his sidearm. The look on my face must have been convincing, because he didn't resist. I felt the cold metal thing nestle itself into my hand as I turned back to face the girl I'd sworn to protect, and the woman who was threatening her life.

I was through with talking.

Without even thinking I raised the gun and fired a single shot, taking the soldier right between the eyes and spraying her brains all over Mrs Atkins' best floral pinny.

The soldier's legs crumpled and she fell in a heap on the floor as Lucy screamed and screamed and screamed.

It was the first time in my life I'd ever killed someone and enjoyed it. I felt a glow of satisfaction. It felt good.

The vomiting quickly put an end to that.

When I'd finished spraying my lunch all over the cobbles I turned and walked back to Barker, wiping my mouth with my sleeve and noticing that it came away covered in blood from the gash on my cheek.

"On your fucking knees," I said.

Barker knelt down and begged for his life.

He fell silent when I pressed the gun barrel into his forehead.

"It's in the best interests of everyone here for me to shoot you. You know that, right?"

Next morning, I sat in front of the school and waited.

It was so silent. All the kids had left, the staff too. I lay on a glorious lawn, in the warm spring sunshine, listening to the birds and the first crickets. There were rabbits nibbling the grass not twenty metres from where I sat, and sometimes the breeze carried the distant cry of a peacock from the gardens behind the house.

I lay back on the grass and closed my eyes, rested my hands on the cool ground. I tried to visualize how fast I was moving – around the sun, around the Earth's core. It sounds strange but it's the closest I've ever come to meditation. Lying on grass and trying to feel the Earth move calms me down.

I needed a lot of calming down.

I thought back on my decision and I knew in my heart that I'd done the right thing. With everyone relocated and in hiding, all the blame for the slaughter would fall on me. It was the only way to make sure everyone was safe. The buck stopped here, and that was only fair. But that didn't mean I wasn't scared to death

So as I lay there, a row of bodies draped in sheets beside me, waiting for the rumble of army vehicles, I felt okay with my choice. I was ready to accept the consequences.

My thoughts went back to that day at the swimming pool, all the ideals Kate had when she'd started my medical training. The Hippocratic Oath seemed like a sick joke to me now. I wondered what the woman at the swimming pool would have thought of me, lying here surrounded by bodies. The thought caused a sharp pang of loss.

"Your cheek looks a lot better. I don't think it's going to be a bad scar," said the man sitting to my right. "You stitched it really well."

"Thanks, Barker," I said. "But I don't really think I'm going to have to worry about my good looks much longer, do you?"

He didn't answer and I didn't open my eyes to see the look on his face.

"I'll tell them what really happened," he said.

"But you weren't there, were you? Not in the cellar, not in the surgery. I appreciate the thought, but your word's not going to carry much weight when you stack it up against all these corpses."

He didn't say anything else, so we sat and listened to the birds.

"Do you ever think things will get back to normal?" he asked eventually. "I mean, telly and buses and elections and stuff?"

"Not in our lifetimes," I said.

"The king says it will."

"The what?"

But before he could answer I heard the sound of tyres on gravel.

"You're on," I said.

I heard him get to his feet and begin walking away, towards the fellow soldiers he'd radioed yesterday. I just lay there, eyes closed. I caught snatches of conversation, and the sound of boots on gravel, then someone walking towards me.

I sighed. Time to face the music.

"Miss Jane Crowther?" The man's voice was deep and strong, it was the voice of someone accustomed to being listened to and obeyed. I'd tried to develop a voice like that over the last few months, but my efforts in the courtyard suggested I'd probably failed.

The voice was also oddly familiar.

"That's me," I said, and I opened my eyes. The soldier was standing over me, and the sun behind his head made a halo and shadowed his face. I winced at the brightness.

"No, it's not." The voice had changed. It was softer, surprised, almost friendly. And definitely familiar.

"Pardon?" I said, as I sat up. I rested my weight on one arm and raised a hand to shield my eyes so I could get a look at the man who'd come to serve justice on me. It took a second for my eyes to adjust.

"Hello, Miss Booker," he said. "What have you got yourself into this time?"

CHAPTER TEN

Katherine Lucy Booker – Kit to her family, Kate to everyone else – died five years ago in a warehouse on Moss Side.

Then she gave herself a bit of a makeover. She dyed her hair, got that nose ring she'd always secretly craved, dumped the Jigsaw wardrobe and went a bit more casual. She even started listening to different kinds of music – out with Kylie, in with Dresden Dolls – and stopped watching thrillers and horror films altogether, preferring inoffensive romcoms and bodice rippers. She walked differently too, but only because she stopped wearing heels.

Her sleep patterns altered. She used to sleep like a log for eight hours straight, preferring early nights and cosy jim jams. Now she was more likely to crawl to bed in the early hours in her knickers and t-shirt, cuddling a bottle of chianti, before waking, sweating and alarmed after four hours fitful rest.

She moved to a different part of the country, broke contact with all her friends and family, abandoned her career as a doctor and became a far less illustrious type of medic, ministering to spotty boys and institutionalised teachers with bad breath and nicotine fingers.

Kate Booker became Jane Crowther.

Then, one day, lying on the grass surrounded by corpses, Jane was visited by the ghost of Kate.

And I couldn't think what to say to her.

"I'm sorry, do I... do I know you?" I stuttered as the ground which had been so solid beneath me only a moment ago, began to spin.

"Lieutenant Sanders, Miss," he said cheerily. "I was part of the team that oversaw your training."

I wracked my brains. Sanders? I didn't remember any Sanders.

He reached down a great paw. I took it and he pulled me up without the slightest effort. The man radiated strength.

Once I was upright the spinning was even more pronounced and I stumbled a bit. He caught me in his arms like I was some kind of swooning schoolgirl. I blushed red with embarrassment. This, of course, made it even worse. I shook him off firmly and regained my composure with a brisk cough.

"It's been a long time since a man's made me dizzy, Lieutenant," I joked.

He laughed awkwardly as I took a closer look at him. He had the tanned skin of a man who spends time outdoors; thick black eyebrows topped deep-set brown eyes that sat either side of a classic Roman nose. His large chin jutted out slightly, making him look like a weird mixture of toff and bruiser. It was a striking face rather than a handsome one.

"Wait a minute," I said, as realisation dawned. "I do remember you! You were one of the soldiers Cooper took me to train with out in Hereford. You were the judo guy, weren't you? Spent a whole day throwing me round a gym like I was a, oh, I don't know what."

"That's me, Miss. I was part of the assault team at the warehouse as well. Nasty business. I'm sorry about... you know."

"Yeah, right. Wow. It's, um, it's been a really long time since anyone's called me Miss Booker. You threw me there for a minute."

He nodded. "What exactly is the reason for the name change, Miss?" The shift from friendly reminiscence to polite officialdom almost went past me. Almost.

"Witness protection," I replied. "They made me into a boarding school matron, would you believe. I was only supposed to be here 'til they caught up with The Spider, but I never heard anything. And then, The Cull, obviously."

"Kept the name though."

"Kate's a distant memory now. It's Jane who looks after the kids. I'm not sure Kate would have been up to this kind of thing."

He was looking at me oddly, trying to suss out whether I was delusional or just weird.

"I know," I said. "It just helps me if I keep them separate in my mind, lets me focus on the here and now. And it would only confuse the kids if I introduced them to Kate after everything we've been through. They trust Jane, they might not be so sure about Kate."

He nodded again. "I've been undercover, Miss, I get it. So, Lance Corporal Barker says you've evacuated the school and he doesn't know where they've gone. That right?"

"Yes."

He looked at the row of bodies and his cheeriness faded. Our surprising reunion lost its novelty and the reality of his job reasserted itself.

"It was just an awful misunderstanding," I said.

He regarded me coolly. "I'm sure it was, Miss. But it's not me you've got to convince, it's Major General Kennet."

More soldiers had arrived now, and Sanders set them to carrying the bodies into one of the three trucks they'd brought, expecting to have to transport all the children and staff to safety.

"What's he like?" I asked as we walked away.

"I've served under worse," he replied.

"But you've served under better?"

"Oh yes."

We reached the first truck and he took a pair of handcuffs from his pocket.

"I don't want to cuff you, Miss," he said. "So if you promise that..."

"I promise."

"And I'll keep an eye on her, Lieutenant," added Barker, who was already sitting on one of the hard wooden benches that lined the metal-bottomed, canvas-topped transit vehicle.

"All right then," said Sanders briskly. "We've got a long journey ahead of us. A lot of the road has been cleared but not all, and there are some unswept areas on the way. We took some fire on our trip here, but nothing too serious. Of course they could be waiting for us on the return journey, but we'll vary our route, just in case. If we do run into trouble, then Barker, your job is to look after Kate here. I spent a lot of effort keeping her alive once upon a time. I'd hate all that work to be wasted."

"Sir," replied Barker, resting his rifle on his lap.

"What do you mean, unswept areas?" I asked.

"I'll let the C.O. answer that, Miss," replied Sanders. "Now if you'll excuse me."

Sanders left and I could see him poring over a map with the three drivers, plotting a route.

"Where are you lot based, Barker?"

"Operation Motherland HQ is at Salisbury Plain," he replied.

"Operation Motherland? What's that?" I asked.

"Top secret," he replied, tapping the side of his nose. "Look, I was expecting you to get some pretty rough treatment, but the Lieutenant was all pally. You got really lucky, knowing him, otherwise you'd be on the floor, in shackles with a sack over your head."

"I know. I can't quite believe it myself."

"My point is that it isn't always going to be like this. The C.O. is not a very flexible boss, if you know what I mean. Me and the Lieutenant speaking up for you might not make a lot of difference."

And with that happy thought, the engine sputtered into life

and we rumbled away.

I looked out the back of the truck at my beloved school. I'd worked so hard to build something special, to make it a safe, happy place. It was my home and the people who lived there were my family.

I wondered if I'd ever see it again. Probably not. I shed a tear as it receded into the distance. Not for myself, but for the loss of a dream. Nowadays it seemed like every good, clean thing had to end up covered in blood.

As we slowed to turn the corner at the end of the drive I saw two small figures burst from the bushes by the side of the road and leap quickly over the duckboard of the third and final truck.

I didn't know whether to curse or smile. It seemed like I still had two psychotic guardian angels looking after me.

In the eighteen months since The Cull had burned itself out I'd not moved outside a twenty mile radius. With one notable exception, who was now God knew where, people just stayed put. The days of travelling long distances for work or pleasure were long gone. This was a parochial world of small, paranoid communities. Apart from some mad American religious broadcasts, which I wouldn't allow anyone at school to watch, there was no TV, no newspapers to keep people up to date with events taking place outside their immediate circle of family, friends and neighbours. Horizons had narrowed, and life had focused on the local and familiar. So it felt weird to pass a battered metal sign at the side of the road which read 'You are now leaving Kent'.

It might as well have said 'Here Be Monsters!'

We moved down quiet country roads, deserted for the most part, until we came to the A272. Barker told me this had been cleared about a month ago, which is why the soldiers had only just shown up at my school. Their sphere of influence was expanding along reclaimed A-roads and motorways. But this road still ran through large unswept areas, which I took to mean places not yet brought under military control. This, it turned out, was not entirely correct.

The A272 had once been a nice wide road, but now there was only a narrow path through the thousands of abandoned vehicles. Londoners had fled the capital as The Cull took hold, hoping to hide away in the country until things calmed down. Soon all the main roads and motorways were gridlocked. Of course many of those fleeing were already infected, and they began dying in their cars. It soon became clear that the traffic was never going to move again, so those still alive just got out of their cars, vans and trucks, and walked away.

The path through the debris, which Barker told me had been cleared by huge diggers salvaged from a quarry, was wide enough that we could get up to a reasonable speed, but with so much raw material available for use as obstacles, the risk of ambush was great.

We travelled this graveyard highway for about an hour until we pulled off the road and into a small market town, empty and forgotten, slowly decaying. The convoy stopped in the middle of the narrow high street, littered with abandoned cars, and Sanders gathered everyone together at the bonnet of the lead truck.

"Change of orders," he told us. "Since we've got more room than expected, the Colonel wants us to recce a site near here and sweep it if possible."

Barker sighed softly and shook his head, but when I tried to ask him why he just rolled his eyes.

"The site is half a mile south-east of here," continued Sanders. "I'm going to take Patel here and we'll scout around. The rest of you stay here and stay alert. If we're not back by oh two-hundred hours, I want you to radio for support and then come looking for us."

"Sir, isn't this Midhurst?" asked one of the squaddies.

Sanders nodded.

"But we swept here. Remember, the gang war we sorted out? Bossy bloke with red hair running things."

"I remember," said Sanders. "But this new site was top secret, apparently. All hush hush. HQ have only just identified it. We went right past it last time."

The squaddie shook his head. "That's not my point, Sir. This town's inhabited and we made it safe. So where is everyone?"

Sanders shrugged. "I dunno," he said. "Moved on somewhere better? It's not our problem. Just stay close to the trucks and keep an eye out for trouble, all right?"

Sanders and his colleague checked their weapons and left, leaving me with Barker and five soldiers whose idea of staying alert turned out to be lighting up and playing cards. Barker was not invited to join them.

"They don't trust me," he explained.

"Well I need to pee, and I trust you not to peek, so that's something, eh?" I said, and I linked my arm through his and led him towards Woolies in search of privacy.

"Ooh," said Barker as we approached the ruined store. "I wonder if they still have any Stephen Kings."

We heard a jeer from behind us.

"Great," moaned Barker. "Now they think we're shagging."

Woolies had been comprehensively looted, and there was crap all over the place. Literally – someone had smeared their own shit on the windows.

"Euw, that's gross," I said, looking around for a quiet spot. "I'm going over there." I pointed to a brick flower bed that housed a large ugly bush. Barker nodded and walked into the shop while I scurried behind the bush.

Sometimes, when I'm feeling especially morbid, I wonder what my last words might be. I picture myself lying in some grand four-poster bed, surrounded by fat, happy grandchildren as I fade away, elegant to the last, imparting pearls of wisdom gleaned from a long, fulfilling life. I bet that Barker, if he ever gave it a second's thought, never considered "great, now they think we're shagging," as particularly likely or desirable last words.

But we don't get to choose, do we?

As I started to unbuckle my belt I heard a tiny metallic 'sprang' and a soft grunt. I assumed Barker had trodden on a toy car or something, and I sighed gratefully as I emptied my bladder.

When I emerged a minute later I went towards the shattered doors of Woolies and peered into the gloom.

"Find anything good?" I shouted.

No reply.

My eyes adjusted to the darkness of the shop interior and it became clear why that was.

The metallic twang had been poor old Barker stepping on a tripwire. The grunt, the only sound he'd managed to make as the six foot long spring-loaded metal spike had leapt free of its housing and swung down from the ceiling, skewering him and lifting him off his feet. And there he remained, dangling in mid air, a huge sharpened girder sticking out of his back, blood everywhere.

Dammit, I liked him.

I staggered back with an involuntary scream and the next thing I knew someone slammed into my back, shoving me hard up against the store window, pushing my right arm up behind my back, and grazing my stitched cheek on a streak of hard, dried shit.

"You fucking do, cunt?" yelled a squaddie in my ear.

It would have been impossible to reply with my face pressed against the glass, so I didn't even try to respond.

"Easy, Col," said one of his mates. "It's a booby trap."

Col wasn't inclined to let me go, though, and he kept me pinned there for another few seconds, pressed up against me. He let me go by pushing himself away from me with his groin, so I could feel his erection, snorting his disgust as he did so.

The wise thing to do would have been to let it go. But I turned like a flash and slapped him as hard as I could.

He snarled and raised his hand to hit me, but his mate intervened, grabbing his wrist and staring him down.

"Fuck's sake, Col, get a grip," he said. My assailant gave a sick laugh, pulled his arm free and walked away backwards, giving me the evil eye.

"Thanks," I said as I spat on my sleeve and wiped the shit and blood off my face.

"Shut the fuck up," replied my rescuer, "and get back in the fucking truck before I shoot you myself. And don't even think of doing a runner."

Leaving the squaddies to their grim task I stepped away and

walked back to the trucks. Before stepping out into the road I instinctively looked left and right for oncoming traffic, then paused, realised what I'd done, and laughed at my own stupidity. Then something registered, and I looked right again.

At the far end of the street stood a figure. I think it was a man but it was hard to be sure because they were dressed in a bright yellow hazmat suit, their glass visor glinting in the sun, hiding their face. The figure just stood there looking at us, seemingly content just to watch.

I looked back at the soldiers. Two of them had taken up positions in cover and were scanning the opposite buildings. I was pleased to notice that Col had chosen the bush to hide behind, which meant he was kneeling in my piss. Ha. The other three were inside the shop attempting to pull Barker down. None of them had seen our visitor. I looked back and now there were two of them, both in the bright yellow suits. And I could see that they both carried shotguns.

"Um, guys," I said quietly, but they didn't hear me. Snatches of their conversation floated across to where I stood.

"No, not that arm, dipshit..."

"Jesus, now I'm covered in guts..."

"Oi, careful I just washed this bloody uniform..."

I spoke more clearly. "Guys, we have company."

The nearest man on watch heard me and called the others. They dropped what they were doing and I heard Barker hit the floor with a thud. Weapons raised, they scattered to positions of cover and vantage, all the while keeping their eyes on our two –no, three now – visitors.

I turned to see where the soldiers were taking up positions, about to move myself, and over their shoulders I saw four more of the yellow-clad figures standing motionless outside a ruined hardware store at the other end of the road. Before I could shout a warning, one of them raised a megaphone to his visor and a tinny voice echoed up the wrecked street.

"You shall be cleansed," he said flatly, his voice altered by a distorter that made him sound like a Dalek. "All shall be cleansed."

"Ah shit, cleaners," yelled the squaddie nearest to me.

"Masks!"

"They're in the bloody trucks," yelled someone else.

Then there was a dull pop, I heard something metal hit the tarmac, and then a soft hiss.

There was a second's silence before I heard Col shout "gas!" and then I ran like hell for the truck where Rowles and Caroline were hiding. A cloud of thick yellow smoke billowed out from the area where the soldiers had taken up positions. I heard screams and then indiscriminate gunfire. A burst of rounds whipped past my head, punching holes in the nearest truck's canvas covering.

The hazmat guys just remained where they were.

Staying just ahead of the drifting cloud, I reached the truck and looked inside. Empty. They must have slipped away. No time to look any closer, the thick yellow cloud was nearly at me. I ran for the opposite side of the road and straight through the shattered doors of a branch of Lloyd's Bank. I was so panicked that it was only once I was inside that it occurred to me to look for tripwires. And there one was, about a centimetre from my right toe. Unfortunately I was still moving and my left foot was just about to hit the thin metal strip. I dived forward, clipping the wire as I did so. I hit the damp, mouldy carpet hard and heard the clang of something big and metal above my head. I rolled on to my back and saw enormous metal jaws, cut from what looked like car bonnets. It was a sort of huge, upside down mantrap and it would have taken my head clean off.

"They really don't like giving overdrafts," said a boy's voice to my right.

"You armed?" I asked.

"Natch," said a girl's voice to my left.

"Spare?"

"Catch."

I caught the browning semi-automatic handgun, chambered a round and sprang to my feet.

"There a back way out of here?"

"Nope," replied Rowles. "Already checked. How d'you know we were in here?"

"I didn't."

"Cool, woman's intuition," said Caroline.

"Yeah, right," Rowles laughed.

"Enough," I snapped. "Quiet."

We listened but could hear no noise at all from the street outside. The shooting was over. Through the door I could see the cloud of gas had nearly dispersed and was being blown towards the other side of the road. As the mist cleared a figure emerged. It was Col, with his hands over his face, staggering like a blind man. He walked into a car and his hands came away from his face. taking most of the flesh with them. His cheekbones shone white in the sunlight as he slumped forward across the car and lay still.

"I think I'm gonna puke," said Caroline.

"Are they all dead?" asked Rowles.

"Looks like it," I replied. "But Sanders and another one, Patel, they're off doing a recce. They should have heard the gunfire. They'll be back any minute."

"And do they have gasmasks?" asked Caroline. "'Cause if not..."

"Sanders is SAS. He'll sort it. We just have to sit tight and wait for..."

A yellow suited figure stepped into the doorway holding a gas grenade in his left hand.

"You shall be cleansed," he said.

And he pulled the pin.

CHAPTER ELEVEN

The men in yellow suits had come to the school during The Culling Year, a month after we closed the gates and instituted quarantine.

They pulled up to the gate in their trucks and got out, sealed inside their protective shells, eyes hidden in shadow beneath Perspex visors, mouths covered by bulbous gas masks. There were four of them, and two had cylinders strapped to their backs. Long tubes snaked out of the cylinders to metal spray guns with tiny pilot lights flickering beneath the nozzles. Flamethrowers.

We'd heard reports of their activities. They were roaming the country in teams, burning any houses that contained dead bodies, carting away anyone they found alive. We'd been waiting for them. Bates was still running the school then, so he and I went down to the gate to talk to them. We took guns.

"We hear you've got kids cooped up in there. Any of them blood type O-Neg?" asked the spokesman, his voice distorted by the mask.

"A couple, why?" I replied.

"They'll need to come with us, Miss. Government orders. All O-Neg citizens are to be taken to special hospitals. They're immune, you see."

"These children are under our protection," said Bates. "They're going nowhere."

"Look, don't make us get rough, mate," said the weary official. "They won't be harmed, they're immune, ain't they? We just need to take some blood samples and then take them to a special camp where all the O-Negs we round up are being looked after. We keep 'em safe, okay? Either of you O-Neg?"

Neither of us replied.

"If you're not, then you're going to die unless you got one of these," he gestured to his suit. "Simple as that. It's airborne. Animals carry it, birds carry it, it's in the water, and it's in the rain. There's no escape. Quarantine won't work. And who'll look after the kids then, eh? Best thing for everyone if you just hand 'em over to us."

"And if we don't?" said Bates, nervously levelling his rifle at the quartet.

"We have the authority to take them by force."

"There are two of us with guns, and there are more back in the main building," I said. "There are only four of you and two flamethrowers, which don't reach as far as bullets. I don't fancy your chances."

We stood there, facing each other.

"You really don't want to pick a fight with us," said the spokesman eventually. His voice was quiet, the threat clear.

"I think we just did," I replied.

"I'm sorry you feel that way, Miss."

I gripped my gun harder, waiting for the inevitable fight. But it never came.

"We'll be back," said the spokesman. "You can count on it."

And they got back in the truck and drove away.

We spent that night and the whole of the next day erecting defences at the main gate, breaking the weapons out of the armoury and rallying the few boys still not sick.

But they never returned. They were the final representatives of bureaucracy and government we ever encountered. When they left, they took the last traces of the old order with them. Or so we thought.

We weren't sure whether they encountered some other group who gunned them down, or they succumbed to the virus.

But as I stood in that bank another possibility occurred to me.

Maybe they just went mad.

The cleaner who stood in the doorway had seen one unarmed woman run into the building. He wasn't prepared for three of us, with guns. We all opened fire at once. The blood flowed slickly down his yellow protective suit as he jerked and shook, then he collapsed in a heap. The grenade rolled forward a few inches then stopped on the threshold.

Without thinking I jumped up, ran forward, and kicked it as hard as I could. I was always more of a netball girl, but Johnny Wilkinson would have been proud of me. The grenade soared away across the street and landed in a bin. It popped and a column of evil poison smoke rose up, only for the wind to take it and blow it away from us.

I ducked back inside the bank, knowing that our victory was temporary.

"We need to get out of here now," I shouted.

"This is a bank," said Rowles, exasperated. "The back door is armoured, we can't kick it down."

"Shit."

"There is the vault," offered Caroline, sounding scared for the first time since I'd met her.

"The what?" I asked.

"There's a vault, a walk-in thing," she explained. "It's not huge, but it's probably airtight."

"And once we're in there how do we get out? Or breathe?" said Rowles.

"Fine," she shouted resentfully. "So what's your plan, genius?"

I didn't have time to waste watching a lover's tiff. "No, that's a good idea Caroline," I said, "and it might work as a last resort but..."

"Look!" screamed the girl.

I turned to see a yellow arm withdrawing from the doorway and a gas grenade rolling towards us, making a nasty squelching noise on the sodden carpet.

"Up!" I shouted. We ran through the door that said 'No Entry' and headed for the stairs. Even as we scrambled up that narrow staircase I knew that all I'd done was buy us a few minutes. We were trapped. Where the hell was Sanders?

This building was one of the few new ones on the main street of town, and it only had two storeys. We came to a landing and a series of non-descript offices so dull that nobody had even bothered to trash them.

"There has to be a fire escape," I said. "Check all the rooms."

None of the windows had been shattered, so cracking open these doors was like walking into a time capsule, breathing pre-Cull air, still with the faint tang of PVC chairs, air conditioning and carpet fumes. One of the desks had a framed picture of two blonde toddlers on it, next to a desk tidy full of neatly arranged pens. I didn't know which was creepier – booby trapped Woolies or this strange museum.

"Here," shouted Rowles. Caroline and I ran to the office he was in, which had a fire exit with a push-bar in the wall facing away from the street. Caroline and I stepped back and raised our weapons then I nodded to Rowles, who crouched down and shoved the door open.

The exit led on to a metal staircase in a dim courtyard. So dim, that the figure standing outside was just a silhouette. I held my fire, unsure, but Caroline panicked and squeezed off two rounds. I yelled at her to hold her fire but it was too late.

The figure grunted, staggered back against the metal railing and toppled backwards into space. We heard him hit the concrete below with an awful thud.

"Dammit Caroline," I yelled. "We have no idea who that was."

"But..."

I ushered her and Rowles out of the door and they clattered down the fire escape. As I turned to pull the door closed behind me I caught a flash of yellow on the landing and fired through the plasterboard walls at where I thought the cleaner was standing. I didn't wait to see if I'd hit him.

I pelted down the loud metal steps and found Rowles and Caroline standing, appalled, over the body of Patel, the squaddie Sanders had taken with him. Caroline had got him clean in the chest. He was stone dead.

In the dank concrete-floored courtyard, with the interior walls of buildings rising all around us, their small staircase windows looking out on this joyless scene, I could see her face was ashen white. Rowles was holding her hand tightly.

"He must have been coming to help us," she said softly.

"No time," I barked as I reached down and grabbed Patel's machine gun.

Then there was a loud clang. And another, and another, as something metal bounced down the fire escape behind us.

At the same time we heard the distant echo of gunfire from the main street. That had to be Sanders.

I threw my arms wide and herded the children towards a small brick alley that led beneath one of the buildings and out of the courtyard. As they ran I turned, slipped the safety off the machine gun, and sprayed the fire escape with bullets, hoping to discourage pursuit. Then I ran after the kids as I heard the loud hiss of escaping gas behind me.

We emerged into a car park littered with wrecked vehicles and shopping trolleys. But no cleaners, thank God. I strained to hear the gunfire and tried to identify where it was coming from. As soon as I was sure that it was coming from our left I turned and ran right, urging the children ahead of me as we ran behind the row of buildings.

"I think we're parallel to the main street," I explained as we ran. "If we can get to the opposite end of the street to Sanders we might be able to trap the cleaners in a crossfire."

The buildings ended at the car park entrance road, which turned right to rejoin the main street. I flattened my back against the wall and indicated for the kids to do the same, then I risked a quick glimpse around the corner. Nothing but a burned-out bus.

I turned to the children.

"Rowles, you stay here and make sure we aren't followed. Caroline, with me."

Why did I do that? I've asked myself a hundred times since then. Why didn't I take Rowles? But at that instant I was sure that it was safer to come with me, to approach the cleaners from behind with the element of surprise. I was certain that Rowles would be in more danger than she would be, and I knew he could cope with that.

So I ran around the corner, waving the traumatised girl along behind me. Guns raised, we moved slowly along the side of what had once been a small branch of Boots. There were sporadic bursts of gunfire ahead and to our right, so it sounded as if Sanders was still in the fight at the far end of the street.

I reached the next corner and again flattened my back against the wall and glanced around. The trucks were about thirty metres away. The gas had cleared and the bodies of the dead soldiers lay on the pavement and in the road.

Beyond the trucks were three cleaners, crouched behind available cover – a car, a brick flower bed, a phone booth. All were now armed with machine guns taken from the squaddies. They leaned out, took their shots, and then ducked back under cover, obviously involved in a firefight. But none of them spared a glance behind them.

I turned to Caroline.

"Okay," I said. "We go quickly and quietly. Move from car to car, stay in cover as much as possible. When we're close I'll give the signal and you take out the one on the right. I've got the machine gun, so I'll take the other two. OK?"

She nodded but I could tell she was having to work very hard to keep herself under control.

"It wasn't your fault, Caroline," I said gently. "But we can talk about it later. Right now I need you to focus on what we have to do. Can you do that?"

She nodded. "Yes, Miss."

I put my arm around her shoulder squeezed. "Good girl. Now come on."

We moved out of cover and ran into the road. It took us only a minute or so to get close to the cleaners. They were so preoccupied, and the noise of gunfire was so loud, that they had no idea they were being stalked. Both Caroline and I, on opposite sides of the road, took up firing positions behind cars.

I was just about to give the signal when it all went wrong.

There was a burst of gunfire from behind us and to our right. I ducked instinctively before I realised it was echoing across from the car park. A cleaner must have bumped into Rowles. One of the men in front of us heard the exchange of fire and turned to look back. He saw Caroline. I turned to the girl and yelled at her to get down and as I did so I saw, over her shoulder, another cleaner emerging from the bank.

And then there were bullets everywhere. The one in the bank doorway raised his shotgun as the man in front of us turned and raised his machine gun. Caroline, unaware of the cleaner to her right, opened fire as I dived sideways and shot around Caroline at the man in the bank.

Caroline hit her man. He missed her and fell backwards, shot in the arm. I hit the man with the shotgun and his arms flew up as his gun went off. This saved Caroline's life; only the edge of the shotgun's pellet spray hit her, and those pellets were slowed by the glass in the car behind which she was standing.

But it was enough. She fell, screaming.

I continued firing and the cleaner in the bank disappeared back into the gloom, full of bullets.

The two remaining cleaners turned to see what was going on. One of them foolishly allowed his head to pop ever so slightly out of cover. A single shot from Sanders, still out of sight down the street, took the top of his skull off. I rolled on to my back, brought the gun up to my tummy and turned the middle cleaner's chest into mincemeat before he could get a shot off.

That left the wounded one. I stood to see where he was, but he was out of it – the bullet had hit an artery and he was lying in a widening pool of blood, not long to live, no threat to anyone.

I ran to Caroline. She was lying in the road, breathing hard, teeth gritted, whimpering.

Before I could bend down I heard pounding boots approaching and I spun, gun at the ready. A yellow suit passed in front of my eyes but the helmet was hanging down. It was Sanders. He casually put a bullet in the wounded cleaner's head as he ran past, without even slowing down.

"Easy, Kate, easy."

I lowered my weapon.

"First aid kit?" I asked.

"Truck," he replied, and ran to get it while I knelt down to tend to Caroline.

She was barely conscious.

She had been lucky. When I rolled her over I could see that pellets had hit her from the waist up, including five that were embedded in her right cheek, one that looked like it had damaged her right eye socket, and a couple above the hairline. If I could treat her quickly, and if I could prevent any of the wounds from becoming infected, she should survive.

"Hold on sweetheart," I said, grasping her hand tightly. "Hold on."

We set up camp in a house near the centre of town. It had been lived in until very recently so it was clean and had everything we needed. I set up a workspace in the living room and did my best to patch Caroline up. Once I'd finished, I went into the kitchen and gratefully accepted the mug of hot tea that Sanders offered me. The kitchen had been installed some time in the seventies and had escaped renovation. The table had a chipped Formica top, like a greasy spoon café, and the chair was cheap moulded plastic.

"Well?" he asked.

"I got all the pellets out, sterilised the wounds, stitched the ones that needed it, dressed them, put her to bed. She should really have some antibiotics, but there's nothing I can do about that. The vodka you found helped, thanks."

"Any left?"

"No, sorry. I wish."

"You lush," he smiled.

"I couldn't save her eye," I said quietly, "and her face will be horribly scarred. Rowles refuses to leave her side. He's just sitting there, holding her hand and stroking her hair. I never really thought he had a tender side. Funny how people can surprise you."

"He's not people," said Sanders. "He's an eleven-year-old boy. Who you took into combat."

I laughed bitterly. "Like I could have stopped him! Trust me, Sanders, the boy's a law unto himself. I'm just trying to keep him contained and alive."

"And Caroline?"

"Goes where he goes. Always."

"And which of them shot Patel?"

Shit, that took me by surprise.

"Sorry?"

"I found his body where you told me," he said. "He wasn't killed with a shotgun, he was shot with a sidearm, and you three had the only ones in play."

"There was a fight upstairs at the bank," I lied. "One of the cleaners got my gun off me. Patel burst in and got shot. Then Rowles hit the cleaner over the head with a chair and in the confusion I snatched back my gun and ran."

Sanders shook his head slowly. "Nice try. If I thought you shot him trying to escape custody..." He left the threat unspoken. "But no, I think one of you shot him by accident. Caroline, at a guess."

I stared intently at the swirling patterns on the surface of my tea.

"He was a good lad," continued Sanders. "Would have made a good officer."

"Look, she just panicked, that's all."

"And that's why you don't take children into combat."

I looked up at him angrily. "What, like we seek it out? Are you joking? I just want to keep them alive and teach them to read. But people keep pointing guns at us. People like the cleaners and you." I jabbed him in the chest with my index finger. "We have no fucking choice. Do you think I like seeing what it does to them? You know, Rowles used to be the sweetest kid in the world. I mean Disney sweet, saccharine, cutesy. Now look at him! He's terrifying. But he's alive, and one day, maybe, if I can keep him alive long enough, he can stop fighting and grow into a man. That's all I want, to see him grow up safe, to see all my kids grow up safe. But as long as there are nutters with guns strolling around telling everyone what to do, that's not going to be possible. And now Caroline. I was supposed to keep her safe."

I stood up and threw my mug across the room, full of fury that had nowhere to go. It smashed against the wall and then, before I knew what I was doing, I was crying my eyes out and Sanders was holding me tightly as I pounded my fists against his chest and wept for the girl lying shattered in the bed upstairs.

Then there was kissing.

Then there was sex.

Then there was sleep.

When morning came I woke refreshed, warm and mortified.

Not because I'd slept with a guy who was about as far from my type as it's possible to get, but because as I lay there feeling him breathe, I replayed the night's events in my mind and realized something awful.

I felt guilty.

Which was, of course, ridiculous. I wasn't seeing anyone.

(Do people still 'see' each other after an apocalypse? 'Seeing' someone makes me think of flirty text messages, bottles of wine, dinner in fancy restaurants, making your date suffer through a romcom as a test of their forbearance. None of those things were possible any more. I found myself drowsily wondering what *Sex and the City* would say about the rules of dating in a post-viral warzone. Of course, with society entirely gone away, every woman who wanted Jimmy Choos could have them, as long as they were prepared to fight their way to a lootable store. And then I had a vision of Sarah Jessica Parker in a sequined dress, with an AK47, mowing down hoards of Blood Hunters, screaming "if you want the strappy sandals you'll have to go through me, motherfuckers!" That was Kate thinking. Jane told her to shut up and focus.)

I had no ties. Since that thing with Mac and the sixth formers last year I'd not been within arm's length of a man I felt like getting to know better. Still, there was nothing to prevent me bedding the entire male population of the UK if the mood struck me.

But as I replayed the night's exertions I realized that at a very particular moment I was thinking of a very particular person. It wasn't as if I was thinking of Sanders at any point. It was a comfort fuck at the end of an awful day; it wasn't about Sanders at all. Neither was I fantasizing about anyone else. It was all about me, about being alive while people were dying around me, about wanting to feel something other than pain for a moment.

Yet at one moment, as I arched my back and dug in my fingernails, I had a crystal clear picture of Lee in my mind, just for a second. And I lay there in the morning with a sinking feeling. I knew what it meant, but I refused to accept it. I banished it from my mind. As Lee was so fond of saying: "no time, things to do".

But, really, damn.

When he woke, Sanders was brisk, businesslike, unsentimental. He didn't want to cuddle or talk or any of that, which suited me fine.

Kate had never had a one night stand, but Jane had had plenty. Of course, Jane had never bedded a guy who knew Kate and that collision did strange things to my head. He was detached come daylight, the kind of behaviour that would have thrown Kate into despair and angst but which was a blessed relief to Jane.

He wasn't cold, though. He smiled and cracked a few lame jokes. Don't worry, his behavior said, I don't expect or require anything else. Ironically, that made me like him a whole lot more than I had the day before.

I checked on Caroline and Rowles. They were curled up on the double bed in the main room, spooning, fast asleep. They looked so peaceful and innocent lying there that I decided to let them sleep. Sanders found some tinned spaghetti and a calor stove, and we sat down to breakfast. We ate our food out of china bowls with old, dull forks and listened to the harsh wind battering the open doors and windows of this deserted little suburban cul-de-sac.

"You said you swept this town," I asked as I wiped tomato sauce off my chin with my sleeve. "What does that mean? What is exactly is Operation Motherland?"

"Our orders are pretty simple," he replied. "We're emptying every armed forces base in the country, gathering all the weapons and ordnance in a series of huge depots on Salisbury plain. The idea is to disarm the population, take guns out of the equation. Then, when we've got all the hardware, we can start to re-impose law and order, raise a new army, take back London, put the king on the throne, get back to some sort of normality."

I gaped. "You're just collecting weapons? That's it? That's your masterplan?"

He nodded. "Yeah, for now. We've got more kit than we know what to do with, to be honest. Take this town for instance. There was a TA base nearby and a gang of kids had broken in, got themselves all tooled up, and they were running this place. It was ugly, what they were doing. So we rolled in, executed the worst of them, took all their guns away so it couldn't happen again. Job well done."

"And where is everyone now?"

He shrugged. Not his problem.

"Jesus, Sanders," I said. "Didn't it occur to you that it would have been better to arm the people here? The sane ones, the adults?"

"Our orders are to disarm everyone, Kate."

"It's Jane, and those are stupid orders. Obviously these cleaners came to town, found the people here defenceless and either drove them out of their homes or massacred them. And that's your fault. If they'd been armed, they'd have been able to defend themselves."

Sanders put down his bowl and stood up suddenly. "Time to ship out," he said brusquely, and he left the room.

Kate was always a good girl at school. She studied hard, got good grades, excelled at science, biology especially, and made her parents proud.

She only got in trouble once, and that wasn't her fault. Her friend April had started a fight – she never really understood what about – and Kate had tried to break it up. But in the struggle to keep the peace she ended up getting thumped, hard, by a nasty little bitch called Mandy Jennings. So Kate thumped her back - the first and only time she ever threw a punch. Well, until Moss Side. Unfortunately, her aim was true and Mandy wore glasses. So when the screaming and hair pulling finally ended, Kate was marched off to see the headmaster, who gave her all that guff about letting herself down. And Kate bought it, 'cause she was a good girl, and she felt ashamed and she cried and said "sorry, Sir".

As Sanders drove the truck through the gates of Salisbury HQ I felt an echo of what Kate had felt when she was about to be brought up before a figure of authority – a sick, hollow, butterfly ache in the stomach. The only difference was that Jane would have told the headmaster to go stuff himself. And the headmaster was unlikely to have Kate lined up in front of a firing squad.

Salisbury had been the centre of British Army maneouvres for decades, and all the facilities had recently been given a 21st century facelift, so the main base at Tidworth was modern and sprawling, with barracks aplenty and facilities for the maintenance of all sorts of vehicles. But there was so much stuff gathered here that it had spilled out of the base perimeter and on to the plain itself. Row upon row of trucks, tanks, armoured vehicles, jeeps, fire engines, both Green Goddesses and the conventional red ones, ambulances and police vans. Not to mention the hundreds of oil tankers, lined up in rows stretching off to the horizon.

Sanders had undersold the operation's ambitions. They weren't just hoarding weapons, they were collecting all the resources they could lay their hands on. After all, resources meant power. If they had all the service vehicles and all the fuel, married to a well drilled force in possession of weaponry vastly superior to anything else out there, they would be unstoppable.

As I looked out of the truck window and saw all that hardware I felt both excited and scared. All that power, just waiting for someone to give the order to move from preparation to implementation. Operation Motherland was a sleeping giant. When it awoke nothing and nobody would be able to stand in its way.

We drove past a parade ground where at least 400 men were doing drills, and groups of soldiers in full kit marched past us at regular intervals, heading for trucks or armoured vehicles, off to round up more guns, fuel, Pot Noodles or whatever. The place was buzzing, full of organized, purposeful activity.

So as we drove into that awe inspiring place I felt insignificant and afraid, and I wondered what the headmaster would be like. Because with all this at his command, he could do pretty much anything he wanted with me.

Sanders pulled up outside the medical centre and carried Caroline inside. We'd made her a little bed in the back and Rowles had sat with her during the journey. He'd not said a word to me since she'd been shot. I think he blamed me for letting it happen, and an angry Rowles was not someone I wanted to confront, so I left him alone to brood. Caroline herself was conscious and cogent, but complaining of sharp pains in her head, which worried me. There was a possibility that she was bleeding into her skull, and I wanted her x-rayed as quickly as possible. I let Sanders sort out the formalities and I sat in the truck feeling guilty, useless and scared.

I caught myself wishing Lee were here, but I banished that thought as quickly as it appeared.

Sanders emerged five minutes later and opened the cab door for me, indicating that I should get out.

"They think she'll be fine, but they're going to give her a full work up. Rowles is staying with her," he said as I clambered down. There was an awkward moment as he put his hands around my waist to lift me down. I stared at him, not unkindly, and he removed his hands and apologized with a smile.

He led the way to the regimental HQ.

"The doctors here have lots of practice treating injuries like hers," he explained. "The one I saw said to tell you that you'd done an excellent job on her."

I nodded, trying to take pride in the compliment, but I felt nothing but shame.

We came to the steps of the main building and Sanders put one of his huge hands on my shoulder. I stopped.

"Let me do the talking, okay?" he said.

I looked at him curiously.

"I think I can sort this out," he explained. "But you'll have to trust me."

"Sure," I said, allowing myself a flicker of hope.

We walked up the steps and through the double doors. There was a notice board on our left as we entered, plastered with timetables, orders, a poster for a karaoke night. It was so normal, it reminded me of school. Down the long corridor which stretched ahead of us men and women in uniform were bustling from room to room carrying clipboards and folders. A drink machine, actually powered up and working, was frothing a coffee for a bored looking army clerk. That corridor was the closest thing I'd seen to pre-Cull England in two years. Nobody was scared, nobody was hungry. There was an air of ordered, peaceful activity, like any office, really. I wondered if this was the way forward for us survivors, or whether the military machine was just hiding itself away inside a secure compound where they could pretend nothing had happened, that routine military life was just the same as it had always been, running like clockwork, all hierarchy and structure.

We walked down the corridor and Sanders knocked on the door at the far end. The nameplate read Maj. Gen. J. G. Kennett. This was the big man. I braced myself, but when a stern voice barked "Enter!" Sanders turned and pointed to a chair in the corner.

"Stay there," he said. "I'll only be a minute."

I nodded, aware that my life, and the lives of my kids, rested entirely upon what this man, who I hardly knew, was going to say next.

As Sanders opened the door, I sat down to wait. I'd only been there for a minute, twiddling my thumbs and staring at the patterns on the carpet, when a young woman brought me a cup of tea in a saucer, with biscuits.

"There you go, Miss," she said with a smile.

Cup and saucer, tea and biscuits. I shook my head in wonder.

About ten minutes later, long after I'd exhausted all the entertainment possibilities of sitting on a chair in a corridor, the door to Kennett's office opened and Sanders popped his head out.

"Jane," was all he said by way of summons.

I felt a pang of butterflies in my tummy as I rose and entered the office of probably the most powerful man in the country. The room was plush but not opulent. Regimental photos lined the walls, and there were even a few paintings – Waterloo, the trenches of the Somme. The floor was polished wood with a huge, deep rug laid across most of it. There were old wooden filing cabinets, upholstered wooden armchairs, a sideboard with decanter and glasses. The room was old school privilege and power; comfort, security and authority embodied in the trappings of tradition and duty.

Major General Kennett was standing in front of his desk, leaning back against it, his arms folded across his chest. He was about forty, plump, red cheeked and bald, with a strong square jaw, and was dressed plainly in green trousers and jumper. He regarded me with calculating green eyes. I was unsure whether his air of easy authority was innate or whether it was bestowed upon him by the room itself and all the cultural and social respect it represented.

Sanders stood to one side, hands clasped behind his back. He wasn't at attention, but he was formal. I think they call it 'standing easy'.

"Miss Crowther, welcome to Operation Motherland," said Kennett, leaning forward and offering me his hand. His voice was high and nasal, with a strong southern accent, kind of like Ken Livingstone. It didn't suit him at all.

I took his hand and he shook it once, firmly.

He didn't offer me a seat, so I stood there, unsure what was required of me.

"The lieutenant has been telling me what happened at your school and on the journey here. There'll have to be an investigation, of course." He folded his arms and pursed his lips, assessing me.

I couldn't think of anything to say, so I just said "right."

There was a long pause.

"I'm not entirely sure I believe everything he told me," added Kennett.

"Sir..." began Sanders, but Kennett silenced him with a look.

"But I've known him a long time, Miss Crowther. He's one of my most trusted officers. So I choose to believe him. And I feel sure that everything the investigation discovers will corroborate his story. Won't it, Sanders?"

"Sir."

"Yes," mused Kennett. "Thorough. I like that in a soldier. So I shall continue to believe him, and by extension to trust you, unless you give me reason to do otherwise. Do you think you're likely to do that, Miss Crowther?"

"No, Sir," I said, surprised by my instinctive deference.

"Good. In which case you are welcome to remain here while the girl in your care recuperates. After that you will escorted safely back to your school. We will, I'm afraid, have to disarm your merry band, but I'm sure you understand that's for the best."

"Actually, Sir..." I began. But the warning in his eyes was clear and unambiguous. I fell silent again and nodded. Jesus, this really was like talking to my old headmaster.

"Excellent." Kennet clapped his hands and smiled. Business concluded. "Sanders will find you a billet, and maybe we'll see you at our karaoke night tonight. Sanders does a very good Lemmy, I'm told." With that he turned his back on us, picked up a file and began to read.

A second later, almost as an afterthought, he said "dismissed."

Sanders saluted, said "Sir" and ushered me out of the door.

"What the hell did you tell him?" I asked incredulously as we walked out of the building into the crisp air of a spring evening.

"What I needed to. I'll brief you properly later, so we can get our stories straight for the investigators. Essentially, the child traffickers killed our guys, and you killed the traffickers."

At the bottom of the steps I stopped, took his hand, leant up and kissed him on the cheek.

"Thank you," I said.

He squeezed my hand and smiled. "You're welcome. Now let's get you billeted, then you can start thinking about what you're going to sing tonight!"

"You wish! I've got a voice like a strangled cat."

The billet was a room on the first floor of a simple barrack building. It had a single bed, wardrobe, wash basin with clean running water, a TV with DVD player and plug sockets that had power. Plus, central heating! I leant my bum against the radiator enjoying that slightly too hot feeling that I'd almost forgotten. Log fires are nice, but give me a boiling hot radiator any day of the week.

After Sanders left me alone I went to the communal bathroom at the end of the landing, drew myself a hot bath and soaked all the aches away. Sanders had scraped together some toiletries from somewhere, so I washed my hair, soaped myself clean, shaved my legs, plucked my eyebrows, waxed my top lip, and did all those things I used to take so completely for granted. When I was all done, I lay back in the water and watched the steam rise and curl as the stitches in my cheek throbbed in the heat.

I closed my eyes and imagined I was at home, that Gran was downstairs making tea, and that after I'd dried my hair I'd go downstairs and eat her corned beef pie with mash and we'd watch trashy telly.

It was a nice, warm daydream.

I felt safe for the first time in two years.

When I woke, the water was tepid and night had fallen. The light was off so the bathroom was dark. I suppose that's why

Sanders hadn't found me and dragged me off to karaoke. I looped the plug chain around my big toe and pulled it out, then I rose, pulled my towel off the hot radiator and wrapped it around me. Back in my billet I found that Sanders had left me some clean clothes, bless him, and although the short black dress he'd chosen for me was perhaps not quite what I'd have opted for, I decided to indulge him, and myself. There was fancy underwear as well – nothing crass, just good quality – and the shoes were nice. He'd almost guessed my size right in all respects.

When I was all dolled up, I put on some slap and looked at myself in a mirror. Bathed, well dressed, made-up. Nothing out of the ordinary a few years ago, but the woman staring back at me seemed like an old stranger, someone I'd known very well once upon a time but had lost touch with. I was glad to see her again, but I knew she was only visiting briefly

I looked like Kate.

Well, no matter. I was about to walk into a room full of soldiers, looking pretty damn good, if I said so myself. It had been a long time since I'd turned any heads, and I was looking forward to it.

Pulling a coat around my shoulders, I left the room, turned off the light and walked downstairs, listening to my heels clicking on the lino. Again, a sound from the past – high heels on a staircase. One small detail of a forgotten life, once commonplace now extraordinary to me.

I opened the door and stepped outside. The camp was dark, but the roads were lit with orange sodium lights. I stopped and listened. From somewhere off in the distance I could hear a chorus of drunken voices singing Delilah. I followed the sound, enjoying the sensation of once again being able to walk alone at night without fear.

Which is why it was such a surprise when the man dropped out of the sky on a parachute and landed on the path in front of me, and hands grabbed me from behind, muffling my shouts, dragging me into the shadows.

CHAPTER TWELVE

I kicked and struggled, but the man holding me was too strong. I'd have bitten his fingers off if he hadn't been wearing heavy leather gloves.

I was pulled off the path and into the bushes, where I was pushed down on to my knees and held firm.

"If you do exactly as I say, you won't be harmed," said a soft voice in my ear. The accent was unmistakeably American, an exotic twang after two years of Kentish brogue. I felt cold metal at my throat.

"If you cry out, I'll slit your throat, Limey bitch. Understand?"

Limey? Who the hell called Brits 'Limeys' anymore?

I nodded gently. He removed his hand from my mouth.

I've been in worse spots before, but I was completely unprepared for this. I was in the safest place in Britain, in my bloody party dress! So unfair. Anyway, I was more scared than I'd been in a long time and I momentarily lost my cool. My terror, I'm embarrassed to admit, made me compliant. I didn't make a sound.

"Good girl," said my captor. "Now, which way to the main gate?"

"I only got here today, I'm not sure. I can't direct you. I could probably walk you there, though."

He tightened his grip. "Not good enough."

He fell silent, thinking it over. As he did so the bushes rustled and another man, the parachutist, joined us. He was dressed entirely in black, almost invisible. It was only when I saw his thick leather gloves that I realised that both men had fallen out of the sky. My captors shared a brief, whispered conference.

"All right," said the new guy, also a Yank. "Here's what we're going to do. You're gonna walk us to the gate. We'll stay in the shadows, but we'll be watching you. If you try to shout out or run, you're dead."

To illustrate the point he pulled out a handgun and slowly screwed a silencer into the barrel.

"Joe's a really good shot," added the man holding the knife to my throat, and I could hear the smile in his voice. "You should remember that. Now go."

He withdrew the knife and released me. I knelt there for a moment, composing myself, then I got up and walked back to the path, brushing the dirt from my knees. So much for karaoke, I thought, as I stood in a pool of orange light, rearranging my dress and getting my bearings. I didn't doubt the ruthlessness or ability of the men who were threatening me. Plus, they'd bloody parachuted here. I'd not seen a contrail in two years, so that implied all sorts of things. I decided to play along until something clever occurred to me or an opportunity presented itself. Which it did almost immediately.

"There you are," boomed a voice to my left. I turned to see Sanders striding towards me wearing shirt and jeans, a bottle of lager in his hand. "I wondered what was keeping you. Lost?"

I nodded. Shit, would they just kill him? Sanders walked up to me and held out his arm. I slipped mine through his and said "let's take a walk."

He seemed unsure, eager to get back to the singing, but his guard was down, he wasn't expecting trouble, and a woman wanted to spend time with him. He smiled. "All right," he said. "But there is no escape, sooner or later you get to hear my Ace of Spades."

"I've already seen your ace in the hole, Sanders. It wasn't all that."

"Hey!"

As we began walking, I caught a tiny flash of movement out of the corner of my eye, a shift in the shadows, black on black. We were being stalked.

I gripped his arm way too tightly and increased the pace. He gave me a curious look and I tried to signal with my eyes that something was up. But it was dark and he was slightly drunk. Sanders the soldier was off duty, this was Sanders the boozed-up Motörhead fan. I wondered how long the two Yanks would allow this to continue before they got trigger happy. I needed to stall.

"Let's take a walk to the medical centre," I said. "I want to look in on Caroline."

"Okay," he replied, giving my arm a squeeze of sympathy.

"It's by the main gate, isn't it?" I asked, slightly too loud.

"Um yeah, it's this way," he answered.

He led the way and we walked in silence for a minute or two. I caught no hint of our pursuers. They were good, whoever they were.

"You look beautiful," said Sanders as we passed a row of silent tanks.

"Well, thanks for the clothes and stuff," I said, lamely.

"You're welcome. You wear them well."

For the love of Mike, Sanders, you dope.

We ambled on a bit more, then I had an idea. If I pulled him into an embrace the gunmen would know I was up to something. But if he pulled me close they wouldn't be sure, and I could whisper in his ear.

"Well," I said, as if suddenly shy, "I'm only wearing them for you." I moved my hand along his forearm and laced my fingers through his. He looked down at me, surprised, as I stroked his thumb gently with my index finger.

"I'm honoured," he said, smiling but a little awkward.

"You should be. It's not every day I make such an effort." Oh this was painful. I was spouting bad dialogue from a Meg Ryan movie.

"You don't need to make an effort, Jane." Now he was at it.

I moved fractionally closer, so our thighs brushed together as we walked.

"Look, I can't keep calling you Sanders. What's your proper name?"

"Neil."

"Neil, I want to make an effort for you. Last night was... special."

"That's a relief. It's been a while. I was, um, married. Y'know, before. My Chrissie."

No, this is supposed to be a seduction, you twit. Don't get drunk and maudlin.

"Kiss me," I whispered urgently as we walked around a corner into the road that led to the medical centre. He kept walking. He hadn't heard me. Oh fuck this. I never was much of a femme fatale. I dug my fingernail into his palm, hard, and he stopped, baffled.

"Kiss me," I whispered again. Finally the great lunk wrapped me in his arms and stuck his tongue down my throat. We were lucky – the men following us must have thought he'd done it on the spur of the moment. They held their fire. Sanders tasted of Grolsch and Marlboro, which brought back hazy memories of another life.

As soon as I was able, I broke the liplock and hugged him hard. Then I whispered in his ear: "Two men. Silencers. Bushes. Main gate." He stiffened and then relaxed, on duty again. He disengaged, wrapped his arm around my waist, and we continued walking. He didn't seem to be looking around, but I was sure he was trying to get a bead on our stalkers.

"Y'know, Jane, you're a piece of work," he said, slightly too loud. His acting was pitiful, I only hoped the darkness would compensate.

"Really?"

"Yeah, Once you turned the corner, after you left the school, I really thought you'd fall in with a bad lot."

Ah-ha, I thought, so that's why he was never recruited by MI5. I rolled my eyes.

"Yes, but I had you to keep me on the straight and narrow, didn't I?" I improvised. Then, as we turned the corner on to the road that led to the main gate, I fell to my left, rolling off the pavement and on to the grass verge. Sanders turned and ran to his right. I heard the soft *phutt phutt* of a silenced automatic, and saw a tiny muzzle flare from the spot Sanders was running towards ("rush a gun, flee a knife" said Cooper, in my head). He held out his hand as he ran, smashing his lager bottle on a lamp-post and then bringing it up to use as a weapon. The gun fired once more, then Sanders vanished into the undergrowth, which rustled and shook.

I heard a cry of "stitch this!" and a grunt.

I leapt to my feet and ran for the main gate, forgetting that I was wearing heels. My right ankle went from under me and I sprawled on to the concrete, scraping my knees and hands. I reached down to undo the straps and as I did so the other Yank was on me, straddling me, rolling me over on to my back and bringing his knife down to my chest. I grabbed his descending arm with my right hand as my left continued to fumble with the strap on my shoe and pulled, releasing the catch. Then I grabbed the sole, brought my arm up and plunged the heel of my shoe into my attacker's ear as hard as I could.

He toppled slowly to his right, falling into the road. I got up, reached down, and pulled the shoe. It came out with a wet sucking sound. Waste of a perfectly good pair of shoes.

The camp was quiet, no-one aware of the struggle that had taken place. I needed to raise the alarm. I looked over my shoulder, and saw that the bushes Sanders had run into were still and silent. I got my bearings – I was right outside the medical centre. There were bound to be people in there, I was about to run and start banging on the door when I felt a hand on my shoulder. I yelped and spun around, swinging my shoe as a weapon. Sanders caught it in his great paw and I sighed.

"Sorry," I gasped.

He shook his head as if to say "it's nothing". His other hand was holding his side, and I could see a red stain spreading through his fingers.

"You've .been shot," I exclaimed. "Let's get you inside." I wrapped my arm around his waist and tried to drag him towards the medical centre, but he resisted.

"No," he said firmly. "It's just a flesh wound. First we search the body and find out who these guys are and how they got in here."

He shrugged my arm away and knelt down beside the body, grunting as he did so from the pain of his wound. I knelt down beside him.

"They're both Americans and they parachuted in," I said.

He looked up at me sharply. "You sure?" I nodded.

He reached down and pulled open the dead man's jacket, searching his pockets. His hand was on the man's chest when he mumbled "oh fuck" and ripped open his undershirt. Strapped to the man's bare flesh was a little metallic gizmo.

"What's that?" I asked, but Sanders was already up and running for the main gate. I pelted after him.

"Life sensor," he yelled back to me as he ran. "It means whoever sent them knows they're..." His final word was lost in the scream of an approaching missile. We were caught in the shockwave of an enormous explosion, which picked us both up and flung us backwards on to the hard tarmac, knocking the air out of us and singing our eyebrows. The main gate and the guard post beside it vanished in a huge fireball and I felt the scorching air blast across me and cook my lungs as I gasped for air.

The perimeter was breached. Operation Motherland was under attack.

My senses were scrambled. I didn't know which way was up, my eyes couldn't focus, my ears were ringing and I felt like I was going to be sick. As I tried to clear my head I felt the world lurch and start bouncing. It took me a moment to realize that Sanders had actually picked me up, slung me under his arm, and was running away with me. I heard sharp cracks all round us, which must have been gunshots, but they sounded distant and dull.

Then I landed on soft grass with a thud and felt large hands running themselves up and down my body. Odd time to cop a feel, I thought, feeling disconnected and out of body. Then he slapped my face and the world got sharp, hot and focused.

"Oi!" I shouted, and slapped him back.

"You're not hit." He was leaning over me, black smears on his face, his carefully combed hair wild and frizzy. "Can you run?"

I nodded. "Come on then." And he was off. I shook my head, rose to my feet with a groan of protest, and staggered after him. Even after being shot and blown up he was making good speed. But he was running away from the sounds of gunfire and explosions. Shouldn't he be in the thick of the fighting? We ran through the base, which was suddenly full of shouted orders and running men, all heading in the opposite direction. Sanders grabbed one man as he ran past and relieved him of his weapons, sending him back to get re-equipped. I caught up with him and he handed me a sidearm.

"What the hell are we doing?" I asked, shouting to be heard over the sirens that were now ringing out. "What's going on?"

"In situations like this, I've got standing orders. Now come on." And he was off again, his wound not even meriting a wince. He wasn't even breathing hard as he ran past the mustering troops. I was gasping for air and trying to ignore the stitch in my side.

"But don't you want to know what's happening?" I bellowed as I chased after him.

"I'm a soldier, Kate... sorry, Jane. I never know what's bloody going on. I just do what I'm told."

It seemed pointless to argue, but I couldn't really wrap my head around it. I never followed orders, never did what anyone told me without being given an explanation first, always made sure I knew the big picture before making a decision. But I was a free agent, always had been. Sanders was a soldier, conditioned and trained to be a cog in a machine. He didn't need to know the whys and wherefores, he just did as he was told, immediately, without question, confident that by following orders he was doing the right thing. I couldn't imagine allowing anyone to have that control over me, or allowing myself to trust someone so much that I'd take their word for anything without being given proofs and reasons.

That said, I was running after him, so I suppose I trusted him that much. I really wanted to be running back to the medical centre. Rowles and Caroline were there, and they were my responsibility. But I knew the fight would already be at their front door, and it would be suicide to head back there now. I just had to hope they'd be safe. After all, no-one would attack a hospital. Would they? I told myself not to worry about it. Rowles could look after himself and Caroline, and as soon as I was able I'd be back for them. For now, I kept following Sanders, hoping he had a plan.

We ran across the base to a barracks that sat at the heart of the compound. It was a low building, brick built, with two guards on the door, one of whom greeted Sanders.

"Lieutenant," he said, businesslike in the face of sudden chaos. "What's going on?"

"He in there?" asked Sanders as he slowed and stopped.

"Yeah."

"Okay, stay here, no-one comes past. Understand?"

"Sir!"

"Come on," he said to me, and I followed him through the doors and into the barracks.

We came to a door and Sanders knocked and entered.

It was a simple bedroom, nothing too fancy. A single bed, a desk, a cupboard and a wardrobe. A bookcase full of *Alex Rider*, *Young James Bond* and Robert Muchamore. There were posters, too, of the Pussycat Dolls and Slipknot.

Kneeling on the bed was a young boy, fourteen or thereabouts, oblivious to our presence, listening to a CD player with his headphones on, the volume so loud it was drowning out all noise. His face was ravaged by acne, his hair was greasy and unkempt, and he was wanking over a porn mag. He looked up in horrified alarm as Sanders tapped him lightly on the shoulder.

"What the...?" spluttered the boy, his face turning red as he realised he was not alone. He pulled his headphones off and dragged the quilt over his erection.

"You need to get dressed and come with me right now," said Sanders.

"What do you mean? What's going on?" the boy whined, spluttering in embarrassment and fear.

"The base is under attack. We need to get you to the safe house. Get dressed. Quickly, Your Majesty."

The boy didn't move, he just stared at Sanders and nodded his head sideways at me, indicating that Sanders should remove me. I grabbed Sanders' arm and pulled him towards the door.

"We'll, um, wait outside," I said, trying to keep a straight face. "Sire," I added, and snigered as Sanders pulled me out the door and slammed it shut.

"That's him?" I giggled. "That's the king?"

But Sanders wasn't laughing. His face was white and he was leaning against the wall. I glanced down and saw that the blood from the wound in his side had soaked his clothes right down to his knees. Suddenly things didn't seem quite so amusing.

"I need to get you stitched up."

"No time," he said, forcing himself to stand upright. "We need to get the king to safety."

"I'm the doctor," I said firmly. "Is there a medkit or anything in this building?"

He glared at me and then reluctantly said: "Try the kitchen."

I ran off down the corridor, looking in all the rooms until I found a small kitchen with a fridge, microwave and a Baby Belling cooker. There was a red plastic medkit on the wall, so I pulled it open and rummaged inside. I pulled out sterile dressing, elastoplast, alcohol and a needle and thread, then I ran back to Sanders, dragged him into the room opposite the king's and set to work.

"So this is your job, huh?" I asked as I worked. "You look after the king?"

"Yeah. Ow!"

"Big baby."

The bullet had gone clean through him, just missing a kidney, but I couldn't be sure whether his guts were punctured or not. I thought they probably were, and if so he'd need proper surgery sooner rather than later or there'd be a great risk of infection. In the meantime I did the best I could. I sterilized the wound, stitched him up, slapped a dressing over it and gave him a huge dose of painkillers.

"I train him, keep him safe," explained my patient. "I don't get out much. They only let me come to the school to get you because I begged and it seemed like a milk run. If the perimeter is ever breached, I'm to get him to a safe house we've set up about ten miles away. He's my only priority."

"But shouldn't he have, like, a whole team of men guarding him?"

"Just me. That's the best way. Keep it low profile, don't draw attention to ourselves. Chances are that whoever is attacking us doesn't even know he exists. We've not exactly gone public with him yet. He's not ready."

"He seemed to have things well in hand a moment ago."

"Jesus, Jane," he said, exasperated. "He's fourteen all right. Cut him some slack. You know what teenagers are like."

"Of course I do. I run a school, remember."

"He's all right, he's a good kid."

"As long as he doesn't expect me to curtsey, I'm sure we'll get along fine."

Sanders and I grabbed uniforms from the cupboard and quickly changed into combats. My uniform was ridiculously oversized, and the only way I could get the boots to fit me was to wear four pairs of socks, but at least it was better than my party dress and heels. All the time we could hear the sounds of battle outside, steadily getting closer. There were explosions, constant gunfire, the rumbling of tanks and, just as we finished getting ready, the roar of a fighter jet, swooping low overhead and the whooshing sound of a missile being released. Sanders was agog.

"F-16?" he said, incredulously. "We really have to go."

At that moment the door to the king's room opened and he stepped out. He was dressed head to toe in black and his face was smeared with boot polish. He handed the tin to Sanders and as we blacked up, he interrogated us.

"Attackers?"

"Americans," I answered. "Trained soldiers, I think."

"And you are?" His air of authority was impressive, but I thought it was an act. I'd seen a fourteen year-old boy really take control, and there was a quality of certainty that Lee possessed that the king lacked. He was trying hard though, I gave him that. And it must have been difficult for him to try and regain any dignity in front of me after what I'd just witnessed.

"Jane Crowther, I run a boys' school, Your Majesty."

"She's with me, Jack," said Sanders, passing the boot polish to me and checking his SA-80.

"Good enough for me, and please call me Jack, Miss Crowther" said the boy, drawing his sidearm. "Shall we go?"

"Both of you follow me," said Sanders. "Stay low, we keep to the shadows, we don't engage the enemy unless forced to. We make straight for the exfil and leave. Is that clear?"

The king and I both nodded. (No, I needed to stop thinking of him as the king. It was ridiculous and it made me think of Elvis. I would follow Sanders' example and call him Jack.)

"All right then," said Sanders. "Come on."

Without another word, we ran out into a battlefield.

CHAPTER THIRTEEN

I always seem to be running away from fights.

The last time I was in a proper pitched battle – on the day St Mark's was blown sky-high – I grabbed a gun and ran like hell. In my defence, I was going to locate the girls who were in my care, and we did come back later and save the day. But my experience of being in a proper battle was of running as fast as I possibly could in the opposite direction. As we ran out of the barracks I was reminded of why that had seemed such a good idea last time.

The two men guarding the door were still there, and we all stood for a moment, getting our bearings and identifying where the heaviest fighting seemed to be.

The night sky was bright with orange flames and the blinding flashes of explosions. The noise was deafening, like a hundred fireworks displays going off at once all around us. The fighting, which had begun at the main gate, had moved quickly, and I could see a group of British soldiers using the buildings in front

of us as cover. They were firing around the corners at the attacking forces.

One man readied a fearsome looking missile launcher, which
he hoisted on his shoulder, and then he ran out between the
buildings, straight into the line of fire. He knelt down and took
careful aim at what I presumed must be a tank. It was an act of
such bravery and madness that I stood riveted to the spot, trying to understand what would make someone risk their lives so
foolishly. The only answer was training and necessity. It was the
kind of thing that would be unthinkable in a skirmish, but in the
heat of war it was almost commonplace. This was true soldiering.
It was awe inspiring, actually. And doomed.

A swarm of bullets thudded into the soldier, and he toppled
backwards, arms flailing. The rocket launcher flipped over his
fragmenting head, still held in his right hand, until it was pointed straight at us. Then his dying fingers twitched and the rocket
screamed free of its housing.

Someone must have shouted for us to run. We scattered and
kept moving. Sanders, Jack and I ran one way; the two squaddies
ran the other. They drew the short straw. The rocket slammed
into the far corner of the barracks, hitting an oil tank used for
heating. I was much closer to this explosion than I had been to
the one at the main gate and it was stronger than anything I'd
ever felt before. I lost consciousness in mid-air.

When I came to, I was lying on a hard metal surface, being
bounced up and down. My head felt like someone had filled it
with nails, and every bone in my body ached.

"Where..." I started to say, but my voice was drowned out by
the sounds of a revving engine and a machine gun. I looked up
and saw that I was in the back of a jeep. Next to me crouched
Jack, SA-80 at his shoulder, firing out the back at a similar vehicle
which was pursuing us. The enemy jeep had a white star painted
on its bonnet, and a bloody great machine gun mounted above the
driver's cab. A soldier was standing in the back, firing at us as we
drove far too fast along a muddy track on Salisbury Plain.

I was about to reach for my gun and join the fight when our tyres exploded. The jeep lurched to one side then another as the driver – Sanders? – struggled to keep control. But it was hopeless. The jeep swayed from side to side with increasing velocity, then we hit a rock in the road and we rolled and span. Everything around me whirled and crashed as I was flung up and down, smashing every part of me into the four sides of the jeep's cab as the vehicle tumbled down a slope. We were still falling when my head met Jack's with an enormous crack.

I slipped into the darkness again.

The next time I woke I felt like I'd never move again. My head was beyond painful. I couldn't focus my eyes, which were as full of blood as my mouth and ears. I was lying on my face in thick wet mud.

It was like that moment when you get home from the pub, drunk. Your head hits the pillow and you realize that even though you're lying down, your senses think you're still moving and you feel the first inklings of the nausea and awfulness that's going to take up the next day or so of your pathetic drink-sodden excuse for a life. The only sense that was working properly was my sense of smell. And all I could smell was petrol and blood.

I could hear an engine idling nearby, footsteps approaching, and two American voices shouting: "Show us your hands! Get down on the ground!" That kind of thing. So that told me at least one of us was alive and moving.

I blinked and concentrated until I began to make out shapes. I wiggled my fingers and toes, trying to work out if anything was broken. My limbs felt okay, but every movement sent shooting pains across my ribs, at least three of which were definitely fractured. The pain was excruciating and all I could think about was that I'd be lucky if I'd only punctured a lung.

When the world stopped spinning again and the pain receded slightly, I gently lifted my face clear of the mud and saw that I was lying in a ditch. I must have been flung clear as the jeep rolled. It also meant that the bad guys probably didn't know I was here. Slowly, agonisingly, I got to my knees and lifted my splitting head over the edge of the ditch. Our jeep was lying on its back about twenty metres away from me, directly ahead. Its lights were still on but the engine was dead. The American jeep was parked on a ridge above it, and the man in the back had a spotlight, and his huge machine gun, trained on the scene below him. Sanders was on his knees with his hands behind his head, an American soldier standing over him. Another soldier was pulling Jack out the back of the jeep by his boots. The boy was a dead weight and he left a deep groove in the mud behind him.

That galvanized me – an injured child needed my help.

I reached down and cursed. My sidearm had been lost in all the confusion. I was unarmed and concussed, with broken ribs, dull hearing, blurred vision and nausea, and I was wearing a uniform too big for me and boots that dangled off my ankles like weights. Yet somehow I had to take out three armed American soldiers.

I'd have been better off in the heat of battle.

The obvious target was the man in the jeep. With the spotlight shining down, I couldn't tell if there was a driver in the cab. If there was only the gunman, I maybe had a chance, but if there was a driver then I was screwed. To my left the ditch led around a small hillock, so I crawled through the cold mud on my hands and knees, sure that at any moment the squelching noises would bring a soldier running. But I was lucky, and I rounded the hillock safely. Now I could move. I dragged myself out of the ditch, grinding my ribs together and groaning with pain in spite of myself. I couldn't run, so I shambled as best I could down a small depression and into a copse of trees which provided cover as I climbed the ridge down which our jeep had tumbled.

When I got to the top I collapsed in a heap, crying in agony, unable to make myself take another step. But I had to. I gritted my teeth and breathed short and fast, hyperventilating to help ease the pain – after all, the world was already spinning, a little extra lightheadedness couldn't make much difference, could it? Then I pulled myself up and staggered on. I approached the American jeep from behind and saw, to my relief, that there was nobody in the driver's compartment.

With no gun, I would have to get very close in order to put this guy out of commission. There was no point walking up to the jeep, he'd shoot me down. I couldn't vault up on to the flatbed and struggle with him – I wasn't capable. I had to get him down somehow, and I needed a weapon. I cast around until I found a large piece of jagged flint which I grasped in my hand tightly. Then I just improvised.

"Help," I muttered, shuffling towards the jeep with my hands to my head. "Someone help me, please!" I didn't look up at the gunman. Instead I gazed vacantly left and right, as if blind. "I can't... I can't see. Oh God, someone please help me."

It didn't need much acting to sell the guy; I was barely functional. I made sure not to look straight at him, but as I gazed around, pretending to be sightless and confused, I saw him get down from the jeep and walk towards me, machine gun levelled. If he decided to shoot me, there was nothing I could do. As he got within a few metres of me I slipped and fell. I wish I could say that was part of my plan, but I genuinely lost my footing and went sprawling on the stoney track, crying out as I hit the ground. I lay there and cried. "Oh God, please help me, someone, please God." But I kept hold of my stone.

The gunman, completely convinced by my impression of a concussed, bleeding wreck who could barely stand, did the damnedest thing. He took pity on me. He swung his gun over his shoulder so it rested with the muzzle pointed skywards and he reached down to help me up.

"Take my hand, ma'am," he said.

I reached up with my left hand. "Oh, thank you, thank you. Who's that? Where am I?"

He grabbed my hand and kneeled down to put his arm round my chest and lift me up. As he did so I swung my right hand as hard as I could and smashed the rock into the side of his head. He grunted and fell sideways, dragging me with him. We splashed down into a puddle in a tumbling heap. I was weak, though, and the blow didn't knock him out, it merely stunned him. He tried to crawl away from me but I held on to his belt and pulled myself up his body, each movement causing awful pains in my chest. He tried to roll over and fight back, but he was too badly hurt. After what seemed like an age but was probably mere seconds, I managed to get myself into a position where I could grab his head. I pushed hard on the buzz cut hair, pressed his face into the puddle, and then collapsed on top of him, holding his face under the water with the weight of my whole body as he writhed and bucked and struggled to throw me off. But I just lay on top of him, crying with pain and anger and horror at what I was doing, until his struggles weakened and, eventually, stopped. I lay there for another minute, just to be sure, and then I rolled off him, lying flat on my back in the mud, breathing hard.

There was no time for rest, though. I bent double, levered myself upright and walked to the jeep. I couldn't climb into the flatbed, I was just too weak, so I flopped on to it and then lifted one leg over the edge and dragged myself on to the hard metal surface. Then I used the machine gun's column to pull myself upright, and I looked down the ridge. Sanders was still kneeling, and Jack was lying beside him. I could see his chest rise and fall, so I knew he wasn't dead, but he was unconscious. The two soldiers were still standing over them. Which certainly made things easier from my perspective.

The gun was not unlike the GPMGs we had at St Mark's, so I checked that the safety was off, sighted carefully, held my breath, tried not to worry about the fact that I was starting to see double, squeezed the trigger and held on for dear life. It took a few seconds for the vibrations of the gun to throw me off; I was so weak I couldn't cope with the recoil. I collapsed to the floor.

If that hadn't done it, then so be it. I had nothing left in me.

I heard shouting, the crack of small arms fire, but it was distant and not my concern. I felt as if I was falling into cotton wool. The world stopped spinning, which was nice. Then Sanders' face appeared above mine. His mouth moved but I couldn't hear what he was saying.

Then he faded away, and I was warm and safe and gone.

The next thing I was became aware of was a distant voice. It was deep and rich, male, unfamiliar. American. It was saying my name.

"Miss Crowther. Jane. Wake up, Miss Crowther."

I struggled to open my eyes and, when I did, I immediately scrunched them shut again. The light hurt. My hands felt soft cotton sheets beneath me and everything was soft and warm. I was lying in a bed.

"Welcome back," said the voice. "You've been away for quite a while."

The ache in my limbs was gone, my chest felt sore but not agonising, and my head was fuzzy and muddled, but not painful. I knew this feeling; I had been drugged.

I opened my eyes again and winced. Things slowly came into focus through the glare. The first thing I saw was the man sitting beside my bed. He was African-American, with a lined faced and short grey hair. He wore an army uniform. The room swam into view and I saw familiar cream walls. I was at Groombridge. This was my sick bay. I was home. I tried to speak, to ask him what was going on, but I couldn't form the words.

"Don't," he said. "You've been drugged for some time. You took quite a knock and there was severe swelling of the brain. My medics put you in a drug-induced coma and nursed you back to health. But you've had three lots of surgery, you died on the table twice and I'm sorry to say you don't have any hair right now."

I felt my scalp, shocked by the smoothness of it.

"They tell me you're going to be okay," the general said. "They called me this morning and I flew down so I could be here when they woke you."

It took all my effort and concentration to croak: "How long?"

"Three weeks."

"Who...?"

"General Jonas Blythe, at your service, ma'am. I command the US forces here. I gave the order to attack the British Army on Salisbury Plain, and I gave the order to take control of your school. Sit her up."

I heard someone walk across the wooden floor in heavy boots and felt strong arms lift me into a sitting position. I was propped up on some pillows so that I could see out of the window. It was a bright, sunny day, cold but clear. Next to the window stood a TV set with a camcorder plugged into it. The general nodded to the soldier who'd propped me up, and the young man went to the camcorder and fiddled with it until it began playing. The screen crackled with white noise and then solidified into a picture.

Lee. Bruised, bloodstained and terrified, sitting tied to a chair in front of a blue sheet with Arabic writing on it. A man in a black hood stood behind him holding a sharp knife. I gasped in horror. I knew what this video was. Everyone did.

The sound kicked in and there was Lee. Kind, lonely, brave, broken Lee, sobbing into the lens. "My name is Lee Keegan. It's my sixteenth birthday today, and I'm English. I flew here to find my dad, a sergeant in the British Army, but my plane crashed and these guys found me. If anyone sees this, please let Jane Crowther know what happened to me. You can find her at Groombridge Place, in Kent, southern England. It's a school now. Tell her I'm sorry."

And the screen went blank. Tears streamed down my face and my stomach felt empty and hollow. Oh God, Lee. Poor, sweet Lee.

"He's dead, Miss Crowther," said the general.

Now I found my voice. Dry throated, I croaked between sobs: "How did you get this?"

"Recovered it from an insurgent hideout in Basra about a month ago."

"Did they...?" I couldn't say it.

"Not them. Believe it or not your boy made friends with them. They let him go."

"I don't understand."

"He joined them, Miss Crowther. To fight me."

I stared at him. "You killed Lee?"

The general nodded. I screamed and tried to fling myself at him, reaching out to scratch his eyes and bite his face. I wanted to pull him apart. But I was too weak, and my limbs wouldn't obey the instructions I was sending them. I just fell forwards and slid off the bed on to the floor, collapsing in a heap at his feet, a pathetic, tear-stained, wailing, wreck.

The young soldier lifted me up. I tried to shake him off, but I was helpless. Instead of placing me back in the bed, he sat me in a wheelchair and pushed me so I was face to face with the general. I stared into his pitiless eyes, summoning all the defiance and fury I could muster.

"Why are you so important?" he asked. "What is it about this school?"

I didn't understand what he meant, but my face betrayed nothing but anger.

"A young soldier from this school flies to Iraq and almost succeeds in destroying my operations," he explained. "The one name he gives us is yours. Then, when we attack British Army HQ you're there in the thick of it, with your very own SAS bodyguard, whose sole purpose, as far as I can tell, is to ensure your safety and bring you here. Why? Why are you so important? What's your game, Miss Crowther?"

Sanders had brought me here. So where was he? And what had become of Jack?

"Shall I tell you what I think?" continued the general. "I think you're a spook. MI5 or 6, back before The Cull. I think this school is a front for all that remains of your British Secret Service."

I started to laugh silently. It hurt my healing ribs but I couldn't help it. I held my sides and laughed and laughed till more tears flowed.

"You fool," I said. "You stupid, pathetic, paranoid fuckwit. I'm not a spy. I'm just a boarding school matron." I could hear the hysterical edge to my laughter but I couldn't stop. "If you want spies, you're barking up the wrong tree, General. All I've got is TCP and sticking plasters."

He sat there and let me laugh for a while, then he stood, grasped the handles of my wheelchair and pushed me to the window.

"Let me show you what I do to people who waste my time, Miss Crowther," he said quietly.

I looked out of the window at the lawn below. It seemed like only yesterday that I'd lain on that grass with Barker, feeling the Earth move beneath me. Now, in the exact spot where I'd passed that quiet moment of contemplation, was one of the most awful things I've ever seen. It was Sanders - strong, gentle, musclebrained Sanders, my sometime lover. He lay facing the sky, impaled on a huge wooden stake which jutted, bloodied and obscene, from his shattered chest. A crow pecked hungrily at a gaping eye socket and then flapped away, as if ashamed of being seen.

Had I anything in my stomach, I would have been sick.

"Now, Miss Crowther," said the soft, menacing voice behind me. "Let's start again, shall we?"

PART THREE

Lee and Jane

CHAPTER FOURTEEN

Lee

CHAPTER FOURTEEN

Lee

"Does this thing have a loo?" I asked eventually.

"No," said Dad.

"Well, I'm sorry guys," I said, "but I really, really have to pee and unless you want to sit in here and breathe ammonia all the way home, I'm going to have to get out to do it."

"Don't we have a bottle or something?" asked Tariq.

"All full of water, which we'll need," replied Dad. "Lee, you can't hold it any more?"

"You remember when I was little and we went on that road trip to Rhyll? How much did it cost to get the car seats cleaned?"

Dad didn't need any more information than that. "Should be all right. Just go quietly, okay?"

I nodded, then reached up and turned the wheel to open the hatch. I pushed up and peeked outside. The noise of the engines was deafening, and there was hardly any light.

"All clear. Back in a sec," I said. I put my right foot on the back of the main bench seat and pushed myself up and out, on to the roof of the LAV III Stryker Engineer Squad Vehicle. Designed for minesweeping and road clearance, it was squat, solid, armour plated and boasted a mean looking set of guns on the roof; this was state of the art kit. It also had nice comfy couches, which is why we'd chosen to stow away in it for the flight back to England.

The fuselage was literally freezing; the US Army obviously hadn't considered the health and wellbeing of stowaways when they designed the in-flight heating system for the C-17 Globemaster III cargo plane. I clambered down on to the metal floor. The only light came from the small round window in the door to my left. I walked across to it and peered out, careful not to trip on the numerous metal tracks that ran the length of the fuselage. We were above the clouds, and the full moon cast a brilliant, cold light. Our vehicle was at the very back of the plane, its rear hanging just above the ramp, which would be lowered to allow it to drive out when we landed in England. Other vehicles and pallets of supplies and ordnance were queued up behind it in the dark and cold.

I walked up the body of the plane a little bit and unzipped my fly, letting rip against the side of a pallet full of bags of flour. Little bit of flavour for your bread, you bastards. I sighed in relief and smiled as I did the zip back up again. Better.

I turned to walk back to the others and then something hit me in the face and I was flat on my back, seeing stars. Before I could get my bearings I felt someone sit on me, straddling my chest, wrapping their hands around my throat and holding my head against the metal. I looked up to see who had attacked me. All I could see were the whites of his eyes. Dressed entirely in black, and with shoe polish on his face, this guy was practically invisible.

"Is this the way to Business Class?" I asked.

He hit me again and my head made a clanging noise against the floor.

"You're that Limey kid," said the man.

"Limey?" I said, playing for time. "Do people really say Limey? Isn't that a bit out of date now?"

"Where are the others?"

"Others?" Suddenly there was a knife at my throat.

"We were given orders not to kill you," said the man in black. "The general wants that pleasure himself. But hey, he's not here so if I drop you out the back no-one will ever know."

In the confusion of disembarkation there was every chance that he wouldn't have heard about any skirmishes that took place, so I said: "No others. Just me. They didn't make it."

"Right," he replied mockingly. "Hey Joe, check around. He must've come out of one of the vehicles."

I couldn't see who he was talking to. It was impossible to know how many of them there were. I wondered what they could have been doing lounging around the unheated fuselage of a cargo plane full of vehicles and supplies, then I registered that his black clothing was a jump suit.

"So you're, like, American parachute ninjas or something?" I asked.

"Or something."

There was a loud thud and a groan from the end of the plane then a floodlight came on, momentarily blinding me. The man atop me rolled sideways and ducked behind a pallet, seamless and silent.

I blinked at the light and realised it was the spot on the top of the stryker.

"Come on, Lee," shouted my dad. I pulled myself upright and ran for the vehicle, past the stunned body of another man in black. I vaulted up on to the stryker, where Dad was standing behind the spotlight and mounted gun emplacement, his eye pressed up against the huge sighting lens. "Get inside."

I slid down into the belly of the vehicle, where Tariq was waiting, gun at the ready.

"You couldn't fucking hold it?" he said, witheringly.

"The sights on this thing are great," said Dad loudly. "I mean, I can only see your right foot, but if I..." There was a loud report as he squeezed the trigger, then he ducked back down to join us. "They'll be considering their next move for a minute or two. Lee, how many are there?"

"I don't know," I replied. "I only saw two. I think they're parachutists, and they're blacked up, so I reckon they're dropping from this plane before we land. Advance guard, maybe."

"And we thought it was only kit in here. Bloody hell," said Tariq.

"We don't want to get into a firefight," said Dad. "Pressurised cabin, all sorts of bad things happen."

"But you just shot at him!" I said.

"Calculated risk. Just to make a point. Let's hope he doesn't call my bluff, or things will go wrong very quickly."

A voice echoed down the plane, barely audible above the roar of the engines.

"Hey, Limeys!"

Dad popped his head back up and shouted: "Yeah?"

"Hold on!"

There was a clunk and a whirr of machinery.

"Oh shit," shouted Dad and he ducked back inside the vehicle, pulling the hatch closed behind him. He looked white as a sheet.

"What?" asked Tariq and I, in unison.

But Dad wasn't listening, instead he scrambled past us and into the driver's seat, where he started pressing buttons frantically. Tariq and I followed, taking up positions either side of him, looking down at the various touchscreens which were illuminating one by one as the vehicle powered up.

"What are you doing?" I asked again.

"Got to initialise the CBRN, it's our only chance," he muttered. Tariq and I looked at each other and shrugged. Suddenly the plane lurched to one side and began to descend. The noise from outside the vehicle began to get a lot louder.

"Oh fuck me, no," I whispered as I realised what was happening. The look on Tariq's face told me that he'd worked it out too.

"Got it!" yelled Dad. There was a hiss of compressed air and the sound of bolts locking. "I've turned on the CBRN system. We're airtight and pressurised." He pulled the seatbelt across, strapping himself in.

"Lee, strap yourself into the other seat," he ordered. I sat down and did as I was told. "Tariq, you're going to have to find something to brace yourself against back there. I think I saw some straps you could use. Just lie flat on one of the couches and try not to let go. This is going to be rough."

Tariq nodded wordlessly, and disappeared into the back.

"CBRN?" I asked, trying not to think about what was about to happen.

"Chemical, Biological, Radiological, Nuclear warfare system," he replied.

"Cool."

The vehicle shook.

"Tariq, you strapped in?" Dad shouted.

"Yeah," came the tremulous reply from the back.

"They must have decided we were too much trouble to flush out," said Dad.

"They're right," I replied.

"Remember that time at Rhyll," said Dad, "when I took you on the rollercoaster?"

"Jesus, do I ever."

"Fifteen people with your sick in their hair. I thought they were going to lynch us. This is going to be much worse."

"Oh, thanks for the..."

The vehicle flew backwards at enormous speed, flinging Dad and I forward against our straps and squeezing the air out of us. Time elongated, and the g-force was overwhelming. I tried to breathe but couldn't force my lungs to inflate. My eyes watered, my ears roared and popped, I would have screamed if I could. Then my stomach flipped and we were falling, weightless. The seat fell away from my arse and the straps dug deep into my shoulders as I was dragged down by the dead weight of the plummeting metal cage that surrounded us. It went on forever until there was an almighty snap as the cords on the 'chutes went taut and our descent slowed. Now the pressure went the opposite way, as the deceleration forced me down into my seat, crunching my spine and pressing my chin down in to my chest as I suddenly felt twenty stone heavier. Eventually we hit our descent speed and returned to normal. I gasped like a fish on dry land, hyperventilating.

I looked across at Dad. He was stunned, but okay.

I craned over to see if Tariq was okay. He was lying on the couch, tied by thick straps designed for holding equipment steady on rough terrain, grinning fit to burst.

"Again! Again!" he shouted, like a demented Tellytubby.

The vehicle rocked from side to side in the winds, making me feel seasick.

Dad unbuckled himself and tried to stand. His legs went from under him, though, and he fell forwards on to the console. "Woah, dizzy," he gasped.

"What are you doing?" I asked.

"Need to see where we're coming down," he wheezed in reply, then he staggered back into the belly of the vehicle, bracing himself against the walls as it swayed.

"Are you mad?" I asked, unbuckling myself and tumbling after him. "You don't know how high we are, whether we're even in breathable air yet. If you go too soon, we'll depressurize. If you go too late, you could be unbuckled when we hit the ground and that would not be good." I grabbed his arm and held him back.

"Lee, we might not even be over land."

"Shit," said Tariq, who hadn't bothered to unstrap himself, and was still lying there. "You mean..."

Dad nodded. "We could hit water and sink like a stone. We could be over the Med or the Channel, I don't know. Or maybe over a mountain range. For all we know, we could hit the top of a snow ridge and tumble all the way down the bloody Eiger."

"And what would we do if we were coming down over the sea or somewhere worse?" I asked. "What good would knowing do us? I doubt this thing has a life raft, or skis. Does it have retractable skis?"

Dad glared at me and then smiled in spite of himself. "No, no skis."

"Shocking lack of foresight, that." Dad held my gaze as I shrugged and said: "All we can do is strap ourselves back in and hope. I didn't come rescue you so you could take a nose dive out of an armoured vehicle at 20,000 feet."

He paused and then nodded. "When did you become the grown-up?" he asked as we strapped ourselves back in.

"Ask Mom," I replied and then instantly wished I hadn't. I avoided his eyes and didn't say another thing.

"All right," said Dad a few minutes later. "We've got lots of parachutes holding us up, and the pallet we're on is slightly cushioned, but it'll still be a hell of a jolt when we land. So be ready." We sat, rocking gently, listening to the wind whistle by outside, feeling the hollowness in our stomachs as we fell.

"Do you reckon..." began Tariq, but he was interrupted.

We hit something but we didn't stop falling. The vehicle spun 180 degrees around its centre axis until we were upside down. Then there was another crash and we spun the other way, facing nose down, still falling. Loud cracks and bangs echoed through the metal structure as we fell, swivelling and spinning wildly.

"Trees!" shouted Dad.

Our stop-start, rollercoaster descent slowed as we crashed down through branches and bowers until finally we came to a halt, swinging, facing downwards at 45 degrees. We all caught our breath. The only sound was the creak of wood from outside.

"Everyone okay?" asked Dad.

Tariq groaned and lifted a thumb. I tried to nod, but my neck hurt in all sorts of interesting new ways. "Yeah," I said. "Nothing two years of intensive physiotherapy wouldn't fix."

"Good." Dad breathed out heavily. "Fuck me, that was a bit drastic wasn't it? Remind me never to do anything like that again. And next time, son, bring a bloody gazunder. Anyway, we're stuck. Which is good."

"Huh?"

"If we'd just hit the ground cold, it would have been the equivalent of falling twelve feet. In a chair. We'd have been lucky not to break our backs."

"Now you tell us," groaned Tariq.

Dad activated the driver's side periscope, but the view was obscured by parachute silk, so he unbuckled himself and clambered down the cabin to the gunner's periscope, which was also blocked. He climbed to the hatch, pulling his knife from its sheath as he did so.

"You both stay here, buckled up. I'll go see what state we're in."

The vehicle swung perilously as he moved around in it, making me feel seasick. He opened the hatch and shoved aside a swathe of silk.

"We're in a forest," he said. "Pitch black, no lights, could be anywhere."

He climbed outside and we could hear him scuttling around on the shell of the vehicle. "We're only about six feet off the ground and we seem pretty well braced. I think you should unbuckle and jump down."

Tariq and I unstrapped ourselves, climbed to the edge of the roof and jumped on to a soft bed of pine needles. Dad stayed on the vehicle.

"Get clear," he shouted. "I'm going to cut some of the parachute straps and see if I can get this thing on the ground the right way up."

"Don't be daft," I replied. "If you cut the wrong cord, the Stryker could flip and land on you."

"Just get clear, Lee," he said impatiently.

I knew that tone meant no arguments, so I walked away and watched, nervous as hell, as Dad sawed away at the various parachute cords that were holding the vehicle in a complex swaying web. Each cord gave way with a loud twang, huge amounts of tension being released as they snapped. The vehicle lurched, first one way, then the other, then forwards, then backwards. It was like Dad was playing some vast, lethal game of Kerplunk. Cut the wrong cord and it was all over.

Bit by bit the vehicle came free, swinging more wildly as it hung by fewer threads. Then Dad made a mistake, cut the wrong cord and the whole thing pivoted and pointed nose down. Dad was flung forward and was left hanging off the gun turret. Tariq and I gasped, but Dad pulled himself up the roof until he reached the rear bumper. Reaching up with his knife, he cut the last cord and the vehicle dropped on to its nose. Then it slowly toppled backwards and landed the right way up, flinging Dad off it like a bronco rider on a bad day. He landed in a heap, but he was fine.

He stood up, brushing the dirt and pine needles off him. "Right" he said, "let's get this show on the road!"

We cut the straps that bound the vehicle into the pallet, and disconnected the final straggling parachute cords. Then we climbed inside and Dad booted her up. Even after that insane descent, she started first time. The touchscreens came to life. Dad pored over them for a minute or two and then announced: "It's Bavaria."

"What?" I said, incredulous.

Dad turned around, facing Tariq and I with a big smile on his face.

"It's Bavaria. We're just outside Ingolstadt."

"How the hell do you know that?" I asked.

"The satnav's working!" he replied with a grin. "All right, what's your postcode?"

The Stryker was designed for road clearance, and Dad drove like a demon, so we made good time. Germany's autobahns and France's highways proved impassable, but the satnav steered us down side roads and country lanes, always heading for our next stop – Calais station and the Channel Tunnel.

A couple of times we encountered roadblocks manned by gangs of marauders, but we kept driving straight through them as the bullets pinged harmlessly off our carapace. I knew that the Americans would have attacked England by now, and the knot of fear and anticipation in my stomach wound tighter with every mile. What would I find when we got to the school? Would it be a smoking wreck, ringed by the impaled corpses of my friends? And if so, how could I ever live with myself? I grew quiet and sullen, eaten up with stress, so it fell to Tariq to pepper our journey with anecdotes and nonsense. Sometimes he managed to get a smile out of me, but not often.

Dad and I didn't talk much, but the silence was less charged than it had been in Iraq. Perhaps he was starting to accept that I was more man than boy now, whatever my age. Or perhaps I was just enjoying being with him, watching him be heroic and confident, enjoying having someone look after me for a change, instead of me bearing all the weight. Either way, it was better. Not right, but at least better.

Eventually, after four days of negotiating our way across Europe, we arrived at the station in Coquelles, near Calais. We knew that the Chunnel might be blocked, but we fancied holding on to the Stryker, and if the tunnel were passable it would be a quick and easy trip. What we didn't reckon on was the welcoming committee.

From my position at the gunner's post, I kept lookout using the periscope as the Stryker nosed its way through the station entrance and on to the concourse. Burnt-out trains stood at the platforms, shattered glass everywhere.

On a bench in the middle of the concourse, a solitary man sat watching us.

"You see him?" I said.

"Uh-huh," replied Dad, slowing to a halt and putting on the handbrake.

"What do you reckon?"

Dad didn't answer, I glanced over my shoulder and saw that he was using his periscope to scan the windows of the buildings that overlooked the concourse.

"What you looking for?" I asked.

"Anything. Keep an eye on the guy. What's he doing?"

I pressed my eye against the periscope and zoomed in.

"He's smiling."

"Like a 'hi guys, good to see you' kind of smile?" asked Tariq, frustrated that he couldn't see what was going on.

I zoomed in closer, until the man's face filled my vision. He was dressed in black and grey combats and was wearing sunglasses. I couldn't see his eyes, but there was a cold malevolence about his smile; something feral yet amused.

"No," I said. "More a 'come into my parlour said the spider to the fly' kind of smile." I described a circle, checking for snipers or traps. I saw nothing, but I wasn't reassured.

"I can see the way to the tunnel," I said. "Should we just drive?"

Dad considered it, and shook his head. "No. I dunno who this bloke is, but he could have booby traps anywhere. The tunnel might be exactly where he wants us."

Before we could decide what to do, the man took the initiative. He got up and walked towards us, stopping just in front of the vehicle. He removed his glasses to reveal jet black eyes.

"Bonjour," he said affably.

Dad stroked the touchscreen and spoke into the mic on his helmet. "Parlez vouz Anglais?" His awkward schoolboy French echoed around the empty concourse and he stroked the screen again, turning down the loudspeakers.

"Ah," said the man in a strong French accent, his eyes full of calculation and surprise. "We thought perhaps some Anglais might come through the tunnel. We were not expecting any to go the other way."

Dad put his hand over his mic. "He said 'we'. Lee, keep looking, he's not alone." Then he took his hand away and replied: "We just want to go home. We've travelled a long way."

"I can see that," said the man. "This is not a British fighting vehicle." It was not a question, which told me that he knew his stuff. Military background, perhaps? "My name is De Falaise," said the man, rather more grandly than seemed appropriate. "My colleagues and I control this station. If you wish to pass, we would expect some form of consideration."

"Here we go," said Tariq.

"What do you have in mind?" asked Dad.

"Information."

"What kind of information?"

"Have you been in contact with Britain since The Cull? By radio perhaps? Can you tell us anything about what is happening on the other side of that tunnel? My friends and I, you see, are thinking of relocating."

I caught a glint, just for an instant, in a window behind us. I thumbed the zoom button and sure enough there was a man in position there; tripod, sniper rifle, telescopic sight. I didn't think he could do us any damage, but there might be more.

"Sniper, three o'clock, in the hotel," I whispered.

Dad covered his mic again. "Get ready, Lee," he whispered back. "When I give the word, fire a warning shot. Just a warning shot, mind. I don't want to start a war."

"'Kay."

Dad took his hand away and spoke again. "No contact. It all went dead long ago."

I couldn't see De Falaise's reaction to this, but I imagined it was either disappointment or disbelief.

"That is what I thought," he said. "Then perhaps we could trade something else. I think, perhaps, I would like your armoured car. I think I would like it very much."

"Fire," said Dad.

I gently squeezed the trigger and the gun mounted on the roof burst into life, spraying heavy rounds around the window where the sniper was poised. I saw him leap backwards, arms raised to protect himself from the chips of stone that were flying into his face. Once he was out of sight I squeezed again, destroying the rifle and taking him out of the game. Then I swivelled my periscope to see how our Frenchman would react. He hadn't moved an inch. Cool customer.

The sound of gunfire reverberated around the empty space, fading away gradually. Only when silence reigned once more did De Falaise speak.

"That is a disappointment," he said. "I was planning on letting you go."

Dad didn't wait to hear what he said next, choosing to slam his foot on to the accelerator and drive straight at De Falaise. But the Frenchman was too fast, diving out of the way to reveal the smoke trail of an approaching rocket-propelled grenade.

"Shit!" yelled Dad, and he yanked the wheel hard right, flinging Tariq and I to the floor. We skidded to a halt sideways and before we could get underway again the grenade hit us broadsides.

To this day, that explosion is the last thing I ever heard in stereo.

It's impossible to describe a noise so loud that it blows out your eardrums. It was like a physical blow; like someone jamming a sharpened pencil in my ear and then wiggling it for a bit as the aftershocks bounced around. I screamed and wrapped my hands around my ears, feeling blood pouring from them. Then all I could hear was a deep throbbing tone, like a dead TV. My sense of balance was gone too. I rolled about on the floor of the vehicle trying to stop everything spinning. I vomited all over myself and I didn't become aware of anything else until Dad sat me up and jabbed a needle in my arm. Then I passed out.

I was deaf. I knew that before I even opened my eyes. I could feel the bandages around my head. I opened my eyes and there was Dad, leaning over me. I was on the couch in the back of the Stryker. Tariq lay on the couch across from me. He also had dried blood on his ears, but wasn't bandaged. Dad, I realised, had been wearing the driver's helmet, which would have protected him from the worst effects of the sound, and Tariq had obviously been hurt, just not as badly as me. So it was just me that got unlucky. Great.

Dad stroked my hair tenderly. I could see his lips moving but all I could hear was that dead TV tone in my right ear. My left ear registered nothing at all.

"I'm deaf," I said. Or at least I think I said it. I may have shouted it, or said "I'm cleft" for all I know. It was weird, knowing I was making sounds but being unable to hear them.

Dad nodded and turned away. I think perhaps he was trying to hide his emotions. After a moment he turned back, and mouthed some words slowly. It took a moment for me to work out what he was saying but eventually I got it.

He was saying: "We came through the tunnel. We're home. England. We made it."

CHAPTER FIFTEEN

Jane

It sounds strange to say it, but I was lucky that I was so badly hurt.

General Blythe was convinced that I was some sort of post-apocalyptic spymistress running covert ops at home and abroad, using specially recruited and trained kids like Lee.

"One boy, about eleven-years-old we think, single-handedly killed seven of my men during the attack on Salisbury," drawled Blythe in his broad American accent.

"Is he alive?" I said, dreading the answer.

"Oh yeah. We captured him. He's a tough little nut – the only person I've ever had in my custody who lasted more than fifteen minutes of waterboarding. And of course you know how effective that method is at extracting information."

"No I don't, you sick fuck. Because I'm not a spy!" I shouted.

"When he did break, he told us a pack of lies that had us chasing our tails for a week. Someone trained him, Miss Crowther. You don't expect me to believe that a eleven year-old gets that kind of resilience out of nowhere, do you?"

"Believe what you like."

"Thank you, I will. And I believe that you are a player. My first instinct was to kill you. But I need to know the details of all your current ops. Do you have people in Russia, the US?"

"Go to hell," I spat.

"Undoubtedly, Miss Crowther, but hopefully not for a while yet. Having instructed my surgeons to save your life, I find that you are too weak to endure our interrogation techniques. They tell me that a single session on the waterboard would kill you, that you need at least a month of bed rest before undergoing any kind of strenuous activity. I'm not willing to sit around waiting for you to get better, but neither do I want to kill you until I'm absolutely certain you've told us everything you know. What to do, what to do?" He was smiling as he said this, toying with me like the sick sadist he was.

"Ah-ha!" he snapped his fingers and smiled. "Got it! I'll torture your friend. Why didn't I think of it before?"

"What friend?" I tried to make it sound mocking, but my fear was too strong to conceal. Had he got Jack? I hardly knew the boy, but I wouldn't sit back and let him be tortured. And what if the others from the school had got tired of waiting for me to come back? Were all the children and staff being held captive somewhere in the house, the guards taking their time choosing which of them would be first for the rack?

The general nodded to the soldier on the door and he left, returning a moment later pushing a woman. She was chained with one of those American prison chain things that loops from feet to hands to neck, so she could only shuffle, and she had a hessian sack over her head. But I knew instantly who it was. The soldier pulled the bag off to reveal Mrs Atkins, our beloved dinner lady. She had a black eye and a bruised mouth, but she stood defiant, her eyes blazing with fury. Then she noticed me, and her reaction told me everything I needed to know about what kind of shape I was in.

"Dear Lord, Jane, what have they done to you?" she whispered.

"We saved her life," said the general. "You'd better hope she's going to save yours." Then he nodded again, the sack was replaced and Mrs Atkins was led away. As she shuffled away she shouted: "You be strong, love. Don't tell them a thing!" Bless her, but that was the worst thing she could have said, merely confirming in the general's mind that I was hiding big secrets.

"I have a few things I gotta get done back at Salisbury," he said. "So I'm going to fly back there now and give you a night to sleep on it. But midday tomorrow, my men are going to go to work on your friend there, and you're gonna have a front row seat. So you think carefully, Miss Crowther. You think very carefully. Indeed." He rose to leave.

"Where's Rowles?" I asked desperately.

"Who?" he asked as he reached the door.

"The eleven year-old boy you captured in Salisbury. What, you couldn't even get him to tell you his name?" I laughed. "You need better torturers, General."

He flashed me a look of warning. I didn't want to push this man too far.

"He's fine. We got him locked up. Collateral."

"And the girl?"

"Girl?"

I bit my lip. Stupid.

"I'll get my men to look for a girl. Thank you for the tip."

"And the others? The soldiers who were based there?"

But he just shrugged as if to say "what can you do" and walked out.

It took me a second to believe it, but I knew deep down that he'd killed them. All of them. The British Army had been routed.

The guard left the room with the general, and I was left alone in the wheelchair. I'd lost Sanders; Rowles and Mrs Atkins were captured; Caroline was missing, and all that faced us was torture and death.

I tried to rise from my wheelchair, to push myself up, walk

to the door, but I was too weak. I couldn't even muster enough strength to turn the wheels and push myself to the bed. And so there I sat, defeated, broken and scared, watching the general's ugly military helicopter rise from the field where the children used to play football.

As night fell there was a knock on the door. I didn't bother replying, after all I was the prisoner. After a moment, the door was pushed open and I was confronted by a young woman in military fatigues.

She stood in the doorway holding a tray on which rested a steaming plate and a glass of water. The woman seemed unsure about whether to enter or not.

"Miss Crowther, may I come in please?" she asked. Her soft accent, Deep South, made her seem polite and diffident.

"Suit yourself," I muttered.

The woman came in, placed the tray on the small bedside cabinet and switched on the main lights. The soldiers must have refuelled the generator. The woman then pushed my chair to the bed and lifted me out off it with surprising ease.

"You're strong," I said as she wrestled me on to the bed.

"I spend most of my time lifting bodies of one kind or another," she said flatly.

When I was settled and tucked in, she stood over me and offered her hand. "I'm Susan, Sue." I looked at her hand and snorted contemptuously. She withdrew it then sat beside me and lifted the bowl of soup from the tray. "It's beef. You need to keep your strength up. It's going to be a long recovery."

I considered spitting it in her face, but what would have been the point? I opened my mouth and gulped down the broth. We sat there not speaking as I ate the food and drank the water. I studied her. By almost anyone's standards she was unattractive. Her figure was short and square, her hair was muddy brown, and she had a flat nose, receding chin and piggy little eyes. She was flat-out ugly, but her brown eyes were kind and her voice was gentle.

"Is there anything else I can get you?" she asked.

"A gun," I joked.

"Small or large."

I sniffed. But she just sat there, waiting for my response.

"Small, please."

"Ammunition?"

I laughed. "Oh, loads."

She smiled and nodded. "I'll see what I can do, Miss." Then she stood, collected the tray, and left.

What an odd little encounter that was, I thought, as I closed my eyes and drifted into a haunted sleep.

It was still dark when I jolted awake, my heart hammering urgently in my breast. Something had disturbed me. I listened and heard the creak of floorboards outside the door. Someone was creeping about outside. I tried to lift myself, but it was futile; pain ripped through every part of me as I tried to move. All I could do was lie there, waiting to see who it was and what they wanted.

The door cracked open quietly and a shadowy figure stepped inside, pushing the door closed behind them as softly as they could. Then they walked to the bed and stood over me.

It seems odd looking back, and I don't know what I planned to achieve by it, but I pretended to be asleep, squinting up at the person, hoping they'd go away. But they leant down and put their hand on my shoulder and gently shook me. No point pretending now, so I opened my eyes.

"Who...?" I began.

"It's me, Miss. Sue. Please don't make any noise, there isn't a guard outside your door, but they do patrol and I don't want to take the risk. I have a message for you from someone called Lee. He told me to give you his love and to tell you not to worry."

In know it's a cliché, but there's no other way of saying it – my heart leapt. I can't remember what I said, it was probably just a mumble of vowels, I was so amazed.

Sue sat on the edge of my bed and whispered softly. "I was in the courtyard this evening, when I heard someone hissing at me from the bushes. It was a man called Tariq. I knew him when I was stationed in Iraq. It's a long story, but I used to pass messages for him sometimes, to soldiers who weren't happy with the way the general was doing things. My, you could have knocked me down with a feather to see him here!"

She talked with her hands, like a big camp drama queen, her eyes flashed with mimed shock and her mouth formed an O of surprise. "He told me that he's here with Lee and Lee's daddy. Now, they caused quite a rumpus back in Basra before we left, and it seems they stowed away on a plane or in a tank or something. To be honest that bit confused me. But either way, they're here now and they're coming to rescue you!"

She flapped her hands and gave a little bounce of excitement as she said that, almost squealing. I had to smile. Her over the top Southern Belle act was so at odds with the way she looked.

Finally I managed to speak. "Lee's here?" I said in wonder. I'd been so certain I'd never see him again, but he was back. The insane boy had actually flown to Iraq, found his father, taken on the American Army, and made his way home. It beggared belief.

"You betcha!" she said with a huge smile. "He's a little beat up, poor kid, but he's here. Now, if you're still not willing to cooperate with the general by midday tomorrow, then that's when they start torturing your poor friend."

"Is the general coming back to join the fun?" I asked.

"No Miss, I'm told he'll only be returning when you decide to talk. In the meantime, while you're trying to make up your mind, I have the item you requested."

She reached into the pocket of her jacket and produced a snubby little gun.

"It's a berretta, Miss. I hope that's to your liking?"

"Does it go bang?" I asked, amazed.

"It surely does."

"Then it's fine with me."

"Tariq told me to say that the action will begin shortly before midday, for obvious reasons, and that you are to shoot anybody who comes through that door who doesn't say the code phrase first."

"And the code phrase is...?"

"Finally, someone with balls."

I laughed, remembering Mac's final words. "Yes, it would be." I hesitated, but I had to ask.

"Sue. I must say, you're quite a surprise. You are the last person I would have expected to find in uniform."

"I'm a nurse, Miss. I just help put people back together. And the army pays good. Well, it used to."

"But surely you're taking a terrible risk defying the general like this?"

Sue dipped her head, suddenly serious. "I had a fiancée. He was in supplies and, oh, he was so sweet to me. And so brave. When the general started giving orders to attack the population in Basra my Josh stood up to him. Led a mutiny. But, well, he didn't realise how far the general would go. Josh was ever so smart but he could be naïve."

"What happened?" I asked softly.

Sue sighed and inclined her head towards the window. "Like the man on the lawn. Josh was the ringleader and so the general made an example of him. After that most people just fell into line. Some went native, joined the Iraqi resistance, but mostly people were too scared of the general, or they agreed with his methods, or they just couldn't break the habit of obeying orders, even when the orders were so wrong."

"And you?"

"I bided my time, made contact with those few remaining soldiers I thought I could trust. Waited for an opportunity. We're not all like the general, Miss. Some of us joined the army because we believed we were doing good, fighting for something right and true. I honestly believe that if we can just remove the general and those closest to him, then things will change for the better."

I gazed at her in wonder. "Sue," I whispered, "you may just be one of the bravest people I've ever met."

She put her hand on mine, looked up at me and smiled sadly. "That's sweet of you to say, Miss. I should go now. But you've got your gun and you know the code phrase, so just sit tight and we'll have you free in two shakes of a lamb's tail."

"Thank you, Sue," I replied, squeezing her huge, strong hand. "See you when the dust settles."

"I hope so, Miss."

She rose and left. She was so softly spoken, so physically unprepossessing, but so brave and kind. I had a new ally and I had hope. But then I remembered what had happened to the last two people who'd helped me – Barker and Sanders. The people who got close to me kept dying.

I just prayed that Sue wouldn't suffer a similar fate.

Someone else brought me my breakfast, a stoney faced guy who spooned porridge into my mouth without a word. I was strong enough to feed myself now, but I pretended I was still too weak. It might not be much of an advantage, but it was all I could manage.

I watched the sun climb higher, feeling more and more nervous. At quarter to twelve I heard someone shouting outside and an engine revving, then there was an almighty crash, my bed shook, and someone opened fire.

I held the berretta tightly and took aim at the door. Moments later it was flung open and the soldier who'd brought me breakfast backed into the room. I squeezed the trigger and let him have it.

The gun clicked and jammed, a useless chunk of metal. I tried to unjam it, but I wasn't familiar enough with the mechanism to do anything but make an awful grinding noise.

The soldier, unaware of his lucky escape, kicked the door closed and pulled a huge knife from a sheath in his belt. He ran across to my bed, shoved it away from the wall and got between the bedhead and the wall, leaning over me and placing the knife blade to my throat with one hand as he raised his gun in the other.

"I'm under orders to kill you if we come under attack," he growled.

I heard a voice from outside shout, "Finally, someone with balls."

It was Lee.

I tried to shout a warning but the soldier clapped his hand across my mouth and took aim at the door. I bit the soldier's fingers but he didn't let go.

I saw Lee's unmistakeable silhouette through the smoked glass panel on the door as he pushed it open. Then the glass shattered and he flew backwards, out of sight, as the soldier behind me shot him three times in the chest.

CHAPTER SIXTEEN

Lee

It was a day's drive back to Groombridge. As Dad drove, the nausea gradually subsided and my sense of balance slowly returned. The pain in my head helped take my mind off the crippling fear that everyone would be dead before we arrived.

The emergency medikit that Dad had plundered for the injection yielded lots more painkillers, much stronger than anything you used to be able to buy at a chemist's. I began popping Tylenol 3 like it was going out of fashion.

We stopped to rest for the night in a suburban cul-de-sac outside Tunbridge Wells, breaking into Barrett homes until we found one that wasn't full of corpses. The living room was lined with DVDs and sported an enormous widescreen TV. It looked new but it would never show a picture again.

Dad carefully unwound my bandages and mopped the blood off

my ear with water from the tank in the loft. When he'd cleaned me up he put his hands on my cheeks and rested his forehead against mine. "You're going to be okay, I promise."

My left ear was still completely silent, but the dead TV tone in my right ear was subsiding, and I found that I could just about hear Dad if he spoke loudly. I hoped the hearing would recover enough to be functional; I didn't think there'd be that many people left who spoke sign language. Being deaf in this world would be pretty fucking lonely. But I refused to give in to self pity. I had the school to worry about and mistakes to make right.

Dad explained that the Stryker had external fuel tanks which were designed to explode away from the vehicle if ignited. The RPG had hit one of them, hence the unusually big bang, but the defences had held and we'd been able to drive away under heavy fire. Had I been wearing the gunner's helmet my hearing would have been fine; Dad just had a mild ringing in his ears.

Tariq, who had been on the opposite side of the vehicle to the explosion, could still hear a constant ringing in both ears, but he could hear us through the background noise. He joked that he had Kevlar eardrums.

We plundered a store of tinned food that we found in the kitchen; obviously the owners had started panic buying when The Cull started. I wondered what had become of them. I spent the night in a child's bedroom, sleeping underneath a Man Utd duvet surrounded by posters of long-dead sports heroes. Knowing that the morning would confront me with God knew what horrors, my sleep was fitful and disturbed.

We rose with the sun and drove the final leg of our journey in silence. We had prepared all our weapons and I had talked them through the layout of the place as best I could. We left the Stryker in the thick woods north of the grounds and approached the house on foot. We stayed inside the woods, scanning the rear of the building with binoculars. It was still standing, but it was eerily quiet. The gardens are ringed by woods on three sides, so we were able to work our way around, checking the house from all angles. Finally we came around to the front and saw a hum-vee parked next to Blythe's calling card – an impaled man. The man was wearing British Army gear and I didn't recognise him. So the Yanks had been here, some had stayed, and there'd been a killing. But nothing told me what had happened to Matron and the others. I was frantic with worry.

Then Tariq gave a start and pointed to a female American soldier who was walking into the courtyard.

"I know her, she's a friend," he said. Before either Dad or I could stop him he was off, running around the edge of the woods to get closer. We stayed put, watching from a distance as Tariq got the woman's attention and she ducked into the tree line. After a few minutes she walked back out and Tariq rejoined us.

"They haven't got the kids," was the first thing he said, and I was overwhelmed with relief. "But they have got your matron and another lady. The lady is in the cellar, the matron is on the first floor in the south wing. She has been very ill and is recuperating."

"How many men?" asked Dad.

"Five, including Sue, and she says one of the others is not happy with things and would probably side with us if she had a word with him." He smiled. "Good odds, yes?"

We retreated and made our plans.

What we didn't know was that our every move was being watched.

I'd always assumed that one day Dad would teach me to drive, but I thought it would be in a Ford KA or a Mini; I didn't expect my first driving lesson to be in an armoured minesweeper.

I remembered when he'd taught me how to ride a bike. It had stabilisers on the back but somehow I kept managing to fall off anyway. Dad would pick me up, dust me off, dry my tears, and ask me if I wanted to give up. I sniffed and shook my head, checked my helmet was secure, and got right back on the saddle. Learning to drive an armoured car was much easier; if I made a mistake, it wasn't my knees that got damaged, it was whatever car, tree or house happened to get in our way. It was more fun getting it wrong and crashing in to stuff, but I forced myself to concentrate; every minute I wasted was another minute Matron spent in captivity.

"I don't want you out in the open, Lee," Dad had insisted. "You won't hear if I shout you a warning, or if someone's yelling at you to put down your weapon. Going into battle deaf is a sure-fire way to get yourself killed. I want you in here, safe."

"I'm not disagreeing with you, Dad. But this isn't your fight. You don't know these people, they're my responsibility."

He shook his head in wonder. "Listen to you. Son, you're six-teen. The only responsibility you should have is passing your GCSEs. And as for no ties, this is your home now. So it's mine too. If you're willing to risk your life for your friends, then so am I. Okay?"

"Okay," I said with a smile. "And thank you."

"Don't mention it. Now, let's get these gear changes sorted."

My Dad. Cool as fuck.

So at 11:45 the next day, at the same moment that I knew Dad and Tariq were approaching the house from the West, I strapped myself in, revved the engine, and drove the Stryker as fast as I could across the moat bridge and straight into the front doors of Groombridge Place. As soon as the vehicle ground to a halt, jammed in the doorway, I unbuckled myself, ran back to the gunner's seat and pressed my eye against the periscope. Didn't take long. Two of them came running down the stairs, guns blaz-ing and I took care of them sharpish. Wow, I thought, that was easy. Only one left. Dad and Tariq appeared at the end of the en-trance hall, so I grabbed my gun, opened the hatch and climbed out to join them.

Sue was close behind them with another soldier, a young Afri-can-American guy, thick set and jowly.

"We'll get the woman from the cellar," said Sue. "You get Jane."

They peeled away and the three of us ran up the stairs, guns raised, ready for attack from the landing. None came. We turned right at the top of the wide staircase and followed the landing around to the three doors that led off it. The final one, with its thick frosted glass panels, was where Sue had told us Matron was being held. I ran forward but Dad grabbed my arm and shook his head.

He inched towards the door and shouted the code phrase: "Finally, someone with balls."

There was no reply, so he raised his gun and pushed the door open. There was a series of shots from inside the room, the glass shattered and Dad flew backwards, shot in the chest. He hit the ground hard and slid back against the banister, mouth gaping, blood splattered across his face and hands. His gun fell from his useless hands and he gasped for breath as I heard Matron scream "No!" from inside the room.

Why I reacted the way I did, I don't know. Maybe it was second nature to me now. But I didn't run to help my dad. Even though I was in shock, and screaming in fury and pain, I didn't go to help him. Instead, I took the necessary steps to neutralise the threat first. Just like a proper soldier.

I flung myself forward, rolled on the landing and came up crouching, gun raised, in front of the swinging door. I saw a tall soldier standing behind a bald woman in a bed. Without hesitation I put a bullet right between his eyes, spraying his brains all over the wall. I didn't stay to watch him fall. I threw my gun aside, spun around and grabbed my dad, who was blinking in shock.

I wrapped my arms around him, trying not to look at the gaping holes in his chest and the thick blood pouring from them, staining his combats. He looked up at me and mouthed something I couldn't hear. I leant closer with my good ear, trying to catch the words, but his eyes rolled back in his head and he became limp and unresponsive.

I cradled him, rocking him back and forth, stroking his hair, crying. I don't know what I said, but I was speaking to him, trying to keep him with me, trying to talk him out of dying.

I was aware of a commotion behind me but I ignored it. There were people running up the stairs too, but I didn't spare them a glance. Then there were hands on me, pulling me away. I kicked and fought, but they were too strong. I looked up and saw that it was Tariq and behind him there was that weird bald woman with the sunken eyes and grey skin. She was in a wheelchair now, shouting orders at Sue. Mrs Atkins stood behind them, her hand to her mouth. Tariq held me there, shouting that I should let them work. But the dead TV tone was louder now, rising in pitch in response to the gunfire.

The soldier I had seen with Sue lifted my dad in his arms and carried him away, Mrs Atkins close behind. Sue followed, going down the stairs backwards, carefully pulling the woman in the wheelchair behind her. When they had disappeared Tariq let me go, to sprawl on the landing in my father's blood.

I felt numb. All I could hear was dead air and static.

Jane

I saw Lee fly backwards from the door and I screamed. He couldn't be dead. He just couldn't. And then my eyes seemed to play tricks on me, because there he was, shaven-headed and bruised, crouched at the door, shooting the guy behind me and then turning round to grab... who?

A young man stepped between us and reached down to put his hand on Lee's shoulder.

"You!" I shouted. "Come here, get me out of this fucking bed."

The man turned to face me. He had brown skin, black hair and kind brown eyes. This must be Tariq, I thought. He didn't move, stunned, it seemed, by what had happened, unsure which way to turn.

"Quickly," I yelled. "I'm a doctor." That did the trick. He ran into the room, grabbed the wheelchair and pushed it alongside the bed. Then he stood there, hesitating. "What?" I said, exasperated beyond words.

"Um, you're..."

I looked down. I was in my pyjamas.

"Oh for God's sake just pick me up, man."

"Right, yeah, of course."

I could hear a low keening noise coming from the landing as

Tariq lifted me from my bed into the wheelchair and pushed me towards the two people on the floor. It was only when I reached the door that I realised who the shot man must be.

"Is that Lee's dad?"

"John, yeah," mumbled the Iraqi.

I heard heavy footsteps on the stairs and then John croaked: "A school. After all that, I buy it in a bloody school," and gasped. Lee bent over his dying father and moaned, a low piteous wail of pure emptiness and grief.

I looked to my left and saw Mrs Atkins, Sue and a Yank soldier racing towards us.

"Sue," I shouted. "You're a nurse, yes?"

"Yeah," she said as she skidded to a halt beside me.

"Who operated on me while I was out? Was it you?"

"No, Doctor Cox, he flew back to the main staging area with the general."

"Shit. But is the OR still in place? Did they strike the OR?"

She looked at me and gasped as she realised what I was suggesting.

"No, it's still there, hooked up to the generator and everything."

"Right, you," I said, pointing to the Yank soldier. "What's your name?"

"Jamal, Ma'am."

"Right, Jamal, pick this man up and take him to the OR now. Sue, wheel me downstairs. We have to work fast if we're going to save him."

Sue blanched. "I'm not qualified to..."

"No, but I am. I'll direct you. Sue, it's his only chance. We can do this."

She had gone white, but she nodded. "Ok," she whispered.

Jamal shoved himself past us and reached down to remove Lee, but Tariq blocked his way with a sneer and did it himself, holding Lee back as we moved away. I so wanted to stop and hold Lee, comfort him, feel the reality that he was back. But there was time for tearful reunions later.

"Sue, wheel me downstairs," I ordered. "We've got work to do."

The operating room that Blythe had used to fix me up had been erected in the kitchen. Ironically, it was the same room I'd used for my fake surgery on the captain who'd been shot here. I tried not to think about what I'd done that day, about the young soldier dying in my arms after I slit his throat. Too much blood on my hands.

A polythene clean-room had been erected using gaffer tape, and there was a makeshift airlock through which you entered the sterile area.

Jamal was standing inside the doorway, still holding John, looking unsure about what to do when Sue wheeled me in. Mrs Atkins entered behind us.

I saw a rack of scrubs in the corner, a tub of alcohol handwash by the sink and a pile of tissue hats and facemasks beside it.

"Is he still breathing?" I asked as we entered.

Jamal nodded.

"Good. No time for protocol now. Jamal, get him on the operating table then get out again." He did so. "Back upstairs, help the others. Mrs Atkins, you're going to help Sue perform surgery."

She nodded briskly. Did nothing faze her?

"Right, both of you, take your shoes off, scrub up in the sink and get those hats and masks on. Where are the instruments?"

"Over there." Sue pointed to a trolley with a metal tray on top of it. In it rested a collection of surgical instruments, some still covered in blood.

"Shit. I suppose boiling water's out of the question?" I asked. Without a word Mrs Atkins walked behind the polythene sheets and I heard a click. She popped out again. "Kettle's on."

"Then let's get to work."

Lee

I sat on the landing, arms wrapped around my knees, rocking back and forth with my eyes closed, my clothes slick with my father's blood.

I felt a hand on my shoulder but I ignored it. It squeezed, trying to attract my attention. I reached up and batted it away. Then someone put their hand across my mouth. I opened my eyes, ready to shout, but Tariq's nose was an inch from mine and he had his finger to his lips. When he saw that I was with him he held up four fingers and pointed down. I saw past him to Jamal, who stood at the top of the stairs, gun raised, craning across the banister to look down into the entrance hall.

Tariq leaned forward and whispered into my ear.

"Wrong ear," I muttered. He switched.

"Sorry," he said. "At least four coming in the front, probably more out back. It was a trap, Lee. They must have been waiting for us to make a move."

"Dad?"

"In the kitchen. Matron and the others are operating on him now."

"Right, let's go."

"I think we..." he began, but I was already on my feet and moving past him. I lifted my machine gun to my waist with my left hand, took my browning out with my right, and walked past Tariq and Jamal before they could react. I walked quickly, focused and calm, straight down the stairs, peripherally aware of Tariq running to stop me. As I descended I saw two soldiers moving cautiously through the entrance hall, silently checking the rooms. One of them saw me, but before he could warn his colleague or bring his weapon to bear I opened fire with the machine gun.

The bullets raked across his body, flinging him backwards as I crouched and fired the browning, taking the other soldier three times in the chest. I stood up and kept moving.

Tariq fell into step beside me.

"They'll have heard that," he said wearily, like he was too tired to be angry.

"Good." I said coldly.

A stream of bullets flew past our heads. I dived down the last three steps, spinning in mid air and letting off some shots at the shooter in the office door. I missed, but the doorframe splintered, momentarily distracting the gunman. Tariq stepped over me and shot the guy in the head.

I'd hit the hard tiled floor with my bad shoulder but I hardly even noticed the pain. I felt a knot of hatred in my belly as I leapt up. These fuckers had shot my dad and I wasn't going to stop until every last one of them dead.

"Fucking deathwish Terminator shit," muttered Tariq.

I chambered another round and kept moving without acknowledging his sour disapproval. I thought: this must be what it feels like to be Rowles.

"Stryker," I barked at Jamal, who was halfway down the stairs. He nodded and ran to the vehicle, still jammed in the front door. I heard gunfire but didn't look back as Tariq and I walked into the school, guns raised. Past the staircase was a passage that led to the kitchen and the courtyard beyond it. Just as I was reaching forward to open the door, it swung open. I fired without hesitation, putting four rounds into the stomach of the soldier before me. Tariq opened fire beside me, sending a hail of bullets over the head of the falling soldier, wiping out the two men behind him. They fired back even as his bullets hit, but their shots went wide.

The second door on the right was the kitchen, and I ran inside. I could see a polythene tent. Inside it, Matron was directing Sue from her wheelchair as the nurse leaned over the kitchen table working on Dad.

"Time to go!" I shouted.

"We need two minutes to stabilise him," Jane yelled back.

A burst of gunfire came from behind me.

"No problem," I said, turning and opening fire at the soldiers coming towards me.

So help me, I smiled as I took their lives. Then Tariq and I walked on, looking for more.

Jane

The third and final bullet landed with a clang as Sue dropped it into the small metal dish.

"What now?" she asked.

"His left lung's collapsed," I said. "He's drowning in his own blood. We need to aspirate. Have we got a tube of any kind?"

Mrs Atkins stepped across to a metal trolley cluttered with implements. She rifled through it and then waved a piece of clear plastic tube.

"Great. Sue, you need to puncture the lung and shove that in."

Sue took up her scalpel and got to work. I leaned forward so I could shout in John's ear.

"John, John Keegan. I need you to concentrate, John. Focus on my voice. I need you to take a deep breath, okay? Very deep, when I say. Can you do that?"

His eyes flickered and he moaned. I took that as a yes.

"Ready," said Sue, holding the tube, which now stuck out of his side.

"Now, John, breathe deep," I said, willing him to obey.

He gasped, then sucked air in through his mouth. It bubbled and gargled in him, then the tube filled with blood and the lung drained its load on to the floor.

I breathed a big sigh of relief. "Good."

There was the sudden shocking sound of gunfire from somewhere in the building. Sue and I exchanged worried glances, but she shrugged. Not our problem yet.

"What next?" Sue asked.

"Now let's patch and seal. We need some superglue. There's some in a tupperware box under the sink."

The gunfire resumed, louder and closer, as Mrs Atkins retrieved the small tube.

"Now glue the entry wounds together. I've a feeling we're going to be moving him before we're finished."

Sue was a calm and efficient nurse. When all this was done with, if she wanted to stay, I'd train her up as a doctor. We needed all the doctors we could get.

"Done," she said.

"Mrs Atkins, roll him over. Sue, come here."

The door crashed open.

"Time to go," yelled Lee.

"We need two more minutes to stabilise him," I shouted. I think he replied, but it was drowned out by gunfire. Then he was gone.

Mrs Atkins had rolled John on to his side so Sue and I could examine the exit wounds. One in particular bothered me. I reached into it and ran my gloved finger around his insides.

"Shit," I muttered. "Sue, glue the other two but this one you're going to have to make an incision, widen it, then go in and tie-off the artery. Can you do that?"

"Yes, Ma'am."

The sound of gunfire was moving around the outside, to the courtyard. It was relentless and heavy; whoever Lee and the others were holding off, there were a lot of them. A sudden explosion blew in the windows and made Sue scream as one wall of the polythene clean-room came free and tumbled to the floor. She recovered her wits quickly and proceeded, her teeth gritted with determination.

She looked up and said "Done" the second Lee and Tariq ran into the room.

"Can we move him?" gasped Lee.

"Yes," I replied. "Sue, can you..." But she already had the wounded man in a fireman's lift.

Tariq leaned out of the door and let off a stream of fire then said: "Now!"

He went first, Sue and John behind, then Mrs Atkins pushing me in the chair, as Lee brought up the rear, firing short bursts to cover our retreat.

We left the corridor and came out into the main entrance hall. The armoured car was still stuck in the doorway, but the gun on top was pointing outside, laying down suppressing fire at the moat bridge.

Tariq climbed up on to the roof, then Sue and he manhandled John through the hatch and down into the car. I could see Sue talking urgently to Tariq as they worked, then she turned and leapt down, running past us all, back into the school.

"Where the hell is she going?" I shouted.

"Tell you later," replied Tariq, his head poking out of the hatch. "Now get in here."

Lee and Mrs Atkins carried me up as Tariq fired past us, and I made an ungainly entrance to the car. Lee was still firing as he closed the hatch above us.

"Go!" he shouted. Tariq put his foot down and tore us free of the doorway, reversing across the bridge, turning, and sending us speeding down the drive.

The Stryker started to clang as bullets raked the shell, but Jamal kept going and eventually the firing faded away in the distance. Once he was sure we were clear, he switched on the satnav and we headed for Fairlawne.

John was laid out on the bench opposite me and as our pursuers fell away I saw that he wasn't breathing. Lee was already performing CPR as Mrs Atkins held his father steady. Lee's face was splattered with blood and tears as he breathed and beat the life back into his dad. Eventually he shouted "Got him," and I saw John's chest rise and fall as he began to breathe again.

Situated outside the village of Shipbourne, the Fairlawne estate is a huge area of land once owned by the Cazlet family, horse breeders to the crown. Bought by a member of the Saudi royal family in the eighties, the Palladian house was fully renovated and restored. It even had a swimming pool. In many ways it was a better site for St Mark's than Groombridge – bigger, better equipped and closer to Hildenborough, where we had friends. But we chose Groombridge because of its moat, which we thought made it easier to defend. Now that we'd abandoned our second home in a year to enemy forces, it didn't seem like the smartest choice.

We were able to drive up to the front door without Tariq reporting any signs of life. Good, they'd been following my instructions. Secrecy was the best defence.

As long as we'd evaded pursuit – and Jamal, who'd both been watching the road behind us through the periscope, assured us that we had – then we should be safe, for a time at least.

Lee popped the hatch and climbed out, and a few minutes later a gang of boys had gathered to help me out.

I was home.

John had coped well with the journey. He was still unconscious but he didn't seem to be in any discomfort and his breathing and pulse were strong. When I looked up after checking him over I saw Lee watching me anxiously. Just for an instant I could see the frightened boy hiding behind the brutal façade. I gave him a smile of reassurance.

"He'll be fine," I said. But I was lying. I needed to get him into surgery again as quickly as possible, and this time I wouldn't have Sue to help me.

The boy relaxed, the mask came back down. Lee nodded briskly. "Good. Let's get you both inside."

We'd left my wheelchair behind in our rush to escape, so I made an undignified entrance, carried between Lee and Tariq past a sea of excited children, standing around the main entrance hall. Their murmuring faded away to shocked silence when I passed through. I tried to smile and put a brave face on it, but I was a sallow-cheeked, hollow-eyed wreck. I cursed the staff for not keeping them away. I had planned to clean myself up and make a dignified entrance at dinner; now that was blown to hell. I'd just have to make the best of it, but I knew that morale would suffer.

I couldn't worry about that now, though. I began issuing instructions for the creation of an operating theatre.

CHAPTER SEVENTEEN

Lee

I rubbed the sticking plaster that covered the cotton wool patch on the crux of my arm and wondered whether my light-headedness was a result of my ear injury, blood loss following the transfusion, or stress.

The sun was just rising above the horizon as I sat on the grass in the Fairlawne gardens, trying to calm myself and reflect on the events of the last twenty-four hours. So much to take in. Matron had been working on my dad for over half of it, all through the night without a break.

I heard the soft crunch of wheels on gravel approaching from behind. The sound changed as the wheelchair was pushed on to the grass. It came to a halt beside me and I heard someone walking away. I didn't look up, just sat there staring at my feet.

"If you're talking, I can't hear you," I said. "You'll have to speak up, I'm basically deaf."

"I've done all I can," said Jane eventually. "Your blood made all the difference. If he lives through the day, I think he'll be fine. But he's in bad shape."

"I know. And thanks." I looked up at her and smiled.

Her eyes were deep sunken with big brown rings around them and bags beneath. Her hair was all gone, shaved clean, and the left side of her scalp was covered by a large white dressing, which marked the site of her surgery. She was pale and emaciated, gaunt and wrecked, huddled in a wheelchair without even the strength to push herself from place to place.

"Jesus, Matron, you look like shit."

She laughed at me and said: "Look who's talking!"

"I didn't recognise you at first."

"And I thought that your dad was you. He sounds like you. Or you sound like him, whatever. Through the glass, in silhouette, I was sure it was you. When I thought you'd been shot..." She left the sentence hanging.

We sat there in silence for a while, watching the sun rise behind the trees. Then I told her my story, everything that had happened from the moment I'd walked away, all those months ago. She listened patiently and never asked any questions, letting me tell it straight.

When I'd finished she reached down and ran her fingers across my scalp.

"I'm glad you're back, Lee. I missed you."

I didn't meet her eyes, nervous of what I'd see there. I wouldn't admit it to myself, but if I looked up and all I saw was maternal affection, I think that would have been the straw that broke the camel's back. So I kept staring at my shoes, not wanting to know yet what it was she might feel for me. Better to leave it undefined for now. There was still so much to do.

"So where is everyone? What happened here?" I asked. And it was her turn to fill me in. As I listened to her tale I grew more and more angry at myself. Angry and ashamed.

"I should never have left," I said when she finished. "If I'd been here..."

"The same things would have happened, but there'd have been more shooting, probably," she said. "As it is, everyone's safe."

"Not Rowles and Caroline."

"No, not them. We have to decide what we're going to do about that."

"I have a few ideas," I said.

"But look at us, Lee. What chance do we have against Blythe and his army? A crippled matron, a deaf schoolboy and an Iraqi – did he say he was a blogger?"

"Yeah."

"An Iraqi blogger, some guy we hardly know and a man with three bullet holes in him. It's not exactly a task force."

"We have to do something," I insisted.

"Yes, we do. We have to hide. Get ourselves well, build up our strength. Bide our time. Come up with a plan."

"And while we're doing that, they secure their position, terror-ise the populace, establish martial law across the south of Eng-land. No," I said forcefully. "They have to be stopped now. Be-cause once they start setting up bases across the country they'll be too widely dispersed to fight. Our only chance is to take them all out in one fell swoop, while they're still all collected in the one place."

"Oh well, if that's all it takes," she mocked, "I'll call the moth-ership and get them to nuke Salisbury Plain from orbit, shall I? I want Rowles and Caroline back as much as you do, more so, probably. But there comes a point where you have to cut your losses. We can't win this one, Lee. We just can't."

I couldn't believe what I was hearing, and I felt the anger ris-ing inside me as she spoke. I stood up and leaned over her.

"What happened to the Matron I knew, huh?" I spat furiously. "The woman who'd do anything to protect the kids in her care; the woman who'd stop at nothing to ensure the safety of others; the woman who stood up to Mac when no-one else would; the woman who showed me what true courage is? What happened to her? You don't even look like her."

I walked away in disgust, knowing even as I did so that I was out of order, being cruel and callous when I should have been kind and caring. But I couldn't help it. I was brim full of fury that had nowhere to go, so I took it out on her.

If she shouted after me, I didn't hear.

Jane

"Here, take this."

The voice made me jump. I hadn't heard anyone approaching. I wiped my eyes and looked up to see Tariq offering me a hand-kerchief. I smiled gratefully and took it, blowing my runny nose and wiping my eyes as the young Iraqi sat in the spot Lee had vacated a few minutes earlier.

"I saw him walking away," he said gently. "He looked angry."

I nodded.

"He is a very angry boy, I think," he continued. "You should not take whatever he said personally. He is young."

I snorted. "And how old are you, exactly?" I asked, not un-kindly.

"Not so much older, it's true. But I grew up in a very differ-ent world to Lee. I did not expect freedom, I knew it would be something I had to fight for, and I knew the risks. I saw every day what a world run by bullies looked like. It seems to me to be almost the natural way of things. For Lee, freedom is all he has ever known and now to have it taken away from him, it seems unfair. He is a teenager, too. I know he seems older, and he tries to pretend that he is a man. But he is a boy, still, with a boy's anger and a boy's loneliness. He is trying to be his father, you know? I have fought beside his father for a long time and he is strong, resolute, cunning. But he is not an easy man. He never rests, he is always moving. I do not think he really understands happiness. And Lee is more like his father than he knows."

I was taken aback. Here was this person I didn't know, talking to me like we were old friends. I almost got defensive, said "what do you know?" But I stopped myself. He meant well, I could see that. And what he said was true.

"I thought you were a blogger, not a psychoanalyst," I said

with a wry smile.

He nodded sadly. "I think I am now a soldier, Miss Crowther. I think these days we all are, no matter what we may have been before."

"I don't want to be a soldier. Neither does Lee."

"I know. But the truth is, from what I hear of you, that you are both very good at it."

"Ha! Have you looked at the pair of us? We're in bloody pieces."

"But you are still standing." He looked up at the wheelchair, realised his mistake, and actually blushed. "I mean, you know what I mean. Sorry."

I laughed out loud. "Don't worry about it. Look, you may be right but I won't accept it. I'm not a soldier, neither is Lee. We're just normal people trying to get a little peace. That's all. I have to believe that one day we'll be left alone."

He shook his head sadly and said: "Not while General Blythe is in command, you won't. He'll be more convinced than ever that you're a threat now. He doesn't like loose ends. We have two choices: we destroy him or we run."

I was too tired to respond to that stark assessment. He rose and pushed me back towards the main house.

"Come on," he said. "Time for breakfast."

I still wasn't ready to face the school, so we had breakfast in the kitchens. Lee was there, sullenly refusing to meet my eye. He, Jamal, Tariq and I feasted on scrambled eggs with fresh basil, and Mrs Atkins and Justin explained what had happened while I'd been unconscious in the sick bay of the school.

They had returned to Groombridge on their own to make sure it wasn't occupied by another group while the others remained at Fairlawne. Then Sanders, Jack and I rolled up to the door. Sanders insisted that Jack be taken to Fairlawne and kept safe, and Justin took him. Mrs Atkins and Sanders made me as comfortable as they could, but neither of them had medical training and I was in a very bad way. That night the Americans arrived in force. Sanders didn't even try to fight, recognising a lost cause when he saw one. Instead, he changed into civvies and pretended to be a farmer. I'd been in a car crash, he told the soldiers. It might have worked, but unfortunately he used my name as part of the cover story. There was no way he could have known they were looking for me, so why give me a pseudonym?

They started torturing him almost immediately. Mrs Atkins was locked up and I was taken away for emergency surgery. At some point Sanders must have broken enough to tell them he was SAS, but it seemed he'd told them nothing else. The Yanks certainly didn't know about Fairlawne or Jack.

It broke my heart to think what Sanders must have gone through. They didn't kill him for two weeks.

Once the school was secured most of the soldiers had gone back to Salisbury, leaving the school apparently exposed, luring Lee and the others into a trap.

And now the choice that faced us was simple: fight or flight. None of us could make our minds up.

"Run where?" asked Lee. "If what Matron's told us about Operation Motherland is true, Blythe's got overwhelming firepower and resources at his command, not to mention a well-drilled army. First he'll begin by terrorising the local population, like he did in Basra. Then he'll start recruiting and training. It won't be long before he takes control of the whole of southern England."

"We could head for the continent, I suppose," I said. "It might be the best option."

"We stayed and fought in Basra," said Tariq. "And John and I are the only survivors. If we try to fight the Americans it is most likely we will all end up with stakes through our chests. And I would like to avoid that if at all possible."

"Even if we do decide to leave, I won't leave Rowles and Caroline there and that's final," I said firmly. "Tariq, you've no ties here, you're free to go whenever you wish. But I will get those children to safety or die trying."

Tariq held my gaze for a moment then inclined his head, a small gesture of acknowledgment and respect. "Lee?"

Lee stared at me as if from a million miles away, finally acknowledging my presence. I held his gaze and smiled a small, sad smile. His face softened and he nodded.

"Yeah, okay," he said. "I owe Rowles my life several times over. We get him and Caroline out."

"Good," I said. "Then..."

"But that's all," said Lee. "You're right, Jane, we can't win this. I'm not starting a war. I don't care about revenge or justice or any of it. I'll go rescue my friends and then Dad and me are going somewhere far away from all of this. It's not my fight. Not any more."

"Fair enough," I said, hoping that I could persuade him to change his mind but knowing this was not the moment to try. "Tariq?"

The Iraqi sighed heavily and shook his head. "Fucking death wish," he muttered. Then he shrugged. "What the hell. I'm in. Jamal?"

"No, Sir," said the soldier. "I'll be hitting the road in the morning. See if I can't get to London, maybe find a way home."

Lee reached across and shook the American's hand. "Thank you for everything," he said. "And good luck."

"You too." He drained his mug and bid us goodbye.

"So what's the plan?" asked Tariq.

There was a long silence.

"I think we ought to talk to the king," I said. "But first, let's go join the school, shall we?"

Lee

Jane insisted on walking into the dining room but she needed assistance, so I held her arm as she shuffled in.

When the children saw us they all rose to their feet and cheered, clapping their hands, whooping and hollering. Some of the little ones ran forward, arms wide, and I had to help her bend down so she could hug them. Green walked up to me, shook my hand, and told me how glad he was to see me. It was nice to be back amongst friends. When I helped Jane stand up again her eyes were brimming with tears. She waved everyone to sit down and I led her to the high table where she sat to address the school.

"Thank you all, so much," she said, uncharacteristically emotional. She wiped her eyes and laughed. "Sorry. As you can see I've been in the wars a bit since I left. But I'm going to be fine and I'm not going to be leaving the school again any time soon." More cheers. "But we have a problem, and I'm going to let Lee explain it to you."

I stepped to the front of the table and began my story, starting with my arrival in Iraq and leaving nothing out. They were children, but they needed to know what we were up against. Nobody made a sound when I had finished. I then handed the floor back to Jane, who told her tale, bringing the school up to date, omitting only to mention the king, who she had subtly pointed out to me as we entered, sitting comfortably with the senior boys.

"So here's what we're going to do," she said finally. "Lee is going to lead a rescue mission to recover Rowles and Caroline. It's important that you know we would do the same for any and all of you. We won't leave our children behind. But when Lee returns with them – and he will – we don't know what the future may hold. It's not over yet, but we promise we will keep you safe whatever it takes. In the meantime, classes as usual." There were some good natured groans, and breakfast resumed, the hum of conversation rising until it was almost deafening.

"Let's get out of here and go somewhere quieter," said Jane. As we walked to the door she looked over and gave the king a nod. The boy rose and left by another door.

We had plans to make.

"These are the petrol tankers," said King Jack, pointing at the large map he'd drawn for us. "There are hundreds of them, all full. Here we have the tanks, here the non-armoured motor vehicles, and here the fire engines and ambulances. To the north is the parade ground, and this whole swathe of buildings is the barracks. Then we've got the shooting ranges here and here, the training ground here, mess, medical centre and MP station. That may be where any prisoners are being held, in the cells. This is the main admin building, so it's probably where the general has his office. Then out further east you've got the houses and flats, accommodation for married couples and officers."

"And what's this?" I asked, pointing to a red cross next to the admin building.

"That is the main entrance to the tunnels. There's another one here," he drew another cross by a firing range. "This one's disguised as a cupboard, so there's a slim chance they don't know about it. If they don't, then it's our way in. I imagine the Americans have blown the main entrance by now. If so, there's a good chance that the prisoners might be down there."

"What was kept down there?" I asked.

Jack hesitated. "I suppose top secret doesn't really mean anything any more, does it?"

"Not really," said Jane.

"The tunnels have got all the really nasty stuff in them," he said. "The weapons of mass destruction."

I hadn't known what to expect when Jane had told me we had the king in our midst, but Jack was a normal kid. He sounded middle class rather than posh, he didn't put on airs and graces at all, and he insisted we call him Jack.

"Thank you for this Jack," I said. "It'll be helpful."

He looked surprised. "But I can show you myself. I mean, I'm coming with you."

"Out of the question," I said curtly.

"But I know the layout better than any of you. I'm the only one who can lead you safely though that place."

"We've got a woman on the inside," I said. "She's going to meet us and take us where we need to go. We don't need you. Anyway, what combat experience have you got?"

"Sanders taught me everything he knew," said the boy defensively.

"But have you ever actually been in a fight?"

"I was there when the Americans attacked."

"That's true, Lee," said Jane. "One of the few things I remember is Jack shooting at them."

"Look," he said. "At the moment it's just you and this Iraqi guy, right?"

"My name's Tariq," said the man standing beside Jack.

"Right, sorry. Tariq. Neither of you know the compound like I do, and you could use the backup."

I shook my head. "No. This is a mission of stealth. In, grab, out. With luck we'll be gone before they realise we were ever there. The more of us there are, the greater the risk of us being detected. And I'll be honest, I don't trust you not to go and do something stupid, like trying to blow the place up."

Our glorious majesty sulked for a moment and then said something which changed my mind.

"There's one very special warehouse down there...." he began. We listened until he'd finished speaking; all of us with our mouths open in astonishment.

"And you know the codes?" I asked incredulously.

He nodded. "Sanders showed me. I persuaded him it was my royal prerogative. I think he thought it was funny."

We were all silent for a moment and then Tariq clapped his hands and said: "Well shit, now we've got a ball game!"

Jane

That night Justin and Tariq helped me to a downstairs room they'd prepared for me. After they'd gone I lay in the cool sheets feeling the soft cotton pillowcase on my naked scalp.

I was too nervous to sleep, unsure of what I felt. My joy at Lee's return, my fears for his safety and that of everyone in the school who I'd unwittingly put into the firing line, the loss of Sanders. It was all too much to process. So I lay there, unable to sleep, until I heard a soft knock at the door.

"Hello?" I said.

The door cracked open and Lee stepped inside. "Hi."

"Hey."

He came and sat on the bed next to me, avoiding my gaze. "I'm sorry. For shouting at you this morning, I mean. That was out of order."

I reached out and squeezed his hand. "Don't worry about it."

"It's just, with Dad and you... I mean, he might die and you look so ill. I just..."

"He's going to be fine. He's had a good day. He's sleeping it off naturally now. He's over the worst."

"I thought I'd lose him, too," he whispered. "Like Mum."

"No. Not today, anyway."

He bowed his head, took a deep breath and said softly: "I killed her."

"Sorry?"

"She was so sick. She couldn't stop crying. It was awful. Then there were the seizures and she started bleeding from everywhere. And I couldn't help. I couldn't do anything for her. I sat there mopping her brow with a wet flannel and telling her it'd be okay. In the end she begged me to kill her, to make the pain stop. She'd never have asked me to do that if it hadn't driven her mad. And when she said that, when she said 'Please kill me', I stopped crying. Because here was something I could actually do, you know? Here was a way I could help her. So I took a pillow and I smothered her. And you know what? She didn't struggle. She put her hand up and held mine, even as I was using it to choke the life out of her. She held my hand and she squeezed it, just like you're doing now. She was grateful, so it didn't feel like murder. Bates felt like murder, even though I suppose that was a mercy killing too. But Mum? No. 'Cause I loved her so much. She was kind and funny and she used to sing me to sleep when I was little. And when she died I thought, that's it. I've killed the person I loved most in the world, the only person left who loved me. I thought I'd actually killed love and that I was broken now, forever.

"Then I came back to school and found you. And then Dad."

He began to cry great heaving sobs. I pushed myself up and wrapped my arms around him, pulling him down on to the bed beside me. I held him as he wept, stroking his head and shushing him into a deep, silent sleep.

Lee

"Dad, I dunno if you can hear me, but I've got to go. Blythe's got a couple of the kids from the school and Tariq and me are going to get them back. I know what you'd say if you were awake, but if you were in my shoes, you'd do exactly what I'm doing now and you know it.

"I reckon we'll be back in a week or so. By then you'll be up and about, I'm sure, waiting to bite my head off for being so reckless.

"If I don't come back, then you'll be among friends here. Jane will take good care of you, and I want you to take good care of her in return. She's special. You haven't met her yet, but she saved your life and mine. Only she's not as strong as she makes out, sometimes. She's better when she's got someone to lean on. And if I don't come back, that's going to have to be you.

"When you called me from Iraq that time you told me to be strong. For Mum. I didn't let you down. You'll never know how strong I was. Now I need you to be strong for me, and for her. I know you will be. You keep sleeping it off and I'll see you soon. I love you Dad.

"Bye."

Jane reached out and took my hand.

"I would ask you not to go, but you wouldn't listen, would you?" she said with a sad smile.

"No. But I came back last time, and I'll be back again. I promise. And this time I'll be staying. I meant it, you know. No more fighting for me. I've had enough. I just want to stay here and look after the school. With you. In mono."

Jane laughed. "How is the other ear?"

"Almost back to normal now. I'd say about 80%."

"That's what you get for trying to be a soldier."

"You can talk, Davros."

"Oi!"

I leaned forward, put my hands on her sunken cheeks and kissed her. Then I rested my forehead on hers and closed my eyes.

"I'll see you soon, Jane."

"You'd better, Lee."

Then I stood up and walked away.

I didn't look back.

CHAPTER EIGHTEEN

Lee

"Anything?" I asked.

"No. Just static," replied Tariq.

"And you're sure you got the frequency right?"

"Of course."

"And the clock's right?"

"She said three every morning. She'll be here, Lee. Relax."

The radio gave two bursts of white noise.

"That's her." Tariq pressed the speak button on the Stryker radio and squawked back four times. There was a pause and then the radio crackled into life.

"That you, Tramp?" It was Sue, whispering.

"Yes. Where are you?"

"South perimeter. There's a firing range by the fence."

"I know where she is," said Jack. "We can be there in five

minutes."

"Did you hear that, Lady?"

"Sure did. There are perimeter patrols, so go carefully. I'll be waiting."

"See you soon." Tariq clicked the radio off and we primed our weapons.

We had parked the armoured car in woodland close to the base. Although we'd encountered no patrols or guards of any kind, Blythe had begun stamping his authority on the area.

We'd passed Stonehenge on the way to the base; the ancient stone circle was full of staked soldiers, hundreds of them, lined up in concentric circles, staring at the stars, like an offering to an ancient God.

We had no doubt that we'd suffer a similar fate if we were caught. I used the periscope to scan our surroundings. "All clear," I said. We turned off the interior lights and cracked the hatch, climbing out into the cold night air. It was a dark, moonless night, but Jack was wearing a nightsight Jamal had given us before he left.

Leaving the Stryker behind us, we let Jack take the lead. I didn't know what to make of this boy king. He was an uneasy mix of overconfidence and insecurity. He'd been reticent about his royalty, unwilling to explain how he ended up the ceremonial head of state, at least in the eyes of the British Army. Green told me he'd been eager to blend into the background, unwilling to draw undue attention. Yet here he was leading us into the heart of enemy territory on a mission to rescue two children he'd never met. When I asked him why he had insisted on accompanying us he just said it was his duty. I had no idea how he'd fare in combat, but his knowledge of the base, and the ordnance contained within it, was our ace in the hole.

We reached the edge of the trees, where the cover abruptly ended in a fifty metre stretch of clear grass. Beyond this stood a high chain-link fence. Crouching down, Jack scanned the buildings for movement. He saw a patrol and gestured for us to retreat back into cover. Hidden by the shadows, we watched the two guards walk past us and disappear past the barracks.

"That's the firing range." Jack pointed to a high brick wall just inside the fence. I reached behind me and pulled the wire cutters from my back pack.

"Stay here," I whispered.

I broke cover and scurried to the fence. Lying on the wet grass, I cut a small hole at the base, wincing at the noise each wire made as it snapped. I pulled back a flap of the fence to make an entrance and waved the other two forward. Once they had crawled inside, I followed and pulled the fence closed again. With any luck, the guards wouldn't notice the hole on their next circuit. Stashing the wire cutters back in my bag, I followed Jack as he led us round the wall at the far end of the firing range to a sandpit where cardboard cut out soldiers stood like silent sentries.

"Psst." It was Sue, standing at the corner of the wall, dressed in black, her face covered in boot polish just like ours. She didn't waste any time. "There are three perimeter patrols and they pass here about every twenty minutes. There are other random patrols wandering the base. They don't have a set pattern, so we have to move carefully.

"Where are they?" I asked.

"The boy is being held in the tunnels under the main building, which is where Blythe works and sleeps."

"How did they get into the tunnels?" asked Jack.

"They blew up the door by the main building," replied Sue.

"And the other door?"

"What other door?"

Jack turned to me and grinned.

"And the girl, Caroline?" I asked.

"They never found any girl," said Sue. "What's the plan?"

Tariq told her and she pursed her lips in surprise. "That's a bit extreme," she said. But she didn't raise any objections.

"This way," said Jack. He led us down the length of the firing range and across a road to a small outbuilding with a big metal door. He punched a code into the keypad beside the door and it clicked open. We hurried inside and pulled the door closed behind us, then crept down the concrete steps into the system of tunnels that lay beneath the base. The walls were concrete, with electric cables and pipes running along them. It smelt of damp. The lights were on.

"Knives only," whispered Tariq, drawing his blade and pushing his gun back over his shoulder. "A shot down here would be heard through the whole tunnel system."

Jack moved quickly and confidently, sure of the way. He led us past endless doors, all locked tight. "Some of these go down to other chambers, some are just offices. The two places we're interested in are at opposite ends of the complex."

"Okay," I said. "Two teams, as discussed. Sue, we're going to get Rowles. Tariq and Jack, rendezvous back at the door we came in by." They nodded. "And if you hear shooting, just run. Don't wait for us, or come to help. Just go."

Tariq took my hand and shook it firmly. "See you soon."

They vanished around a corner and I turned to the small, squat nurse. "Lead on."

She moved with remarkable grace for someone so solid, and we hardly made a sound as we moved deeper into the tunnels. Eventually she held up her hand.

"One more corridor and a left turn," she whispered. "There aren't guards outside the actual cell; they're up top at the door. So we shouldn't meet anyone." I stepped forward and took the lead, knife at the ready.

"Stay here," I said. I walked down the corridor, feeling my nerves giving way to the calm that comes before the kill. I reached the corner and took a quick look. Nobody. I waved Sue forward. She went past me to a nondescript wooden door.

"I lifted this earlier," she said waving a key in the air and then using it to open the door. We entered a small, bare room. All the furniture had been removed, leaving it a cold concrete box. There was no light and the smell was awful. The light that seeped in from the corridor revealed a small figure curled up asleep in the corner, and a bucket in the opposite corner. It was just like the cell where I'd found Dad in Basra. Blythe's bag of tricks was small but effective.

I crouched down and shook the boy's shoulder. He was awake

instantly. I don't know what I'd been expecting to find. The Rowles I knew was quiet and brooding, utterly self contained and unemotional. He was so ruthless, so terrifying, that I'd forgotten one simple fact: he was an eleven-year-old boy.

His right eye was horribly bruised, swollen shut. His front teeth were gone, as were his fingernails, and his bare arms were covered in tiny cigarette burns. His one good eye wasn't the cold orb I remembered; instead it was full of fear. Rowles scrambled away from me, trying to hide himself in the corner, burying his head in his arms and keening like a kicked dog.

"My God," breathed Sue.

"Rowles," I said firmly. "Rowles, it's me. It's Lee. We've come to get you out of here."

The ruined child couldn't hear me above his petrified whining. I reached out and put my hand on his shoulder, but he flinched away.

"Rowles," I said, louder this time. "Listen, it's Lee. From school. I've come to take you home."

Still no response. I cursed under my breath. We didn't have time for this. I reached forward and grabbed his head, holding his face up and forcing him to look at me.

"Rowles. Come on. We've got to go home."

His eye focused on me then and widened in surprise. "Home?" he whispered. "Home?"

"Yes, home. Can you stand?" His chin wobbled convulsively as he tried to nod. "Good lad. This is Sue, she's a nurse, she's going to help you."

"Hello sweetheart," said Sue. "You take my hands now." Rowles did so, his animal panic replaced by mute acquiescence. I went back to the door and scanned the corridor. Still quiet. I began to think that maybe we'd get away with this.

I turned back to see Rowles standing up. Sue had wrapped her arms around him and he was huddling into her for warmth, snuffling.

"Rowles, this is important. What happened to Caroline? Is she here?" I asked.

"Doctor," he muttered. "The doctor took her."

"So she's not on the base?" He shook his head.

"This can wait," Sue said sternly.

I nodded. "Okay, let's go."

I led the way back through the silent tunnels. We had to move more slowly, as Rowles was weak and disorientated, but we encountered nobody until we arrived back at the door where Jack and Tariq were waiting for us.

"Any joy?" I asked.

Jack shook his head. "I found and primed them but I couldn't find the remote units anywhere. Sorry."

"It was always a long shot," I said. "Let's not worry about it now. We've got what we came for. Let's get the fuck out of here."

And we did. We didn't meet any guards at all on our way back to the Stryker. I leaned against the cold metal hull of the vehicle and breathed a huge sigh of relief. We'd made it.

I climbed on to the vehicle and opened the hatch, turned to the others, smiled and said "let's go home."

And that's when I noticed we were missing someone.

"I won't leave him," I insisted.

"Tariq chose to go back, Lee" said Jack. "He may be planning to detonate. We need to get out of here."

I shook my head. "No. He's gone to get Blythe, and he'll want to do it personally. If I go quickly, I might be able to catch him up. Get everyone inside and batten the hatch. Sue have you got your radio?" She handed it to me without a word. "I'll call if I can but if I'm not back in an hour, you go without me. Understand?" Sue nodded. I looked across at Rowles. He had stopped whining and was sitting on the bench holding a handgun, staring at it intently, almost caressing it. I fancied I could see a flash of the boy I knew.

"You get him back safe to Fairlawne," I said.

"Lee, it's suicide!" said Jack.

"Just give me the door code," I snapped back. Shaking his head, Jack used a biro to write it on my palm.

Then I grabbed the nightsight and climbed out of the Stryker, back into the darkness.

Why did I go back for Tariq? He'd made the choice to go after Blythe without consulting me. He almost certainly hadn't told me because he didn't want me risking my life too. So we'd not managed to wipe out the Yanks, like we'd hoped, but we'd accomplished our primary mission – rescuing Rowles – and escaped. Going back in was foolhardy and, yes, suicidal. So why did I go after him? I've thought about it a lot and the only answer that I can give is that I wouldn't have been able to face my dad if I hadn't.

I snaked under the fence and ran for cover. My best chance of making it to the main building alive was to use the tunnels again. Jack's door code let me in, and I descended once more into the cool, silent passageways. I retraced my earlier steps to the cell where Rowles had been kept and beyond. Eventually I reached a staircase. This was it, the door by the main building. I looked up and saw that the door had been blown clean off. Now there was just a waist-high wooden barrier. I couldn't see or hear anything at the top, but I knew there would be at least one guard. I drew my knife and steadied my breathing. Time to fight.

I crept up the stairs as softly as I could, ready to throw the knife into the chest of anyone who stepped on to the doorway. But nobody did. When I reached the top I risked a furtive glance outside, left and right. The two guards were already dead, lying in pools of blood by the sides of the doorway. Tariq had been here.

I looked to my left and saw a large brick building with imposing steps at the front leading to double doors. This must be the HQ. My nightsights picked out a tiny movement and I realised the front door was just closing. I should have checked the area, but I didn't want to wait. I took a deep breath and sprinted for the door, expecting a hue and cry at any second. None came, and I vaulted up the steps and through the door as fast as I could, wondering how long my luck could possibly hold.

Not, as it turned out, that long.

A long, carpeted corridor stretched out ahead of me. In the

middle of it, Tariq was struggling with an American soldier, trying to get him in a neck lock as the man writhed and tried to shout for aid. Tariq had his forearm jammed into the man's mouth, and was trying not to scream as the soldier bit down. I hurried to his aid, and slid my knife in between the American's ribs, up into his heart. He stiffened and then relaxed into Tariq's arms. We dragged the corpse into a broom cupboard and stashed it.

"We have to go. Now," I whispered urgently, grabbing Tariq's bitten arm.

Tariq shook me off and kept going. "You heard what Sue said, Blythe sleeps in this building. I'm not leaving him alive, Lee."

He began climbing the stairs and I ran after him, grabbing him again.

"Tariq, this is madness. You've seen what he's like. If we go now, we might just make it."

The Iraqi shook his head. "No more running. This ends now. You shouldn't have come after me." He put his hand on my shoulder. "Go, Lee. This is my fight."

This was a different Tariq to the man I'd come to know. The light-hearted geek was gone, replaced by cold fury and suicidal vengeance. Suddenly he made sense. This was a man who would lead a resistance movement, who'd stand his ground no matter what, who'd stage mock executions to terrify enemy combatants into talking. I realised that I hardly knew Tariq at all. The celebrity blogger was the person he had been; this ruthless warrior, the side of himself that he kept carefully hidden, was the person the Cull had fashioned him into.

He turned away and kept climbing the stairs. I stood there for a moment, torn between my loyalty to the man who'd saved my life in Iraq and my duty to Rowles, Jane and Dad. But there was really no choice. I went after him.

The first floor corridor stretched to my left and right. Tariq had turned left, and was standing halfway down, outside the only door that had a chink of light showing around the frame. He drew his gun and opened the door in one swift movement, stepping inside, weapon raised. I padded along to the room, drawing my own gun as I ran. When I entered, I saw Tariq standing with his back to me. I stepped to one side to see who he was aiming his gun at. Sure enough, sat on a large double bed with a book resting on his lap, was General Jonas Blythe.

He was smiling.

"Tariq," I said.

"I know," he replied.

"You're thinking this was far too easy, ain't you, kid?" said the general, still smiling.

"Shoot him and let's go," I urged.

There was the sound of doors being flung open and boots stomping down the corridor. Then a cacophony of voices were yelling at us to lay down our weapons, put our hands above our heads and get on our knees. I don't know why they bothered, since they didn't give us time to comply. I felt a rifle butt smash into the backs of my legs and I pitched forward on to the floor.

I'm unsure whether the next sharp crack was Tariq trying to shoot Blythe, or the big heavy thing that cracked my skull and sent me spinning into unconsciousness.

The first thing I heard was screaming.

I shook my head to clear it, trying to ignore the crippling pain. I was tied into a chair by my wrists and ankles, but I wasn't in a cell or warehouse; I was in an office. Quite a nice one, with lots of wood, and paintings of old battles on the walls. I looked to my left and saw Tariq, also tied up. Blythe was standing in front of him, puffing hard on his cigar, making the tip glow bright orange. Then he stubbed it out on Tariq's naked belly and the Iraqi gritted his teeth, staring at the general in furious defiance, all the muscles in his body straining with the effort of not screaming again.

We were both facing the window, so I could see that it was still dark outside. I scanned the room quickly for a clock and found one on the mantelpiece. Four-fifteen. The others should have driven away by now. That was something at least.

I knew that our chances of survival were nil. I'd overplayed my hand and walked into danger one too many times. There was no cunning plan to rescue us, no force capable of fighting their way in here and overwhelming the entire American Army. The only allies we had for miles were a traumatised child, a boy who would be king, and a nurse. And by now they were driving as fast as they could in the opposite direction. The only thing left was to give them as much time as I could.

"Hey Tariq," I croaked. "I think you were right. I think maybe I do have a death wish." I began to laugh.

The general stepped sideways and punched me full in the face. His enormous fist was like a brick and I felt my nose crack. The momentum knocked the chair over and I toppled to the floor. I lay there and laughed as I spat out the blood.

The general nodded to someone behind me and my chair was uprighted. The general stepped back and sat on the edge of his desk, puffing on his cigar.

"Did you really think our security was that bad?" he asked.

"We hoped," groaned Tariq.

"I'm curious to know how you got into the tunnels. You didn't blow your way in like we did, so you must have had the code. Hook up with some soldiers who escaped?"

"Nah," I said. "Didn't you know? We're spooks! We know everything, don't we Tariq?"

"That's right, 007," said Tariq, following my lead.

"Yeah, top special agents, that's us. I heard you met our shadowy boss, The Matron. Let her slip through your fingers though, didn't you. Loser!"

The general smiled. God, I hated it when he did that.

"It doesn't matter," he said. "I'll have complete control of this whole country within the year."

"Right," I laughed. "Wherever will she hide in this huge and almost entirely empty country, which you intend to rule with a few hundred soldiers? You're right, she hasn't got a chance."

"Yeah," added Tariq. "It's not like me and a bunch of friends managed to evade capture in a city for over a year is it?"

Blythe stood up and walked over to Tariq, leaning forward so that he almost touched noses. "And look at what happened to all of you," whispered the soldier.

"Do you really, seriously, think we're spies?" I said. "I mean, come on. You must have worked it out by now, clever bloke like you."

Blythe turned to me, his face full of barely controlled fury. "I know that you managed to turn my son against me. That's all I need to know."

And there it was, the chink in his armour. In spite of all the coldness and detachment he'd displayed at the time, the murder of David was preying on his conscience.

Tariq noticed it too, and this time he took the lead. "We didn't turn your son, General," he said quietly. "He came to us of his own free will."

"Never," spat Blythe. "My son was a good soldier."

"Your son was a traitor," I said. "And he hated you."

"He approached us," said Tariq. "Said he wanted our help to bring you down."

"Couldn't wait to lock you up and throw away the key."

"Said you were a madman."

"Sadist."

"Psychopath."

"A traitor to everything you'd ever believed in."

"He hated you, General."

"Hated you."

The general roared as he grabbed a pistol from the desk and shot Tariq in the gut and me in the leg.

My vision blurred but I was actually glad. Bleeding out like this would be a hell of a lot easier than being staked or electrocuted. Maybe if I taunted him some more he'd even put a bullet in my head.

I hyperventilated, trying to make the pain subside. I'd been shot in the other leg the year before; I remembered this pain and knew I could master it.

"Don't talk about my boy like that," said the general, his voice full of calm menace.

I looked around and saw that Tariq was fading away. The blood from his gut wound was dripping down his naked torso and soaking into his trousers. His eyes were rolling back in his head.

My leg wound wasn't that bad. It hadn't hit the artery so it wasn't life threatening. I needed Blythe to shoot me again.

"Who, David?" I shouted. "The baby you nursed, the boy you played football with, the man you trained? The man you murdered? The son who loathed and detested everything you stand for? Him?"

The general roared in fury and came at me, pistol whipping me over and over until I blacked out. As the world slipped away, I felt only relief. It was all over. I didn't need to fight any more. My battles were done, my sacrifice made, all my sins paid for. I let the comforting darkness embrace me and I fell into deep, soft, warm oblivion. My last thoughts were of Jane and Dad. I saw them in my mind's eye, standing on the grass outside the original St Mark's. They were holding hands and smiling at me, their faces full of love.

"I'm proud of you, son," said Dad.

"I love, you, Lee," said Jane.

I felt myself floating free of my body.

"Sod this," said the voice in my head, pulling me back to reality. "I'm not having this at all. Pull yourself together, Nine Lives. Don't be such a loser. Wake the fuck up, find a way out of this, and castrate this motherfucker, or I'll come back from the dead and do it my bloody self."

I could hear a voice. I listened carefully, assuring myself that it was external. The accent was American but the voice was unfamiliar.

I was still tied up, my leg was wet with blood and I hurt all over. My head felt like it was going to burst. I tried to open my eyes but found only one of them would respond; the other was swollen shut.

"... spied her rounding up the children," the voice was saying.

Squinting, one-eyed, through the blood, I saw the general standing by his desk talking to someone I couldn't make out.

"I'm sorry, Sir, I don't understand," he said. "What exactly am I supposed to do with the children we capture?"

"Put 'em on a plane to New York, General. We have need of them here."

I couldn't be sure, but it sounded like the voice was coming from a speaker. Of course – he was on the video link, talking to his bosses in America. But it wasn't the president this time, merely one of his subordinates.

"Let me be clear," said the general. "We're in a position to impose rule of law on this whole island, but the primary objective of our occupation of Britain is to capture all the children and ship them to America?"

"Yes, General."

"May I ask why, Sir?"

"You may not," said the man, smugly. "Those are your orders and you will carry them out. Am I to understand that you have an issue with this directive?"

"I just don't understand, Sir. We've spilt a lot of blood getting to this point. I've done some things... some things I'm not entirely comfortable with. A new beginning, he said. A new American empire, won through force of arms but proceeding in justice. Those were the president's exact words to me, Sir."

"Don't quote the president to me, General."

"But how is that to be achieved by rounding up children?"

"That's not your concern, soldier," barked the man. "I possess information that you do not. There is a bigger picture here and you will play your part. That is your job, General, lest you forget. I am your commander-in-chief and I have given you a direct order that you will obey. Is that clear?"

There was a long silence.

"I said is that clear?" shouted the man.

"Yes, Sir," replied the general quietly.

"Then snap to it, soldier."

I tried to turn my head to see how Tariq was doing, but I got shooting pains in my neck every time I tried, so I gave up. Eventually I managed to open my good eye fully and I saw the general turning off the video conference.

"Trouble with management?" I asked, my voice sounding weak even to myself.

The general turned to face me, his face troubled and uneasy. "You still alive?"

"My granddad...." I broke off in a fit of coughing that brought blood up into my mouth. I spat it out, took a ragged breath, and went on. "My granddad was a soldier. Major General. He told me an army is only as good as the orders it receives. Who's giving your orders, General? 'Cause from where I'm sitting, it sounds like your boss is a crazy old fucker who might just be the world's biggest paedophile. And if you're taking orders from him, that makes you the world's biggest kiddie pimp. Ask yourself, General, is that what you signed up for?"

Blythe walked over to me and stared into my face, studying me. He was calmer now, his fury spent. "Who the hell are you, boy? The things you do, the way you talk. I can't decide whether you're the bravest soldier I ever met, or some kind of lunatic."

I laughed, but it sounded more like a dying gasp. "I told you, General. I'm just a boy trying to protect my family."

"I think I'm starting to believe you."

"What are you trying to protect, General? What's your end-game?"

"Same as it ever was, son," he said firmly. "Freedom."

"And this is freedom, to you? Torture, massacre, impaling civilians on stakes, burning them alive in football stadiums, killing your own son when he questions your motives. This is your freedom?"

He shook his head, momentarily allowing the doubt and weariness to show on his granite face. "No, son, it isn't."

"So what's this all for?" I yelled. "Why are you following these orders?"

"Because I'm a soldier, it's all I know how to do. It's what I am, a thing that follows orders, no matter what the cost. I don't know how to stop." He paused and then said softly "'I am in blood stepped so far that, should I wade no more, returning were as tedious as go o'er.'"

He stepped back then, shook his head, took his handgun from

his desk and raised it so it was pointing right between my eyes.

"I'm sorry, son. Close your eyes."

I shook my head as much as I was able. "No, General. Eyes open."

"So be it."

He squeezed the trigger, the hammer retracted, and I waited for the impact that would end me.

CHAPTER NINETEEN

"Hello? Anybody there?"

The voice crackled out of my left trouser pocket.

The general narrowed his eyes. "Thought you'd come alone." He put the gun down and fished the radio out of my trouser pocket. It was slick with blood, and he wiped it clean on my other trouser leg.

"Lee, Tariq, you there?" It was Jack. I cursed inwardly. So they'd ignored my instructions and waited for us, which meant that now they'd be captured and all of this would have been for nothing.

The general held the radio up to his mouth and pressed the transmit button. "I'm afraid the boys can't come to the phone right now. Can I take a message?"

For a few seconds all we heard was the crackle of static and then Jack said "Good morning, General." He was keeping a cool head. Good. "Are they still alive?"

"The boy is. The Iraqi," he glanced at Tariq, "is still breathing.

Don't know if he'll be doing that for much longer. To whom am I speaking?"

"You're addressing the rightful King of England, General. I rule this country, and you are not welcome here."

What the hell was his game? He should know by now that this was not a man you bluffed. I sat there, powerless to intervene, terrified for my friends. I hoped Jack knew what he was doing.

The general laughed. "Son, you sound about fifteen."

"I'm not the first fifteen-year-old king of England, General. And I won't be the last. I'm calling to give you a simple choice."

Blythe rolled his eyes for me, a moment of theatre. Then, grinning, he said "Your Majesty?"

"Leave now. Get in your planes and go back to America. Or I will destroy you and your army utterly." His voice wavered, betraying his nervousness. He didn't quite pull it off, and the effect was awkward rather than threatening.

For a moment the general was too stunned to respond. Then he began to laugh, a deep, rich, booming laugh. "My God, you Brits really know how to raise your kids!"

"Unlike you, General," I said pointedly. That stopped his laughter abruptly.

He flashed me a look of pure hatred and spoke into the radio again. "How exactly do you propose to destroy me, young Majesty? You've got no army left. I've seen to that."

"He's got me, you bastard." That was Rowles, and he sounded anything but nervous. "And that's all he needs."

Blythe shook his head in wonder. "Son, you may have killed some of my men, but... oh, this whole conversation is ridiculous. Where are you, anyway? I presume Keegan let you out of your cell."

"I'm still in the tunnels, General," said Rowles. "In a big underground warehouse with a large nuclear symbol on the door."

Oh.

Oh fuck.

The general saw my eyes widen in shock. He became cautious, my reaction leading him to believe that maybe this wasn't a bluff. He waved at the soldier standing behind me. "Go," he said curtly, and I heard the man open the door and run down the corridor.

"What do you know about this?" Blythe asked me.

I had to think very carefully about what I said next.

"I know that Rowles is a psychopath who doesn't seem to value his own life at all," I said slowly. "I know that he really, really doesn't like people in uniforms telling him what to do. I know that he's been tortured horribly and that probably hasn't left him in the best frame of mind. Oh, and I know that Jack – that's Your Majesty to you – knows the detonation codes for the nuclear warheads collected by Operation Motherland. The ones in the big underground warehouse with the nuclear symbol on the door."

The radio crackled again. "I can hear your soldiers coming down the tunnel, General," said Rowles. "If anybody tries to enter this warehouse, I'll detonate."

"He will, too," I said. "He has... issues."

Blythe narrowed his eyes, thinking hard. He hit the transmit button. "What do you want, son?"

"I want to kill you," spat Rowles, full of hatred. "With a knife, not a gun. Slowly. I want to cut you up, piece by piece. I want to gouge out your eyes, puncture your eardrums, rip out your tongue, slice off your nose, pull out your nails and teeth and hair, cut off your cock and make you eat it, then very, very slowly push my knife into your brain through your eye socket and stir."

Christ.

"I told you," I said. "Issues."

"I'll settle for blowing you up, though. And your army."

"And your friends, and yourself," said the general.

"If I have to."

"Here's what we want, General." It was Jack again. "We are going to drive to the main gate. You are going to bring Lee and Tariq to us and let us drive away."

"What's to stop the boy blowing us up once you've gone?" asked Blythe. "If he is as suicidal as Keegan says he is."

"Nothing except my word," said Rowles. "All you need to know for certain is that if you don't do as I ask, I'll definitely blow us all to hell."

"It's a good offer, General," I said. "I'm done with fighting. Once I leave here, you'll never see me or any of my friends again. We'll just vanish, and you can get on with doing whatever it is your boss wants done. We won't oppose you, we just want to leave. Probably France, maybe Spain, I dunno. But away. Let us go, you live, everyone's happy."

Through the window behind Blythe I could see a thin line of light appear on the horizon. Dawn was coming.

The door behind me opened and someone began giving a report.

"There is someone in the nuclear warehouse, General," said the soldier I couldn't see. "We've drilled through from the corridor and inserted a mini-cam. The boy is sitting next to one of the warheads, and the cover is off."

"So he could be telling the truth?" asked Blythe.

"Yes, Sir."

"Could a sniper take him out?"

"If we can get someone into the ventilation system we believe we could get sight on the target."

"Do it. I want to be informed the second the shooter's in position. Meanwhile, we play along. Get some men in here to clean these two up."

"Understood, Sir." The soldier stomped away.

The general leant down and picked up Tariq's black shirt, ripping it into strips and using it to gag me. Then he picked up the radio again.

"You don't leave me much choice," he said. "Bring your vehicle to the gates now, we'll have the prisoners."

"We'll be there in a moment," replied Jack, sounding surprised.

A stream of soldiers scurried into the room and I was untied and allowed to stand. I'd lost so much blood from my leg that I momentarily blacked out as I stood up. I was caught and sat back down. A doctor patched my leg up as best he could and helped me into a new pair of trousers. I could hear more frantic activity from where Tariq had been sitting. When I managed to look across all I could see was a wall of soldiers, some kneeling down.

"Just patch them up," growled the general. "No need to do too much. They've only got to make it to the main gate, after that they're not our concern."

Eventually a soldier indicated that they were ready, and they lifted Tariq up on a stretcher. He was pale and unconscious, and his breathing was shallow, but at least he was still alive.

Surrounded by soldiers, their rifles raised, we were marched out of the building and on to the main road that ran to the gate. I was unable to walk properly and had to wrap my arms around the shoulders of two soldiers who helped me. The base looked very different in the early twilight, with soldiers running all over the place; some were streaming down into the tunnels, others were lining up beside trucks ready to ship out.

As we moved towards the main gate I saw the Stryker pull up outside. Its gun turret rotated, pointing straight down the road at us. I smiled at the threat. Nice to have some firepower on our side. Then I heard a deep rumbling sound and a tank rolled into view ahead of us. Its gun turret – so much bigger than the Stryker's – rotated until it was pointing straight at the armoured vehicle, which suddenly seemed kind of puny. The general fell into step beside me and made eye contact, holding my gaze steadily, his deep black eyes, so pitiless and cold.

"I want you to know, son, that I'll be coming for you," he said. "I don't care where you try to hide, here or abroad, I'll find you and your daddy one day. And when I do, I'll fry you both alive, so help me God."

I didn't reply, just kept trying to put one foot in front of the other, gritting my teeth against the pain in my leg and focusing on the means of my escape. I had no idea how this was going to pan out, or what plan Jack and Rowles had concocted. Our original plan – for Tariq and Jack to use a remote detonator to set off the nukes after we'd left - had failed when they couldn't find the remote detonators anywhere. So how was Rowles planning to escape?

We approached the gate and the Stryker's hatch clanged open. Jack's head appeared in the opening and he shouted: "bring them forward."

The general nodded, the gate was opened, and Tariq and I were carried through. This was the most dangerous moment. If they decided to take this opportunity, they could kill us all with ease. It was only their fear of Rowles' that stopped them. If their sniper killed Rowles before we closed the hatch and drove away, we were dead.

The soldiers helped me up and through the hatch, lowering me down so that Jack and Sue could take hold of me and drop me on to one of the benches. Tariq was a dead weight when he was lowered in, but somehow they managed to get him stashed away. When the soldiers had gone, Jack closed the hatch.

"What the hell are you doing?" I yelled. "You were supposed to be miles away by now!"

"Not my idea," said Jack as he applied pressure to Tariq's wound and Sue took the wheel. "It was that bloody kid."

"Rowles?"

"He is a scary ass motherfucker, you know that, right?"

I shook my head, confused. "What did he do?"

"Held me to gunpoint, made me tell him about the nukes and the codes, and then threatened to shoot me if I followed him."

"So what's the plan?" I asked. "I mean, does he have a plan?"

"Not that he told me. I've just been doing as he says."

"Great king you are, letting yourself get bullied by an eleven-year-old."

"He had a gun to my head and knife to my balls," he protested. "And his eyes... that kid is not right in the head."

"He was bad enough before the months of torture," I said, shaking my head. "Let me on the radio."

I shimmied along the bench and Sue handed me the radio handset. "He's on setting three," she said. I adjusted the frequency so I could talk without the Yanks overhearing us.

"Rowles, you there?"

"Hey, Sir. You safe?"

"For now, but what about you?"

"Don't worry about me, Sir. Just drive."

"Don't be fucking ridiculous, Rowles. We came here to rescue you, we're hardly going to bugger off now."

"You'd better, Sir, because I plan on detonating as soon as you're clear."

I bit my lip, thinking furiously. How the hell was I going to get him out of this?

"Listen, they've got a sniper coming for you, through the ventilation system. I don't know how long you've got."

I clicked off the radio. "Can you rig up a remote detonator from scratch?" I asked Jack. "Did anyone teach you that while you were here?"

He shook his head.

"Shit." I pressed the transmit button again. "Okay, Rowles, we're going to have to bluff it out. I want you to find some piece of kit there that you can pretend is a remote detonator. If we can convince them you can set off the bomb from a distance, they'll let you walk away."

There was no reply. "Rowles, you there?"

"Yes, Sir. Sorry, I can hear them coming through the ventilation. I don't think I've got much time. I'm not leaving. If we run, they'll just come after us. I know what they do to people, and I'm not letting anyone else suffer like I did. The only way to be safe is to nuke the lot of them, and that's what I'm going to do. So you need to drive away now, Sir. Get to a safe distance."

I was thinking furiously. I couldn't let him die, I wouldn't. But as I was about to try again to persuade him, the Stryker started to move.

"Sue," I shouted. "What the hell are you doing?"

"You heard the boy," she yelled back. "I'm getting us out of here."

"Dammit, turn us around, that's an order!"

"You're not the boss of me, Lee."

"Jack," I cried, "stop her!" But the boy king just sat there looking scared.

I hit the transmit button again. "Rowles, please, don't detonate, just give yourself up. We'll come back for you again, I promise."

"Sorry, Sir," he replied. "I just..." I heard a sharp crack over the radio and Rowles grunted.

"Rowles? Rowles?"

Blythe's voice cut through the static. "Forget the boy. He's gone. Keep driving Keegan, 'cause I'm coming for you, and I'm going to kill you all myself. There's nowhere you can hide, son. This land belongs to me now!" Then his voice was muffled as he turned away and barked "Launch the Apaches!"

I felt sick to the pit of my stomach.

Jack looked at me, terrified. "What do we do now?"

"Faster, Sue," I yelled. She didn't reply; she was concentrating too intently, driving like a lunatic, trying to put as much distance as she could between us and our relentless, unstoppable pursuers.

Then the radio crackled again and I heard Rowles whisper, "I am so fucking sick of people in uniforms telling me what to do."

Shit.

I leapt forward to the control panel and shoved Sue to one side, causing the Stryker to veer wildly. As she regained control, I began hitting the touch screen. "Where is it? Where is it?" I shouted in fury until finally I found the button I needed. I stroked the glass panel and heard the CBRN system sealing us in and preparing us for a chemical, biological, radiological or nuclear attack and then...

The ground shook once, violently, throwing us back in our seats. There was a second's pause and then the shockwave hit. Incredible noise, like the Earth itself was roaring in agony. And then the Stryker was flying. Picked up and tossed through the air at the front of the blast wave, a sealed metal can holding four people who were tumbled and thrown, screaming and yelling, crashing into metal surfaces and edges, tossed against each other like rag dolls in a tumble dryer, cooked and deafened and shaken. I felt the awful lurch of freefall in my stomach as the stryker soared through the air, riding the wavefront, spinning madly, cooking us alive, deafening and blinding us, makes our senses reel and spin.

We began to descend and then an enormous crash as we hit the ground. I smashed, face first, into the metal floor and felt Jack and Tariq flop on top of me. Then we bounced, up again into the air, pitching and yawing and cresting the top of our arc, leaving us floating, momentarily weightless, before we began to fall again and crash again and bounce again. In ever decreasing arcs we leapfrogged across Salisbury Plain for what felt like a lifetime, feeling our bones crack. Eventually we stopped taking to the air and just tumbled along the ground, rolling across the landscape like a kicked toy. First we rolled side over side but then the nose dug in and we pitched across the ground front to back, end over end. It was endless, like the worst fairground ride you could imagine.

But eventually the rear of the Stryker dug into the ground and we gouged a deep scar across the plain, slowing until we stopped with a shattering crash that sent us all flying to the back of the vehicle in a smashing tangle of limbs.

The noise didn't stop when we did, nor the heat. The shockwaves of the explosion, weakened now that its greatest fury was spent but still fierce enough to strip the flesh from the bones of any poor soul caught in its path, swept across our craft, nestled in the soil now, dug in for protection against the onslaught.

But in the end that faded away too. The explosion passed over, leaving us broiled and broken, deaf and burned and shattered, heaps of disarticulated flesh in a hot metal stove, unable to see or speak, barely able to feel.

But alive.

EPILOGUE

Jane

We saw the light in the sky as the nuke obliterated Blythe and his forces. Even though that had been the plan, I knew deep down that something had gone terribly wrong.

When John Keegan left Fairlawne in pursuit of his son, I didn't think I'd ever see him again. Lee should have been back long ago, and John should still have been in bed recovering from his wounds.

I suppose I should have learned by now not to underestimate the Keegan men.

He was gone for two days, but on the morning of the third, he pulled up in a people carrier with the four most broken people I've seen in my life.

I worked on them for two days straight, setting bones, performing transfusions, cauterising wounds, treating burns and stitching them back together. Lee had broken every single rib, punctured a lung and shattered his jaw so badly that I had to wire it up; Jack had broken both arms, legs and collar bones in multiple places; Sue had had both an ear and a hand ripped off.; Tariq's guts were a mess.

A few days after the first round of surgery was completed it became clear that some wounds would not heal properly and I had to make the awful decision to amputate.

I removed Tariq's left arm below the shoulder and Jack's left leg just above the knee.

I kept them all in chemically induced comas for two weeks, eventually rousing them one at a time when the medicine ran out. When she regained consciousness, Sue just wasn't there any more. She could breathe and open her eyes, but she was gone, brain dead apart from the most basic autonomic functions.

I euthanized her as soon as I realised. Another death on my conscience.

John sat beside Lee all day, every day, holding his hand, reading him stories, playing his favourite songs on an old battery-powered CD player. I wanted to sit with Lee too, but I felt I would be intruding. So I busied myself with the day to day running of the school and only allowed myself to sit with my poor damaged boy when his father had fallen asleep. I sat there, stroking Lee's hair, fighting back tears, willing him to pull through.

Then one wet, grey day, John came running to find me. I was teaching a first aid class to a group of juniors when he burst into the room.

"He's awake," he said, and I didn't need telling twice. I ran as fast as I could down to the room we'd put aside for recovery and there was Lee, lying in bed with his eyes open. He mumbled something unintelligible and I felt a rush of fear – what if he was brain damaged? But then I remembered the metal in his jaw.

"Don't try to speak, Lee," I said softly. "Your jaw is wired up to help it repair." I saw the understanding dawn in his eyes and I realised he was still in there.

John hugged me hard, crying into my shoulder saying "thank you, thank you," over and over. I hugged him back, looking down at Lee, knowing that he would live but unsure how he would cope with the long, slow process of recovery and adjustment. Half deaf, crippled, held together with wire and plaster casts; his biggest fight was only just beginning. For Tariq and Jack, too.

But there were no soldiers coming after us, no armies left to do battle with. The land was free of military rule.

We were free.

Free.

THE END

The staff and pupils of St Mark's will return.

SCOTT ANDREWS has written episode guides, magazine articles, film and book reviews, comics, a Stargate Atlantis audio play, far too many blogs, some poems you will never read, and a previous novel for Abaddon.

You can contact him at www.eclectica.info, where you'll find bonus material to accompany this book.

He still lives in London's orbit, though somewhat farther out than last time, and still dreams of escaping to the wilderness with his wife and two children.

THE AFTERBLIGHT CHRONICLES

coming
September
2009...

Now read the first chapter from the next exciting
Afterblight Chronicles novel...

THE AFTERBLIGHT CHRONICLES

DEATH GOT NO MERCY

AL EWING

ISBN: 978-1-906735-15-9

UK RELEASE: September 2009
US RELEASE: December 2009

£6.99/$7.99

WWW.ABADDONBOOKS.COM

CHAPTER ONE

The Duchess

Skrr-rr-retch.

The knife was a combat knife, and it was sharper than a knife had any right to be. Put to use the right way, it'd cut bone, and even in the hands of an amateur, it could gut a man from stem to stern and spill his steaming guts out on the dusty ground.

The trick was, when you sharpened it, to drag the blade over the whetstone, gentle-like. Cade was a man who could be gentle when he had to be.

Wasn't what you'd call his main skill, however.

Right now, the knife was only cutting wood, but Cade gripped it like he was cutting through a man's skull. And a man who was alive, at that.

Skrr-rr-retch.

Cade sat on the steps of his trailer, bringing the knife slowly up against the wood, letting it bite in and then flicking his wrist up so as to carve one small shaving at a time off of the piece in his hand. The work was slow and Cade's body was still – an intense kind of stillness, like that second of quiet before the artillery tears into brick and slate and flesh and leaves nothing but mist behind it. When Cade was still and silent like that, there was a danger about him. That ain't to say clichés like 'coiled spring' could quite apply to the man – even the suggestion of potential motion was missing from him. But put your ear to his chest, the old-timers in Muldoon's used to say, before the bad times came, and you wouldn't hear a heartbeat. You'd hear ticking.

Across the way, the Duchess was laying out solitaire. She'd found a poker set in Bill Aughtrey's trailer after Cade had taken his body out to the back lot for burning and burying – once upon a time she might have felt a little out of kilter about playing with a dead man's cards, but too much time had passed. They were just nice things going to waste, and the Duchess made it a point of pride to never let anything go to waste, especially not now Duke was in the ground more than two years.

Even in her middle sixties, even playing solitaire, looking at the Duchess was like looking into a burning fire. Every move she made, she shifted against her t-shirt – low cut and ugly pink, off the shoulder, what she called her 'show-off' top. She leaned – playing the ace of spades down into the space she'd marked for it – and the bounty of her breasts leaned along with her, heavy and gorgeous against the tight ugly pink cotton, moving just on the edge of Cade's peripheral vision.

She knew what she was doing. They did the same damn thing every day.

Skrr-rr-retch.

The knife cut deep.

Pretty soon, Cade figured, he was going to have to stand up and turn that damn card table over. The Duchess would say something appropriate and Cade would say something appropriate back. Then he'd carry her into her trailer and put her down on the old mattress and they'd get to it. The Duchess knew it. Cade knew it. Hell, the rusty bedsprings in her trailer knew it. It was coming, it was inevitable, and Cade knew it because it happened every damn day.

Not that Cade was complaining, exactly. There wasn't a hell of a lot else for either of them to do.

It was a routine they'd fallen into, on account of how routine was about all that was left for anybody after the bad times, unless you wanted to go stone crazy. But it was a pretty damn good routine for all that.

Cade just hoped she wasn't playing a winning game when he sent the cards flying. Be a shame to wreck that.

The knife handle twitched. The blade cut.

Skrr-rr-retch.

Woody Dupree was due any time. Another ritual. Woody would come and bring the insulin, and they'd maybe play cards a little. Or maybe they wouldn't. Maybe Cade would knock over that card table first, and they'd be in the trailer getting to it when Woody arrived, and he'd just have to sit awhile. Cade wasn't a rude man by nature, but sometimes it happened that way anyway.

But eventually they'd all be sat around the card table with a beer each and they'd talk about the weather, or about something Woody'd read in a book, or maybe about how the vegetable patch was doing.

The last three living people for miles. They'd sit. And they'd talk.

Mostly Cade and the Duchess and Woody Dupree didn't talk about the bad times – mostly they skirted around it, like old rats around poison. But occasionally someone would say something. A subject that big, that black, someone had to say something. Woody might mention his mother, or the Duchess would make an off-hand comment about Duke, and all of a sudden all of those old ghosts would be back in the room and things would get colder. The night would end in silence and pain and a few tears, with Cade left to watch the other two feeling things he couldn't.

Best to leave the past in the past, Cade figured.

Skrr-rr-retch.

More wood shavings fell on the ground, the fresh ones joining with old and rotting ones from the day before and the day before that.

The Duchess shifted and laid down another card, her body shifting on the edge of Cade's vision.

Cade cut.

Skrr-rr-retch.

He didn't even really know what the hell he was carving.

He just cut.

Skrr-rr-retch.

Cade was considering standing up and turning the damned card table over when he heard a rumbling noise from down the track, and turned his head to see Woody's pickup rolling up next to one of the empty trailers, saving him from his thoughts. The Duchess looked over and waved as Woody opened the driver's door and stepped out, then walked around to the back of the truck. Cade figured something was wrong right then.

Generally, Woody brought the insulin a box at a time, on the passenger seat. But now there was a big crate of the stuff in the back of the truck.

The Duchess' smile left her face, and she looked puzzled instead – puzzled and a little fearful.

Woody was breaking the routine.

Woody still lived in the same house over in Muir Beach, about a couple miles away from the trailer park, and he spent most of his time there. He was a solitary man, even before, and since his mother died along with the rest of the folks in Muir Beach he didn't seem to need or want any company, beyond the time he spent with Cade and the Duchess. Sometimes he wouldn't come to the park for days, and when they'd head into Muir Beach to find him and drag him out for a beer in what was left of Muldoon's – another ritual they tried to keep to every week at least – he wouldn't answer his door. Him bringing the insulin to the trailer park every week was a way for the Duchess to keep an eye on him.

Woody was a fella who needed taking care of, she figured.

His hands shook as he tried to get a hold of the big crate. They shook most of the time, these days.

"Gimme a hand with this, Cade? I don't want to drop it."

Cade stuck his knife in the ground, got up and walked over. The crate wasn't that heavy, but Woody wasn't much of a physical specimen and besides, he had the shakes pretty bad. Cade figured it was best he took hold of it.

By now the Duchess was looking worried. She was scratching lightly at the needle marks on her arm, saying nothing as Cade laid the crate down inside her trailer. Cade figured he'd best ask the question.

"Woody?"

Cade was a man of few words.

Woody sighed, looking down at the ground.

"That's the last crate, Cade."

Cade narrowed his eyes. The Duchess spoke up, a tremor in her voice.

"Now, that can't be right, Woody. I – I thought there was plenty left in Brenner's..."

Woody shook his head, not looking her in the eye. "I thought so too, I did. But, uh, the crates in the back room of the store, the ones that have insulin written on the side, they're... well, they're all full of eye drops. I guess they ran out of eye drop crates at the factory, or there was some sort of mix-up or something... anyway, that's the last. There's sixteen boxes in there."

The Duchess shook her head, getting to her feet. She was blinking slowly as it dawned on her.

The Duchess had known the insulin would run out eventually, but she figured they had enough for a year, maybe two. Long enough to work something out.

"Woody, that'll only last about four months. What happens after four months?" There was an edge of panic in her voice.

Cade shrugged. No sense he could see in panicking. "We get more."

The words hung in the air for a moment. Woody swallowed. "Um, yeah, that's why I brought the whole crate up in one go. See, uh... I figure there's going to be more in the city, so I'm taking the truck down that way, and loading some boxes up..."

He tailed off.

The Duchess looked at him, blinking. "Jesus Christ, Woody, you wanna go down to Sausalito?"

Woody shook his head. "Sausalito's gone. I was thinking San Fran."

Cade looked at Woody. Woody who was out of shape, who still lived with his mother's ghost. Woody and his shaking hands and his twitch that wouldn't go away, talking about how he was going to take the pickup truck down all the way into San Francisco.

Ed Hannigan had taken a car down that way to see how things were there, about a couple of weeks after the last broadcasts finished and even the emergency band on the radio wasn't giving anything but static. He never came back.

After a couple more weeks, Woody had driven after him a

ways. He'd stopped when he came to a skeleton hanging from a sign by the side of the road. He told Cade later there was an orange glow lighting up the horizon.

Sausalito on fire.

Since then, the three of them had pretty much given the cities up for lost, and now Woody Dupree wanted to go down and load up a few crates of insulin, because he felt guilty. He was terrified. You could tell just by looking at him.

Cade shrugged his great shoulders once, reaching to scratch the hairs at the back of his neck. It was pretty damned obvious Woody was about to get his fool self killed.

Hell with it.

"I'll go."

Woody looked at him like a drowning man looking at a rope. He shook his head, licking dry lips. "No, it's okay. I should have checked the crates earlier. It's my fault, I'll –"

"I'll go, I said."

Cade wasn't a man you felt comfortable arguing with, at least not when his voice carried that tone to it. Woody looked down at the ground. "Are you sure?"

The Duchess spoke, her voice dry as Martini. The scare had gone out of her, and Cade was glad of that. "If it's my life on the line, I want Cade to go. No offence, Woody."

Woody nodded. "I'll..." He swallowed hard, unable to keep the relief off his face. "I'll leave the truck here. If... if you drive down to the town tomorrow morning, I'll help you load up with stuff." He licked his lips again. Nervous. "You know. From the gun store."

"Sure." Cade said. He didn't smile, but he probably would have made an attempt if he'd thought of it, for Woody's peace of mind as much as anything else.

Cade was never what you'd call the smiling type.

Woody looked at his shoes for a bit, and then waved, feeling foolish. His face was red as wine, and his eyes were wet, and Cade couldn't help but feel a little sorry for the man. The bad times had left their mark on him and he wasn't ever going to be the same, but he was a decent fella who wanted to do the right thing, and Cade knew that he hated himself right then for passing the buck along. Cade almost wished there was a way he could take that off the man's shoulders.

There wasn't, though. Not a way Cade could figure, at least.

Woody finished waving and turned. "I'd... I'd best get moving, if I want to get home before the sun..." The sentence trailed off, and he turned and trudged back down the hill, leaving the truck where it stood, looking foolish.

They watched him leave, and when he was out of sight the Duchess eased the fullness of her body back into the picnic chair she'd been playing solitaire in and made a show of picking up her cards. Her hands trembled, just a little.

Cade went to pick up his knife.

"Hey."

Cade turned. The Duchess was smiling, or trying to. She was still scared, he could tell. It wasn't just the possibility of losing her insulin supply – or her life. It wasn't even losing him – he knew a lot better than that. She didn't much like Cade, except in bed.

What scared her was tomorrow would be the end of the routine.

The Duchess shot a glance at the card table, and then a glance at him. Then she half-lowered her lashes, leaning back and raising her hands up into her dyed-blonde hair. "You want to come turn this over?"

Cade nodded, and went.

THE AFTERBLIGHT CHRONICLES

For more information on this
and other titles visit...

Abaddon
Books

Price: **£6.99** ★ **$7.99**

ISBN 13: **978-1-905437-01-6**

THE AFTERBLIGHT CHRONICLES

KILL OR CURE

Rebecca Levene

ISBN 13: **978-1-905437-32-0**

Price: **£6.99 ★ $7.99**

ISBN 13: **978-1-905437-40-5**

Price: **£6.99 ★ $7.99**

ISBN 13: **978-1-905437-62-7**

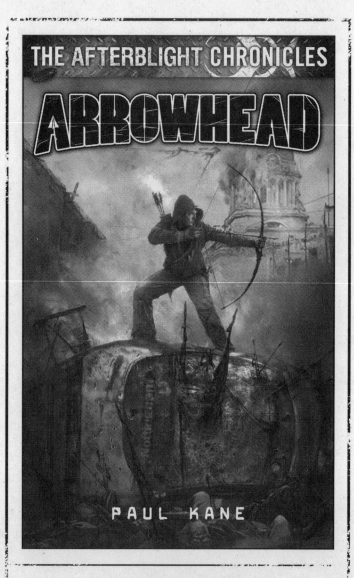

Price: **£6.99 ★ $7.99**

ISBN 13: **978-1-905437-76-4**

Price: **£6.99** ★ **$7.99**

ISBN 13: **978-1-906735-04-3**

Price: **£6.99 ★ $7.99**

ISBN 13: **978-1-905437-10-8**

PAX BRITANNIA

EL SOMBRA

Al Ewing

Price: **£6.99** ★ **$7.99**

ISBN 13: **978-1-905437-34-4**

PAX BRITANNIA

LEVIATHAN RISING

JONATHAN GREEN

Price: **£6.99 ★ $7.99**

ISBN 13: **978-1-905437-60-3**

Price: **£6.99 ★ $7.99**

ISBN 13: **978-1-905437-86-3**